PRAISE FOR THE TURTLE-GIRL FROM EAST PUKAPUKA

"Teeming with outlandish scenarios and bizarre yet deeply compelling characters, *The Turtle-Girl from East Pukapuka* is a veritable feast for lovers of playfully absurd fiction. Who knew cannibalism could be this much fun?"

—Josh McAuliffe, *The Scranton Times-Tribune*

"*Dr. Doolittle* meets *Lost* ... interesting and colorful cast of zany characters on a crash course with fate."

—Michelle Hessling, Publisher, *The Wayne Independent*

"Would a god really eat his own boogers? He might in this wonderful, crazy, non-linear novel filled with a cast of characters floating in and out of a literary universe peopled with pirates, South Sea Islanders named Dante, Jesus, and Butter, and a Loggerhead turtle with cosmic consciousness. Controlled craziness at its best, this novel dazzles with its stylistic inventiveness. And there's an island (or is it?) called Happa Now where... 'the only requirement for entering...was that you become dead...' Part religious allegory, part pirate tale, part fantasy,

Alpaugh's novel gives us hope for the future of fiction. Oh, and there is, of course, the Shark-God …"

—Jack Remick, Author of *Blood* and *The California Quartet*

"Lyrical and yet wonderfully warped, if *The Lord of the Flies* had been written by Kurt Vonnegut, you would have some idea of what to expect from Alpaugh's second novel.

"Heavily outfitted with wry humor and cutting sarcasm, this unique tale doesn't pause for a breath. You are swept into *The Turtle-Girl from East Pukapuka* with the same energy as the tsunami that sparks the critical events leading the reader across the vast South Pacific and at breakneck speeds along a downhill race course, all headed to a place in the afterlife known as Happa Now.

"Characters include a cocaine-addicted god who is half-man, half-shark, an alpine ski racer with a head injury that could cause him to die at any moment, and a young island girl who is rescued from the ocean by a tug boat captain named Jesus who thinks he's reeling in the catch of a lifetime—an authentic Turtle-Girl.

"A highly entertaining read."

—Hua Lin, MLS, Los Angeles Public Library

"*The Turtle-Girl from East Pukapuka* is a story of homecoming, whether it be for a young girl named Butter clinging to hope and the shell of a sea turtle, or a wounded ski racer longing to return to an island he has never visited. Writing with grace and simplicity, Alpaugh reminds us of how home can be both a wonderful and bitter thing. The book begins with a tsunami headed straight for a beach of hand-holding natives, enveloping the reader in quite a ride of suspense, humor and sadness

.... Alpaugh's words dance in the mind and tug on the heart."

—Regan Leigh, writer/blogger

"In his second novel, Cole Alpaugh once again captivates us with words, taking us along on a bittersweet adventure of unusual circumstances and leaving us breathless. Like the opening tsunami, his brilliantly layered plotline immediately sucks us in, making it unlikely that we'll come up for air anytime soon. His characters are so honest, so utterly raw, that we fall in love against our will. In Alpaugh's world, flaws are beautiful, no hero is perfect, and every person—no matter how strange or depraved—has a purpose. And, of course, there's always hope."

—Rhiannon Ellis, author of *Bonded in Brazil*

THE
TURTLE-GIRL
FROM
EAST
PUKAPUKA

THE
TURTLE-GIRL
FROM
EAST
PUKAPUKA

a novel
Cole Alpaugh

coffeetownpress

Seattle, WA

coffeetown**press**

Published by Coffeetown Press
PO Box 70515
Seattle, WA 98127

For more information go to: www.coffeetownpress.com
www.colealpaugh.com

This is a work of fiction. Names, characters, places, brands,
media, and incidents are either the product of the author's
imagination or are used fictitiously.

Cover design by Sabrina Sun
Drawing of Turtle Girl by Tylea Rain

The Turtle-Girl from East Pukapuka
Copyright © 2012 by Cole Alpaugh

ISBN: 978-1-60381-116-3 (Trade Paper)
ISBN: 978-1-60381-144-6 (eBook)

LOC Control Number: 9781603811163
10 9 8 7 6 5 4 3 2 1

Printed in the United States of America

For my mother

ACKNOWLEDGMENTS

Special thanks to Joni Cakobau of Suva, Fiji, who provided his expertise on cannibal history and food preparation.

My gratitude to Tylea Rain, whose love of even the most god-awful animals was inspiration for my character Butter; to Hailey Neales for her help with a specific vision; to my beloved Amy, Kat, and Regan for their support; to Western Wayne High School's Justin Hayden, Alyssa DeKenipp, and Allie Poltanis; and to Catherine Treadgold, the most patient and talented editor on this extremely blue planet.

CHAPTER 1

The birds were gone. The green ones that darted like spears across tree tops. The ones with spindly, old man legs that charged up and down the tideline pecking at leftover bubbles. Gone were the sand burrowers and the dive-bombing frigatebirds that sometimes stole fish right off James Hilton's lines. If something huge and bad was coming to visit, the birds knew first. Birds saw the Bigness from up high. And the Bigness was coming to swallow them.

James Hilton's own spindly legs wobbled, the sudden silence playing with his balance. It was as if both ears were filled with water too stubborn to be thumped out with a palm. He hesitated in the doorway of the empty thatched hut, rubbing at his yellow eyes to make them adjust to the dim light.

"I'm a dirty thief," he whispered, shuffling across the threshold into the familiar stench of rotted jackfish. The smell was another sign that things were not right. It was proper to eat inside, away from the sun, but leftovers quickly turned rancid and invited in all sorts of jungle creepers. The hut's owner knew that leaving food to spoil near your bedroll was akin to swimming in the feeding grounds at dusk. A good neighbor like Hilton would always take the time to scrape the forgotten dinner plates into the sea.

But the Bigness—the giant wave—was coming too fast for courtesy.

Hilton's old knees crackled as he shuffled guiltily past the plates toward the sacred books. He'd called out for the widow—the Keeper of the Books—but his voice had echoed back unanswered. He'd even looked for her crazy child, who wasted days sewing up snakes and lizards the boys had gotten at. The girl made Hilton uncomfortable. Her eyes darted like a goby fish, and were the same mix of colors. She had probably flown away with the birds.

There would be no more "normal," thanks to the coming tsunami. A radio broadcast had warned that they were about to die. This was his one chance to rescue the book that held his unanswered questions. The emergency message following the earthquake played in a loop in the back of Hilton's mind like a catchy slit drum melody. "The tsunami is forecast to reach ten meters in height." Hilton didn't know what a meter was, but from the gravity of the voice, it must at least be equal to the size of a man. The two words, man and meter, sounded similar in his language. Hilton had pictured ten men stacked on one another's shoulders, peckers waggling in the wind, and concluded it would be a mighty wave indeed, worthy of such dire warnings.

The word came back to him again, as if it were a dark shadow swimming circles at the end of a reliable hook.

"Bigness," Hilton whispered. It was one of the words brought to his people by the flying soldier. The soldier used it to describe the ocean, had held out his arms and made the sweeping gesture the elders of the time had taken care to learn. It was a word the villagers had accepted into their language, saving it for the mightiest storms and the ships with three chimneys that passed at the end of every hot season.

Hilton's fingers spider-walked along the dusty shelves and

found the book. Snatching it down, he clutched the copy of *Lost Horizon* to his boney chest, knowing without seeing because an old fisherman had a way of identifying things by weight and touch. He'd only held the waterlogged book a few times in his life, but knew it weighed nineteen shells in one hand. Hilton had been named to honor the book's creator and he had a plan to solve the mystery of the story told inside the moldy leather binding.

Embarrassed about his crime and dripping sweat, Hilton turned toward the daylight and retreated into the salty air, knowing that not much time remained.

Hilton stepped over a pile of splintered bamboo—pieces that would have made sturdy backbones for fine new homes—and gave a wide berth to the five muscular teenagers struggling with a washed up boulder. A powerful storm had deposited the enormous rock in the middle of the beach, and the cocksure youngsters had promised to clear it away. They'd dug in their heels and tried pushing, then secured vines to it and tried pulling. *Heave*, they had cried. And *ho*, they had called.

Hilton shielded the book as they jabbed fresh cut poles into the sand, leveraging with their shoulders until their veins bulged almost to bursting. Hilton was halfway to the lagoon when a piece of bamboo shattered so loudly that he instinctively ducked, searching the sky for thunderclouds. He smiled at the distant shouts and laughter behind him, as the boys dropped their mangled tools and chased each other into the jungle. Over the months, the boulder had been nudged no more than two arm lengths. The surging tides had begun pulling sand from beneath the giant stone, as if the island was trying to swallow it whole before it could escape.

Hilton followed the curved shoreline, the sea and lowering sun off his left shoulder, busy homes lining the way on his right. There were no salutes, no hellos, but Hilton wasn't offended. Just as he had needed to find his book, his neighbors all had last minute tasks to complete before death.

The lagoon was filled with what looked like bobbing heads—coconuts loosened by a heavy jolt inside the earth a few hours earlier. A thousand hard fruits had rained down across the island in a lethal brown hail storm, causing the emergency radio from a supply ship to be switched on for the very first time. The news was ominous, but the chief elder decided his people would accept the sea god's plan calmly and without fear. "There's nothing special for us to do," were his final words on the matter.

Hilton had nodded and mumbled agreement. There'd been no dissent in the meeting, no hysterical desire to paddle away in the village's half dozen boats. Hilton had joined the group of elders in the last few years by no choice of his own. He'd just managed to become old. His only specialized knowledge involved the motion of the tides and the proper way to make and bait a hook. But because he was old, people expected answers from him. He only ever replied with a smile, which was enough.

The ground continued its intermittent shifting under Hilton's feet, a familiar sensation from so many years aboard his small skiff. He watched his neighbors stumble, as if drunk on wapa juice, comforting one another and tidying up what was about to be smashed. Hilton trudged through sand littered with broken palms fronds. Every few moments, a coconut falling from an overhanging tree sounded a heavy kerplunk in the otherwise still water of the lagoon, perhaps the gods' way of counting down the remaining minutes.

Hilton stepped over the mooring lines of the fishing boats one by one. On his skiff's bench was the collection of hooks he'd spent years grinding with coral files and stone tools, meticulously shaping the whale bones and shells. There were a dozen types of hooks for a hundred species of fish. He considered stopping to tuck them into the narrow bow. But everything was to be left behind on this moving day, this pilgrimage from peaceful existence on an isolated tropical island to the next life in a place called Happa Now. Everything but the book clutched in his right hand, he hoped.

Hilton didn't want to miss the wave's arrival. He yearned to welcome it peacefully, not rushed and out of breath. He had no other possessions he cared to save. It was believed that only people made the trip to the next life. No animals, not even a beloved pet. But maybe, just maybe, Hilton thought, the gods might allow an object as simple as a book. He reasoned that if a drowned child appeared good as new on Happa Now, it was possible that his waterlogged book—a gift from the flying soldier during the Great War—would arrive crisp and light again, no longer just a solid brick of paper and ink.

Hilton craved to know what a lost horizon truly was, to learn if perhaps it was a story about a great wave that swept away the writer's people to their version of Happa Now. Or maybe it was something different and wondrous, meant to answer questions Hilton could never even think to ask.

Sweat dried on his chest as the beach angled toward the west, the sweeping panorama of colors mixed by the nearly exhausted day. And there it was, a black curtain rising from the once familiar sea. Tiny white specks swarmed across the growing face of the wave, and Hilton recognized them as curious, scavenging gulls. Every other bird was smart enough to find some distant safe place, while the seagulls could only listen to their bellies. He rubbed his own empty stomach, wondering if he'd ever eat again, then pushed away the dark thought that haunted him. If there were no animals in the next life, what would a fisherman do all day?

Hilton shaded his eyes with cupped hands, the book trapped between one arm and his bony ribs, as he stood on a mound of sun-bleached coral stacked by recent tides. He was perched at the north end of a crescent-shaped cove—the main hub of activity on his people's tiny atoll. The wave was still too far away to hear.

Hilton supposed the teaming flocks of seagulls were drawn

to fish trapped beneath the wave's looming crest. Or were the fish drawn to this safe haven from the churning waters below? Maybe there were no fish at all, only hopeful birds. He knew that if he had wings, he too would be drawn close by such marvelous power, such bigness.

Hilton glanced over his shoulder at the stubborn boulder, sitting there in the middle of the white beach as if waiting, then back at the black curtain hurrying toward him.

"Bigness," he repeated. A smile spread across a face carved by deep wrinkles—hundreds of tiny channels at the corners of his eyes and mouth, usually visible only during the glare of the morning sun. It produced what the islanders called a fisherman's squint. Now, as the wave loomed, it was his smile creating the furrowed brow and sinuous creases.

The people of East Pukapuka made their slow, ambling way to the edge of the lagoon behind Hilton—all one hundred of them, as far as he could tell. They came to accept their fates head on. There was no panic or visible dread, just what seemed like nervous anticipation over the pragmatic issues for which the elders had no specific answers. Would it hurt to die? Or would part of the gods' plan be to shield them from pain as the wave tumbled and drowned them? How long did it take to get to Happa Now?

The briny water of the cove was nearly black this time of day, an hour past supper. White sand was dappled by long shadows of puka trees and coconut palms, and broken shells tinkled underfoot as person after person left off whatever they'd been doing to bear witness to what approached on the distant horizon.

A hush had fallen over the small island—a tiny dot in the South Pacific that had gone mostly unnoticed and unbothered since the Great War, save for an International Red Cross supply ship's intermittent visits. Dusty bags of flour and rice were accepted with tempered gratitude; they were a polite people who took pride in their self-sufficiency. They'd enjoyed more than a half-century of tranquility, at one with nature and in harmony with the gods.

Hilton turned his head away from the rising curtain and searched the faces of his cousins and neighbors. Mostly they seemed curious. He was still smiling at the prospect of learning the story inside the book held against his side, and a few of his neighbors returned that smile.

There was a tug at his fingers. The villagers were holding hands, forming a complete link from one end of the cove to the other. Hilton stepped down from the pile of coral beneath his amber toenails and grasped the hand of a boy whose name he couldn't recall. It felt tiny and soft. He gave it a gentle squeeze.

The evening breeze stirred small ripples on the lagoon and in the mouth of the cove, dancing whitecaps kicked up beyond the reef. Even the creepers had gone silent, another sign of nature's understanding—or at least an appreciation—of what was about to happen, even though its involvement wouldn't go beyond this life.

Many eyes were closed, chins tilted to accept the last rays of orange sun and the cooling air. Most stood naked except for shell jewelry and belts and wristbands woven from coconut husks and sea grass. There was no shame on East Pukapuka and only the least bit of jealousy. In a peaceful society, the greatest warrior was one who could hold his or her breath the longest, spearing fish from the deepest hiding spots. And who could be jealous of an eight-year-old?

Hilton looked down at the boy whose head came to his hip. "My name is James Hilton." He spoke softly, but the boy's eyes were fixed on the horizon, and his only reaction was to clutch Hilton's hand a little tighter. It made the old fisherman suspect there might be more fear buried just beneath the surface.

As the moments passed, the breeze became a wind and the palm leaves rattled behind the chain of villagers. The sun was eclipsed by the rising sea and, with the sudden darkness, there came a chill. The wave began to make itself heard.

"We'll be okay," Hilton said to the boy when he noticed the small hand had begun to shake.

"Bigness," was all the boy said, and shut his eyes.

The one man not part of the human chain at the cove was Franklin Delano Roosevelt, who had shimmied up the tallest coconut palm at the north end. Roosevelt was an expert climber, the best of any male in the village, and thus had claimed the fattest girl as his wife. He'd enjoyed a good, full life thus far, revered for his impressive climbing skills and humble nature.

"Big, big, wave." Roosevelt looked down at his wife, then back over his shoulder toward the highest spot of land on the island—the modest lava knoll to the north. He scanned the rooftops of the thatched huts. "Not good." Roosevelt expertly shimmied down to his beautiful fat wife. His expression of apprehension was not caused by the impending drowning or crushing impact, but at the possibility of losing his standing as the best climber. Would his fat wife still love him if another man climbed faster in the next life? This long-time worry was only exacerbated by the big wave's approach. Roosevelt shared his daily anguish with anyone who'd listen. The fuel for his exceptional climbing abilities was the fear of slick, polished trees in the next life. Roosevelt was bone thin because he was often too distressed to eat, no matter how much food his beautiful wife prepared. She would eat it instead, thus making her even more breathtakingly lovely. It was a vicious, bittersweet cycle for Roosevelt.

"Hold me tight," whispered Roosevelt's wife into his ear, sweeping the lanky rail of a man into her wonderful brown folds. They were both naked and the cool breeze made her shiver, her skin quaking against his scrawny body. "The trees on Happa Now will be like ladders. I promise you will climb like a frightened monkey."

Roosevelt's eyes spilled tears on her soft, round shoulder.

The only child not joined in the human chain already had far too much life and death to attend to in order to calmly appreciate the impending tsunami. The little girl was furiously tearing open the cages of her hospital, coaxing patients out of their warm nests, back to the harsh reality that had already broken their beaks, wings or legs once.

"You have to climb!" Butter shouted at a handful of young rats she'd been nursing from a dropper meticulously fashioned from bamboo and a melted plastic soda bottle. Black mane bounding across her narrow, mocha-colored shoulders, Butter ran the pups to a leaning tree that they might be able to climb. At least now they would have a slim chance of survival. She swiped sand from eyes rounder than the other children's. "Eyes like a scared goby's!" the boys would tease.

"C'mon, hurry!" she pleaded with her sea turtle—a half-century old Loggerhead—whose recovery room had been the bow of a small skiff that had washed up years earlier. The girl had spent an entire day excavating sand, then dragging the boat into the hole and filling it with water. Butter could never have lifted the heavy creature, and the men on the island wouldn't be caught dead helping the ridiculous girl who tended to dying animals instead of playing with other children.

"Please, you can't stay! You have to get to the deep water or you'll die!"

But the sea turtle never went anywhere in a hurry, even in the best of times. Butter gave him a rough push, spilling the warm water she had freshened every morning with coconut shells filled from the lagoon. He extended his long neck to try seeing behind his shell as the girl heaved against his massive weight.

"Go!" Butter shouted. She stood back up and pointed toward the sandy beach before scrambling back to her other animals.

"Fly!" she hollered at the Red-Footed Booby, who had been slow to recover from a terribly cracked beak. Butter had found the booby dehydrated and near death on the north end of the island. She had gathered him up and nursed him back to health with ground squid and fresh water from the dropper.

Diving birds were especially prone to severely damaged beaks. Entranced by the silver flashes of prey below, they zeroed in on the target, misjudging the shallow reef as they crashed from the sky.

"Please go!" Butter begged, her frenzy fueled by the awful fact that animals were not welcomed on Happa Now. There were thirty small cages, most on the ground, while a few rested on stone shelves above. All the doors were open, but most of the patients wanted none of this change. They were content to have three square meals and a doting human to change their dirty nests.

You want me to do what? You want me to fly where? But I love it here!

"The wave is coming. You can't stay!" Butter began plucking birds from roosts, tossing one after another into the darkening sky. A few took flight, tiny splints and all, while others fluttered and fell in puffs of feather dander and indignantly scrambled back toward their doomed homes.

In her hysteria, Butter tore into the Habu nest and was promptly bitten by the fat little viper, who had been grumpy since having most of its tail either lopped or bitten off. *Stupid,* she thought through tears, although it didn't really matter. Not with the wave coming to take them all away. The bite sent searing heat running up her arm and deep into to her shoulder. It kept her muscles from responding, no matter how much her brain pleaded with them. The tendons in her neck clenched and her jaw locked tight. Sweat stung her eyes.

She was able to confirm that all the cages were wide open. It was the best she could do, though not enough. Now the poison was coming for her, just like the wave. Hearing the noise of a jet airplane flying close, Butter glanced upward. She saw nothing but a few clouds and several circling gulls that seemed hesitant to land. Confusion turned to horror as she identified the source of the thundering noise. "Oh, god," she wanted to say, but her mouth was frozen shut. The heat from the toxins reached her forehead, making her dizzy. She stumbled back to the sea turtle, who had made no progress toward the lagoon.

The thunder grew and Butter could feel tremors in the sand as she knelt behind the thirty kilogram turtle. She leaned her good shoulder into the back of its shell and pushed with all her might. It didn't budge. Butter extended her legs, gripped the shell with both hands and dug her toes in for leverage, but one side of her body had gone mostly numb.

This was just too much for a ten-year-old girl, Butter thought, with two small specks of blood on her swollen hand peering back at her as she weakly shoved the recalcitrant, backpedaling turtle.

It was too late.

A second before the wall of water swept the island clear of all living creatures, the great reddish-brown sea turtle retracted its gnarly head and flippers, hiding from the raging sea as best it could. Butter shifted forward, grabbing hold of the sides of his shell in a final loving embrace, her heart already broken.

Bigness swallowed them all.

CHAPTER 2

Dante Wheeler knew where the birds were hiding. He had a rainbow sherbet image of rustling feathers, could hear their nervous bickering, despite being ten thousand miles away and having barely enough bird savvy to distinguish a pelican from a pigeon.

"Sherbet," Dante hissed into the turbulence created by his tremendous velocity on the famed Lauberhorn downhill race course. He'd blasted through the start wand and made great skating strides toward the first gate. Television cameras followed him across the top of the world, expanses of treeless snowfields zipping by, picturesque jagged peaks in the distance. The first jump was thirty second in. Dante's long skis were rifle shots slapping down on icy flats. "And yellow," he chirped happily, despite instincts from a lifetime of training that demanded he rerun the images of his inspections and practice runs.

Dante sensed the huddled birds in his mind were agitated as he came roaring across the side hill portion and bled his speed in the hundred-eighty degree C turn, just before the nightmarish Hundschopf jump. Through the narrow chicane, giant netting on the left and a rock and snow wall a ski-length away on the right, Dante snuck a peek at the barren tree tops that had begun to appear, half expecting a glimpse of one of those birds from the Fruits Loops box.

"Cuckoo for Cocoa Puffs!" Dante shouted giddily, laughing, flashing under the train track bridge and into the speedy Super G turns. His eyes watered behind the yellow goggle lenses he'd chosen to cope with the flat light sections.

The slope fell away and Dante accelerated to a hundred miles per hour, ski bases melting, vibrating madly as they barely touched the snow.

"White," Dante cried out, his voice hoarse from the strain and the icy wind. "I see white!"

Spectators and coaches could practically reach out and touch gloved hands here, where a racer approached the first off-camber turn of Stump Alley, the Ziel-S. And they might have thought the American wearing bib number fifty-five—the hot-shot young cowboy—was referring to the course, or maybe the few fat snowflakes set free from a single dark cloud directly above. But Dante was seeing the curious seagulls framed by a great black monster when he caught a whiff of perfume that had been trapped somewhere in his long underwear since the night before. It was already a fond memory, what with all the wonderfully dirty things the girl had allowed him to do to her. Her smell had been sweet and fruity, and Dante was smiling as he and his skis launched into the frigid Swiss air at sixty miles per hour, headed for a tight grove of pine trees.

"Focus," Dante called out too late, arms flailing, body too far back on his tails to absorb what should have been a harmless, buried mound of earth. Dante was helpless against the mighty wind and roar that began his ascent. He sniffed for the girl from last night, but was distracted by salt on his lips. He licked them and tasted the sea.

A recurring lack of focus was forever his albatross. Precious course inspection time had been wasted when he'd skied over to an early spectator to score a phone number and autograph her breasts as their steamy breath mingling overhead.

"Dammit, boy, do you have a death wish?" The German-accented American coach had railed over muffled laughter from the teammates who'd whipped out their own cell phone cameras. The coach shook a ski pole, pointing at Dante from an especially tricky section of the course. "You are too scatter-brained, Wheeler. A downhiller needs to be focused. A downhiller who expects to live, anyway."

"Big, big wave." Now that his body was fully airborne, Dante's voice was calm. He opened his mouth wide, frigid air puffing his cheeks, and his lips vibrated and tickled insanely.

The orange safety netting protecting the last turn of the Lauberhorn would have done its job had Dante not been soaring out of control, twenty feet above its reach.

"Hit your line perfectly, or very bad things will happen," Dante's coach had said to his most worrisome charge during the morning inspection. He'd smacked the rock-hard snow with his pole. "This is life or death right here."

"Life or death." Dante's voice was a whisper as he flew headfirst, looking skyward at the rogue cloud still spitting flakes. *Like a lawn dart*, he thought, recalling a dangerous version of the game he'd played with his drunken teenage friends during summer ski camp on the Mount Hood glacier. Two puncture wounds, an eye nearly put out. They had been turned in by an Amazonian camp nurse, whose betrayal was almost made forgivable by her spectacular boobs that brushed your naked chest and arms.

"Incoming!" the thrower would shout, sending the heavy metal-pointed dart straight up in the mosquito-filled mountain air. The last to bail out of the launch spot won the point, sometimes paying with his own blood. But it was totally worth it. A little creative twist on a tedious game had resulted in the group having to wash breakfast dishes for the remainder of the session. Any mention of lawn darts disappeared from the following season's camp brochure.

A sudden, buffeting wind forced Dante's chin to his chest, and he took in the awesome view of his Atomic skis overlooking the meringue-covered Alps. He made a mental note to run an idea past his agent—a photo of him launching into the sky over Wengen, showing thumbs up, smiling, knowing he would land safely. Maybe even the girl from last night could be tucked under his arm, Superman and Lois Lane-like, for a new ad campaign. "They make you fly!" Dante mused, his body slowly rotating as if in a space orbit, providing a postcard-quality panorama of snow-topped roofs in the scenic valley.

And then Dante heard the collective gasp from the thirty-thousand spectators below, knowing this life or death thing must surely be only an instant away.

"What was her name?" Dante tried to sniff for another hint of perfume. Her skin was pale as snow, cheeks freckled and nipples pink, eyes a deep green he'd guessed were colored contacts. And even though he only had one final second to recall the young redhead's name, he couldn't. She'd never told him and he'd never asked. She was probably just another energetic ski racer groupie, willing to take on a talented but young second-tier competitor. "Maybe she'd already done all the old-timers," Dante pondered, suddenly melancholy—a brand new emotion when it came to women.

Normally melancholia set in at bar closing times or during visits to the team doctor—the last time in particular, when he had diagnosed the source of the burning when he peed.

"Three times, Wheeler?" The doctor had scoffed at Dante's reckless disregard for his penis, shaking his shiny bald head. "Who catches the clap three times in one season? Put a condom on it, boy, or just keep it in your pants. Are you going for a record?"

But to be melancholy over a girl? Could she have been *the one*? Could he have fallen in love? She did give incredible head and did that cool thing with her left hand. Dante smiled, even shivered a bit at the memory, despite all the dangerous things racing toward him.

Dante suspected she'd only mastered four English words: *yes, okay, sure,* and *again*. But language was no obstacle to true love. To smell her perfume one last time, her warm tongue in his ear distracting him from identifying the familiar song she was humming. She had hummed when he kissed her on the dance floor and when he made love to her in the narrow hotel bed.

"You're disgusting, Wheeler." His new roommate had rolled over in the other bed, but Dante had caught her giving the guy a lingering look. Had she already been with his roommate? Would she be with him tomorrow? Dante thrust harder, hoping to convince her of his own feelings.

Love was confusing for a man who had no trouble finding willing partners for sex, but only with women who invariably developed amnesia in the morning light. He'd first suspected he was doing it wrong, that the Europeans knew things he did not. Like any fearsome competitor, he'd borrowed one of the team's video cameras used for race analysis and studied the surreptitiously recorded tapes he made. He found no major flaws in his technique. Nothing glaring, anyway. He tried hard to excel in all things, even on matters that were not of life and death.

Was he too much of a jerk? Being nicer didn't keep any of these girls around, nor did being an even bigger jerk. Sleepily telling the girl who'd decided she was up for one more go 'round to "feel free to screw his roommate" was probably going too far.

"I love you," Dante called into the frigid wind that made his lungs ache, just before slamming head-first into a tree. His helmet shattered on the first sticky pine trunk, goggles launched and flapped away like a drunken bird, and the wispy, slicing sound of speed turned into the racket of bounding impacts. The sounds made by Dante's body and equipment combined to form a symphony—the high pitch of his snapping poles, the base reverberating from his thumping boots. Dante's bones resonated with the metallic and fiberglass music, soon joined by the cracks of breaking tree limbs. There was a terrible beauty in the shocking reality of pale, splintered bone emerging from gashes in the expensive speed suit.

"I love you," he tried to say again, but his mouth was too filled with blood, and the little sparks of electric messages zipping around his brain were not reaching their destinations. Dante came to rest face up. The great pines, looming like tall, prickly skeletons, surrounded his small crater in the snow.

Dante listened to the faraway birds, and then died for a little while.

CHAPTER 3

It was as if a knit hat was jammed down too low, limiting Dante's vision to two narrow slits. His eyes were being pulled by separate tides, had lost their synchronicity. A wave of nausea rolled over him. Blurry light flickered—a fire, or maybe a movie screen. He seemed to be lying down, but having no point of reference, he was just speculating. He couldn't actually feel anything against his skin, just a vague, detached sense of pressure on his shoulder blades and buttocks. Yes, if he had to guess, he was lying down, looking up at a house engulfed by flames, despite there being no heat.

"Hey, it's time for *The People's Court*!" A queer announcement at the scene of a raging fire. "Which of you wrinkled farts has the goddamn remote?" *Remote?* Dante had to stitch the words together for the sentences to make sense. Capital letters were appearing and disappearing across his field of vision, as if someone was typing them into his brain using an old manual machine, maybe a Smith Corona.

Moments later, a more coherent picture came into focus on the large screen above him. There were black tones from the judge's robe, surrounded by the dark wood interior of the courtroom, and stark music to herald new proceedings. Dante strained to coordinate the direction of his wandering eyeballs, as the judge hushed the chatter of the crowd and the smiling, gray-haired bailiff stood at attention. There was order in this court despite the stakes, which involved a vicious dog bite and a questionable countersuit. Viewers were introduced to the defendant and the plaintiff, and the tension unfolded like the first round of a Vegas boxing match.

"Will somebody please wheel the dead guy out of the way?"

"He ain't dead. Look, he's even pitchin' a tent under there."

"You're just filthy."

"Move your chair and shut your yap. I can't hear shit."

"You shut up! I can't see past his goddamn boner!"

"You're jealous that a dead guy can get it up and you can't!"

"I'd beat the livin' piss outta you if I was thirty years younger."

Dante followed the exchange by reading the subtitles, the angrier tones creating scarlet letters.

"If you was thirty years younger, you'd still be the same limp-dick antique. Only thing the dead guy can move is his pecker, and the only thing you can move is your flapping gums."

"I'm not dead," Dante wanted to say, lowering his eyes to where his erect penis was pointing toward the television from under the white sheet. His penis and eyes were the only functioning parts so far. He tried his feet, but received no answer from his toes or ankles. They wouldn't budge. His knees refused the slightest bend and it was the same for his hands and arms. Just a distant sense of dead weight, of being pushed down toward whatever he was lying on. Gravity seemed to be working exceptionally well. There was a metal bar next to his shoulder, the kind that protects hospital patients from falling out of bed. A hospital gurney?

Is this a hospital? Am I a patient? If nothing but my penis is working, then this had better be a hospital.

Dante went back to inventorying his non-functioning parts. Shoulders wouldn't shrug, neck wouldn't bend. Panic began to well up, as he tried and failed to wiggle one ear then the other and scrunch his nose. He tried clenching his left fist again, but nothing happened. His right was also … Wait! Something happened over there. His right hand had responded. He was pretty sure that his heart continued to function, for this sliver of success caused a warm rush of blood and adrenaline that made Dante's boner wave a little.

"Jesus Christ, that's distracting." It was a voice from nearby. The letters were light purple.

Using every bit of concentration, Dante zeroed in on his right hand. He began at the wrist and then tried lifting each finger, one at a time. Nothing from his pinky or ring finger. He strained to lift his middle, pointer, and … yes! His middle finger had moved. He was certain of it. He tried again: tap, tap, tap. He could hear fingernail on metal. *Woo hoo*! Dante triumphantly raised his middle finger under the sheet, a smaller counterpart to his upward facing erection.

A warm sense of accomplishment flowed through his prone body. If Dante could have managed a smile, it would have been wide and genuine. Could he cry? He felt the tears of joy just on the brink, so he squeezed his eyes, but was disappointed when nothing spilled out. No, it was either too soon or too late for crying.

"Wait a minute." Dante interrupted his thoughts of successful finger pointing to ponder the big picture of his immediate situation. "If I can only move my middle finger and my penis, I'm probably in a boat load of trouble."

"Nurse!" shouted one of the faceless, old man voices. "How 'bout you come jerk off the dead guy real quick so we can see the whole TV screen?"

CHAPTER 4

Dante had never been so squeaky clean in his life, despite only being able to lift a single finger due to his current vegetative state. Nurses and volunteers who were young and old, male and female, enthusiastically sponge-bathed the motionless athlete. Dante's skin spent a lot of time moist, pink, and deeply pruned.

The attention was welcome, even though it interfered with his attempt to determine the exact number of dimples in the section of ceiling tile directly over his pillow. The surface of the tile resembled the craters of the moon that arced outside his window. The tile was about twenty inches by twenty inches, with approximately ten indentations per square inch. The trouble spots were in the middle, where it became hard to keep track of what he'd already counted as opposed to new territory. He had a rough estimate, but was confident he'd come up with an exact number without all the interruptions. There was no longer a typewriter in his brain sub-captioning dialogue, a positive sign, because he could now follow conversations quite easily. He was in some sort of convalescent home, and weeks, if not months, had passed.

"They make me lie here and stink," grumbled Dante's latest roommate, an eighty-year-old former school teacher from Tallahassee. "The turnip gets all the goddamn attention." The roommate rolled away from the current sponge bathing by a tall, dark-haired nurse named Derrick, who sported finely plucked eyebrows and carefully manicured fingernails. His breath was hot and minty, and Dante could hear the candy clicking around his teeth.

"You're next, Mr. Thompson." Derrick didn't look over his shoulder. "If you behave yourself."

The old school teacher let go a wet fart that reverberated in the rubber mattress, sealing his fate of spending another day unwashed.

"I know this feels nice," Derrick cooed, raising Dante's elbow to run the soapy sponge into his armpit. "I added a few drops of wild fig bath oil," the nurse whispered, extending Dante's arm and slowly drawing the soft sponge along his flaccid bicep, down to his wrist. Derrick didn't wear rubber gloves, so that his skin often touched the injured skier's flesh.

"Your skin is so cold." Derrick dropped the sponge into the basin, using a coarse washcloth to dab at wet spots on Dante's chest before heading to the bathroom and running the water hard. "I'll be right back," he called around the corner. "Don't you dare move a muscle."

"Fudge packer," the former teacher barked at the wall.

In the hours after daily medicine rounds, Dante's eyelids became heavy, narrow fissures offering blurry images of the daily parade of nurses and attendants. He only caught glimpses of most of them, while they were busily washing his head and hair, sometimes leaning in close to speak in whispered tones. Some of these whispers were accompanied by quick, surreptitious kisses square on his lips. These kisses confused Dante, since he understood he was in some sort of care center. Could they be relatives? A wife and perhaps an overly affectionate uncle? Dante didn't mind the closeness, only that their attentions were so brief and secretive. He craved being held, or even having one of these people climb on top of him, enveloping his entire body and pinning him down under their weight. He felt physically suspended, motionless, as though caught halfway between the surface and the bottom of a swimming pool.

Not that he was sure he'd recognize a relative. Dante had no recollection of who he was, let alone who might be a family member. Nurses called him by name and often spoke to him as if certain he understood. His world had been reduced to sponge baths, a ceiling tile, hours of television, and countless questions he could only ask himself.

Why am I here? I mean, I know I can't move anything but my penis and a finger, but what the hell happened? Is this punishment? And where is this guy with the plucked eyebrows and minty breath taking me now?

Dante tapped his middle finger on the gurney's metal guardrail as Derrick wheeled the drying ski racer out of his room and down the long, brightly lit corridor. He tapped and tapped, trying to replicate the Morse code signal for help. He had questions that required immediate answers.

Was I in a car accident? Was I in a plane that fell out of the sky? Was I shot? Food poisoning?

Tap, tap, tap! Tap tap! Nothing. The eyebrow guy was humming, oblivious, as they rolled along. Dante didn't actually know any Morse code, but he'd spent hundreds of hours in the community room parked underneath the television in a place chock full of ancient men and women. The programming favored World War Two movies, courtroom dramas, and *The Lawrence Welk Show.*

Dante may not have known what caused his current predicament, but he did know the names of four polkas and how many yards a howitzer shell traveled.

"Hey, Dead Guy's here! How's the pecker today?"

"Don't be cruel, Abe."

"What? He gets the best seat. A little teasing is all."

"God hears you, Abraham Levin. Your filthy mouth right to God's ear."

"Look, we could play ring toss with his ding dong!"

"Grow up."

"Grow up? I'm eighty-seven years this July, my ass wrapped in a diaper and my roast beef spooned out of a jar. And you tell me to grow up?"

"Just take it easy on the dead guy."

"Which of you bastards has the remote?" Abe had begun frantically searching his wheelchair. "*The People's Court* has been on for five minutes. We ain't gonna know who the real putz is!"

Three hours later, the community room had thinned to a few snoring souls. Dante could not see them, only heard the different tones in what seemed like a triangle of calls and answers, like frogs or other creatures staking out territory to lure a mate.

Dante had drifted off at some point. His gurney had been realigned to provide a clear view of the wide-screen television—a positioning he assumed was for babysitting purposes. The attendant assigned to check on him was probably at dinner. Something else was different, and it took him a few minutes to locate the source of change.

Under Dante's one working finger was a smooth, hard object, with a small triangular shape slightly raised from the larger surface. Although he did not know more than his name and a few bits of polka and war trivia, Dante immediately recognized the universal shape and feel of the object at his finger tip.

This time, Dante did not have to fight to bring the tears of joy that blurred the flashing screen above; they simply flowed over his cheeks and into his ears. He'd suffered through a show about a household of old lady roommates called *The Golden Girls* for the past twenty minutes—a program he endured on a daily basis. Before that, a show called *The A-Team* had the room hooting and cheering. And earlier, a female panelist from a black and white version of *To Tell The Truth* had inspired catcall-induced coughing fits.

But now it was Dante's time. A sense of power, a transformation into a gatekeeper rather than mere observer took hold, flushed him with power. The answers to his endless list of questions could wait. No longer was he just some poor sap hopelessly damaged by a bad case of food poisoning or a parachute that hadn't opened, no sir.

Dante Wheeler drew in a deep, cleansing breath and clicked the revered television remote control with his right middle finger.

The whole world unfolded before him.

CHAPTER 5

The intra-axial lesions from Dante's traumatic brain injury made him see fireflies. They blinked inside his catheter tube and from the folds of the thick burgundy window drapes. His eyes followed them in circles above his bed late at night, as he tried to keep track of which was which. It was frustrating when they crossed paths, but he noticed each bug's light was a different intensity.

The fireflies sometimes took Dante's mind off the cold, which lurked barely out of reach, cat-like, preparing to pounce with claws bared. He didn't even mind when the fireflies landed on his closed eyelids, stirring him from a dream. From the way they made speedy little concentric circles, he imagined that their tiny legs must tickle. He longed to feel the energy behind the light. Dante envied how a firefly, like few other creatures, must always be warm, in easy command of its core temperature.

Dante's early vegetative state dreams were restless and unpleasant. Despite the swirling, omnipresent aroma of wild fig bath oil, Dante's mind screamed of a deep forest, with ragged, sharp-limbed pines and an underpinning of decay. His brain registered the cold not as a temperature, but in degrees of sharpness. It made him certain that touching any object would be like handling jagged razor blades and long surgical needles. Breathing this cold air meant inhaling tiny glass shards, opening slices in his windpipe and lungs, setting warm blood free to steam against the flooding cold.

The spiny tipped, razor-sharp cold surrounded Dante's sterile bed and his crisp white sheets. His most mundane dreams—concerning simple tasks performed in a former lifetime—would end on a similarly disturbing note. He would be standing over a sink with soapy water, holding a razor blade and making up and down strokes. Then, suddenly changing course, his right hand would slide from side to side across his cheek until the basin overflowed with blood.

Or he was back at ski camp playing the childhood game of kamikaze lawn darts, but instead of glancing blows and near misses, the darts would impale hands and pierce eyes, even puncture hearts and lungs. Punishment wasn't washing dirty dishes but digging graves for his friends and for himself.

Familiar laughter startled Dante awake. But the ceiling was too high, and there was no wall to his left. Panic surged through him as he fell backwards, dizzy. Naked and exposed, he searched for some landmark for his eyes to lock onto. The flickering television came into focus just as a giant lizard swallowed a man and his automatic rifle whole. It took a moment for his heart to quit racing, for him to recognize where he was—alone in the community room.

Laughter again emanated from the overnight cleaning staff out in the hallway, people used to ignoring time. It was not at all raucous. Their day was simply everyone else's night. Dante liked these women he'd never seen. For one thing, they interrupted his nightmares. And their stories, which he could never really follow, kept him company in the loneliest hours. Sometimes English, but more often in a language like a song. They were his lullabies.

The television remote again in touching distance, he escaped the giant lizard show. He would have smiled—had he been able to—as he held the button down, creating his own firefly of flashing light. Ownership of the remote control was intoxicating. Channel after channel zipped by, and Dante was consumed by the authority one finger could wield, a stark contrast to the complete and total impotence of his daily life.

When his finger grew tired, Dante released the little triangular button. And his overwhelmed senses sought to grasp his current reality.

"Salty," Dante tried to say, in a sudden urge to narrate. "The air is salty and the sun is bright and hot." Dante could feel the sand and small shells under his feet, as the gentle tide lapped over his ankles. The sea breeze ruffled his brown hair, felt delightful on his naked balls. The pressure from the catheter gone, Dante raised his chin to the blinding sun, arms extended, palms facing upward. Goose pimples—from excitement not cold—broke out across his body, and he experienced the glory of each and every one.

There were calls from exotic birds and shrieks from small mammals, all accompanied by crashing waves out near the coral reef barrier. Dante lowered his chin, opened his eyes to the white caps in the distance, and slowly turned to the lazy motion of dark, swaying palm leaves.

"There is nothing cold here." Dante's voice hummed with peace and calm. "There is nothing sharp."

Dante squatted, scooping rocks and bits of shells in his impossibly pale, needle-scarred right hand. The rocks had been tumbled to make smooth jewelry, the shells were polished treasures. He returned the fragments to the shallow water, rinsed the sand from his hand, and splashed warm water onto his hot shoulders.

There were curious, zigzag lines on his legs. He followed them with his fingers as he stood back up, intrigued by how they seemed not to end, as if he'd been stitched together like a rag doll or a winter quilt. Dante's peaceful state was strengthened by this discovery. It answered a question that often nagged his damaged brain as it tracked fireflies across his dark room. It solved the mystery of why he had no memories of family, of a mother and father. It put to rest any terrifying speculation about tragic accidents, any violence that would result in his confinement in a hospital or nursing home.

"Someone made me." Dante's traumatized brain was craving to assemble the puzzle, even if the pieces had to be hammered into place. "Someone sewed me together from things they found."

Dante splashed his way out of the ocean, up onto the white sand beach and into the shade of the heaven he'd found on channel sixty-three.

"Home," Dante said simply. "I am home."

CHAPTER 6

The ninety-foot Gypsy Dancer's diesel engines rumbled in neutral while her captain worked a stainless steel gaff over the port side, hooking pieces of debris left in the tsunami's wake.

For all its death and destruction, its catastrophic human toll, a tsunami provided salvagers with what amounted to a totally awesome Easter egg hunt. These were good days, the best of times for trash-pickers treated to a near endless bounty reaped from other people's misfortune. A salvager might find a hundred dollar life vest or a swamped hundred thousand dollar boat.

Captain Jesus Dobby, a stout, middle-aged man of Texas decent, hauled in a size-four Prada high-heel shoe with leather and snakeskin ankle straps. Dropping the ten-foot gaff pole, Dobby carefully examined the exotic piece of footwear, sniffed it, and looked out at the nearby sea. Calculating the odds of finding the matching shoe was beyond Dobby's first-grade education, but he correctly surmised they weren't all that hot. But Dobby knew a guy in Tang who had a queer thing for women's shoes and figured his friend would swap it for a shot of whiskey, if not a whole bottle. The captain turned and tossed the keeper onto the growing pile of jetsam and flotsam in the middle of his tugboat's main deck.

Climbing the bridge ladder up to the wheelhouse, Dobby scanned the horizon for the most promising debris field, then gunned the engines toward a curious object that seemed to be self-propelled and leaving a slight wake. The seasoned captain took pride in his uncanny ability to identify water-logged, half-submerged objects, but this damned thing made no sense. It was surely a living creature, but not one his mind could place. Fifty yards off the Gypsy Dancer's tire-laden port bow, the strange animal seemed to catch wind of approaching danger and paddle faster.

The sea turtle battled an overwhelming instinct to dive.

"Dive, dive, dive!" shrieked an inner turtle voice, but he knew the kind human girl clinging to the top of his shell didn't like being under water, even for a few seconds. When she'd slipped below the surface, she'd come up scrambling, clambering for a handhold on his slippery back. She had coughed and coughed, her body wracked in spasms as the guilt washed over him. He could feel her pain, wishing he could make it go away the same way she'd banished the pain of his once cracked shell.

The passing of time was a difficult concept for the elderly turtle, but he knew the girl hadn't grown much bigger since she'd rescued him out near the coral reef where he'd spent his entire life. He was only alive because of the girl clinging to his back. He'd loved her from that first traumatic day they'd met. He remembered being upside down—a frightening and vulnerable position for any sea turtle—his own blood forming a growing slick all around. Tiny swarming fish had poked at his head and shell, nibbling small morsels of his body. It went to show just how quickly everything in your life could change.

One minute you have a fat shrimp cornered, the next minute you're bobbing belly up in your own gore. The sea turtle had known it was only a matter of time before the sharks caught the scent and came for him.

When the turtle had heard the splashing, he'd closed his eyes and waited for the second terrible impact. The first had been the passing metal beast. He hadn't noticed it because his full attention was on the fat shrimp. Most of the surface creatures avoided the dangerous reef. This next impact would surely be from a white shark, the meanest of all animals in these waters. They swam with stupid grins on their faces and dead, unblinking eyes. The sea turtle had kept close to escape routes in the reef shelves when the biggest of the white sharks was hungrily lurking. The turtle had seen the shark eat a dolphin mother, orphaning a tiny calf that had disappeared alone into the deepest water. He'd even seen the same big shark attack a human for no apparent reason, biting him in two and then swimming off without feeding.

The splashing had stopped suddenly and the cringing upside-down sea turtle had held his breath. But no heavy blow had come, no horrible chomping or gnashing of giant shark teeth. There had come, instead, a soft voice and a careful touch. He had been turned with great care, slowly propelled, brought to shore and dragged into an alien world. He'd concentrated on the human girl's voice, a sound that lifted him away from his damaged shell, where he looked down from above at the angel who had whisked him away from the sharks.

The young island girl had hand-fed him a stew of ground shrimp and sea grass, after first applying a smelly paste to harden along the searing two-centimeter wide crack. The paste had taken away the sting, allowed him to sleep. He'd entered a comfortable existence in a flooded skiff, napping for extended periods half-submerged in the water the girl changed each day. Was there anything better than a warm sun baking your top half, while your belly was awash in cool water? And the kind little human girl was always there to tell him a story while he recovered from the near fatal wound. Her soothing voice told and retold the story of a magic sea turtle named Kauila, who was born on a mystical place called Hawaii. The magic sea turtle loved children so dearly that she sometimes changed into a little girl, playing on the black sand beaches of Ka'u. What would it be like to rise up naked, with funny round toes and long strings dancing from the top of your head, laughing like a bird and wrestling your brothers and sisters like nesting snakes? Maybe it was weeks, or months, the sea turtle wasn't quite sure. But he grew to love the human girl with all of his heart.

And then the sea rose up and swallowed his flooded skiff and even the trees. It had set free the beast chasing them.

"Dive, dive, dive!" the inner turtle voice shrieked again, but he fought the impulse with new resolve. Out here on the open ocean, swept away from his home with the girl clinging to him for dear life, the sea turtle knew he must out-swim the massive beast hunting them. He maneuvered right then left, then back to the right again. The sea turtle checked the sun's position, confirming it was still hours before darkness would hide them, and shifted into a dead sprint to the north.

Captain Dobby eyed the bizarre mermaid-like creature located off his starboard bow. The girl was not half-fish, like in the stories and pictures, but appeared to be half-turtle. Her round, naked buttocks were as brown as his own rutted face, and her legs seemed to work as a rudder for her oblong shell. Dobby kept popping the Gypsy Dancer in and out of neutral to keep the tug's speed low, not wanting to run over what could be the greatest discovery in the history of marine salvage. How much would a half-turtle girl fetch? Easily the price of a new engine. Hell, maybe the price of a whole new boat!

But Dobby couldn't reel in his prize because he didn't have a deckhand. He'd steer the tug alongside the turtle-girl, cut the engines after a short burst to maintain momentum, then scramble down the bridge ladder and grab his throwing net. But the damn turtle-girl would veer off, first right and then left, and then sometimes back again, always just out of reach.

"No wonder there ain't no friggin' turtle-girls in zoos." Dobby leaned over the gunwale, spat into the water, exasperated. "They're wily-ass bastards."

After five unsuccessful trips up and down the ladder, Dobby's arthritic knees were complaining loudly and his lungs were burning something fierce. He decided on a new plan, which was to track the thing from behind, to tire it into submission. The turtle-girl wasn't capable of submerging and the old railroad tugboat had four hundred liters of only slightly watered-down diesel in its tank. Dobby settled onto his tall wheelhouse bar stool and reached down for the long-necked bottle of Cruzan rum he kept on standby.

"Ain't no turtle-girl gonna get the best of Jesus Dobby," he croaked through the tug's smudged view screen, lifting the bottle of rum and draining half its contents in four swallows.

CHAPTER 7

Butter felt worse than the night she snuck a coconut shell full of wapa juice from Pearl S. Buck's rancid smelling hut. Her empty stomach churned and her aching head pounded from dehydration. Her cracked lips scraped her tongue, and her hands were cramping from gripping the sea turtle's wide shell. The two red fang marks from the Habu viper had turned black, the top of her right hand swollen to the size of a young breadfruit.

The viper's hemolytic toxin had attacked the cell walls of her blood vessels, allowing serum to escape into the surrounding tissue. There was just enough poison coursing through her nervous system to slow her heart rate and respiration, but not enough to cause cardiac arrest. Butter was in shock. She would experience bouts of loud raspy moaning. One moment she'd be lucid, the next, lapse into a coma-like state. She clung to the turtle's shell like a baby marsupial, desperate and vulnerable. Somehow she managed to keep her grip through the many hours of semi-consciousness, perhaps because of some primitive instinct inherited from a pre-human ancestor.

It was Butter's heart that was in the worst shape. In her clear moments, she worried her injured animals had not escaped the wall of water that had punished her village. She knew she'd see Mama again on Happa Now, where all people were reunited after their time on the island was done. Mama had promised. They would meet her papa, who had been bitten in two by a great white shark when Butter was much younger. Her best memories of Papa were of being tossed into the air and then gently caught in his strong, brown hands that were as big as taro leaves. She had trusted those hands, even though she remembered Mama telling him to be careful, not to throw her so high.

Papa had taught her to love lesser creatures, to assume responsibility for the sick and injured. He taught her not to fear poison urchins and venomous snakes, only to respect what made them hunters and defenders. She would never forget the Habu viper Papa had carefully curled into her lap when she was no more than three. It was early morning and Mama was still sleeping when he had woken her, told her to sit up and pull the blanket across her legs. The Habu was fat with eggs, her papa had explained, and probably as tall as she was when stretched out. Butter stroked its slick skin, was tickled by its darting tongue. Her papa crouched above her bedroll, smiling.

"It's beautiful," Butter whispered.

"She's very beautiful."

"Can I keep her? I'll take really good care of her."

"No, honey, she's just here for a visit. She belongs on the far side of the island, away from people. She must have gotten lost while hunting for food."

"Does she bite?" Butter ran her finger along the two horizontal stripes on the side of the viper's sleek head. Its tongue prodded the air, tasting these new surroundings.

"Yes, her bite is very dangerous." He reached under the snake in Butter's lap and gently lifted it, cradling the fat mother-to-be in his arms. "You want to come take her home?"

Papa had led them across the quiet island on an adventure.

The entire village was asleep as they ducked into the thick jungle and followed the narrow path toward the leeward side. The broad leaves and reaching vines were nourished well by the rich soil in the middle of the island. An elder woman who lived in the home next to Butter's family had been smiling when she warned the children not to stay in one place too long while playing hide and go seek here. She told the children the jungle grew so fast that you might get wrapped up in a hungry vine and never be found. Butter watched the back of her papa's head dodge the countless green tendrils that seemed to come from every direction. But he wasn't afraid. Not of the deadly snake cradled in his arms like a baby, and certainly not of the jungle.

The vegetation grew less dense and the sound of the ocean returned as the pair pushed through to the uninhabited side of the island. Birds woke and chirped good morning and Butter said good morning back. Papa knew everything about animals and quickly found a perfect new home for the snake family. He tucked the Habu into a shadowy stone crevasse at the base of a tall palm tree.

"Good protection for her babies and she can come out to sun herself." Papa looked up at the clear morning sky, hands on his naked hips. A few moments passed. "Mama explained that animals don't go to Happa Now?"

Butter nodded, trying to follow exactly where her papa was looking in the sky. Was he looking at Happa Now? Could grown-ups see it? Mama had gathered her against her droopy breasts, held her close for the sad talk. She had told Butter how the gods had other plans for animals, that their spirits were different than the spirits of people. Animals were left behind to enrich the earth, her mother had explained to a tearful daughter.

"That's why we're responsible for taking care of animals," her papa had said, still searching the early morning sky. "This is their one life, not like us. Not like people."

Butter knew she wasn't supposed to cry when the shark bit Papa in half, that it was nature's way, so she was careful to only share her grief with her patients. She believed the shark had made a terrible mistake, as it was Papa who had clouded the water with tantalizing blood from the fish he'd been spearing for supper. According to an elder who'd witnessed the attack, the shark had bitten him and then quickly disappeared, as if embarrassed by its awful blunder.

Butter had her papa's strong hands. They had saved her life thus far, having clamped down on the sea turtle shell, despite the aching snake bite, as the pair were battered and tossed by the angry wave. But her small hands were growing weak, and she sometimes lost her grip and slipped under the water in a daze. The burning saltwater in her lungs snapped her awake, alert but confused. Hacking and coughing, she'd heave herself back up on the turtle.

The turtle seemed to have a plan and Butter was in no condition to question or protest the direction his front flippers were leading them. Had it been two nights? Or three? Butter's long black hair covered her shoulders, splayed out over the side of her face to ward off the brutal sun. She slept in short fits filled with uneasy dreams that ended with the big wave's arrival.

What had angered the gods enough to wash away an entire island of people and animals? Was it something the grown-ups had done that she didn't know about? Butter didn't understand what possessed the men to drink the vile tasting wapa juice late into the night. In slurred, too loud voices, they would use curse words and tell stories of exploring beyond the sight of the island. Butter knew none of the men had ever paddled or sailed their skiffs out of sight of the island. You could never come back. Nobody ever had. Everyone knew you only left sight of the island when it was time for Happa Now. Had the men's cursing and lying provoked the gods?

But if there was no afterlife for animals, what plan could

there be? Butter had dug dozens of tiny graves for creatures too badly hurt or dead from old age. In her curiosity, Butter had exhumed the body of a parrot after nearly a year. She held the corpse in her tiny hands, brushing away sand. Is this what god's other plan looked like?

Butter accepted the job nursing injured animals back to health with fierce resolve. She was their last chance and demanded that they survive their ills and various broken parts. Let Franklin Roosevelt fall out of the tallest tree right on top of his fat wife; both still had the joys of Happa Now to look forward to. No such future awaited a mangled gecko or little brown kakerori bird with crushed wings.

Butter didn't question her mama's wisdom. Mama was the first woman ever entrusted with the third most important job on East Pukapuka, which was Keeper of the Books. Lesser only than the Tree Climber and Head Wapa Brewer, Mama was charged with maintaining the sixteen previously waterlogged books given to the people of East Pukapuka by a flying soldier during the age of great war.

The books were all bestsellers from before the war, the flying soldier had explained. They were the most important stories of the time, although the original Keeper of the Books had made the terrible mistake of washing them and then leaving the books out overnight to dry. A heavy tropical downpour had further melded the pages, leaving nothing more than sixteen hardcover bricks.

The first Keeper of the Books was quickly designated for an early, unscheduled trip to Happa Now, while many of the newborn babies were given the names on the book covers in an attempt to placate whatever gods were surely offended by such recklessness.

Noel Coward was the first child born after the literary desecration. Thomas Wolfe, Adolph Hitler, and Aldous Huxley soon followed, crying and screaming into life on East Pukapuka.

Years later, Butter's mama was named Anonymous, to honor the great author of a famous book called *Washington Merry-Go-Round.*

On the open sea, out of sight of land and therefore with little hope of ever returning, Butter once again nearly lost her grip as the sea turtle became agitated. His flipper strokes jerked her from side to side, changing their direction, tossing her small body across his hard shell. Butter closed her eyes and concentrated on using her wrists and forearms to take some of the pressure off her raw fingers and inflamed hand.

"It's okay, boy," Butter tried to say, but her voice didn't work. And the sea turtle wouldn't have been convinced anyway, not with the unrelenting metal beast bearing down on them from behind.

CHAPTER 8

Fueled by panic and determination, the Loggerhead sea turtle had never paddled faster in his life … except maybe on his hatching night, and those memories were jumbled and a half-century old. He and his hundred or so brothers and sisters had escaped from their leathery round eggs and paddled away from their clutch under cover of darkness.

Hatching night was the first time the sea turtle had heard his inner turtle voice. "Hurry up!" it had shouted, and there was no questioning the urgency of that command, especially for a brand new turtle in such a great big world.

"No, the other way!" came the next command, and the tiny turtle did an about-face, sneaking only the briefest of glances at his brothers and sisters. The waves the voice directed him toward were barely visible under the sliver of light from above. But there had been no mistaking the power behind the crashing breakers, for the sand under his still-soft belly had vibrated with each violent pounding.

"Hurry!" commanded the inner turtle voice, and his flippers had once again gone to work, slapping frantically. Ten meters to go and the sand had been wet and cool, almost refreshing.

Five meters and he was bursting through salty, leftover bubbles. *Good so far*, he'd thought, right before the sliver of moon was eclipsed by a black monster rising over what had suddenly become a suicide mission.

Chaos. The tiny sea turtle was upside down, spinning. The noise was so loud it seemed to be coming from inside his head and his shell. It boomed with such force that even his inner turtle voice was drowned out.

"Swim!" it might have said. Or maybe it was saying, "Good luck, I'm outta here, little buddy."

The baby sea turtle had decided to try swimming, flapping all four flippers with as much strength as he could muster, even though he'd lost any sense of direction. Expending so much energy, he wished he had taken a deeper breath before this black monster had taken hold of him, tossing and tumbling him every which way. The hatchling swam for dear life, straight ahead, worried that he'd been abandoned by the now silent inner voice. "Please help," he said, or was it his inner voice, its commands reduced to desperation? The turtle caught glimpses of light and pushed through the foaming, swirling water toward the flickering rays. The light appeared and disappeared again, each surge of darkness accompanied by an angry roar.

More waves crashed over the little turtle, but each subsequent attack was less disconcerting. The farther he swam into the cool water, the less effect the crashing waves had on his small body. When the black monster backed off, its voice reduced to a distant roar, he allowed himself to drift to the surface, his tiny head bobbing just out of the water. He took a few deep breaths and floated quietly, his body still, his flippers relaxing in the swaying current. Under the dim light, he noticed dozens of his brothers and sisters who had also come to the surface to rest after their ordeal with the black monster. But they were all floating upside down, asleep perhaps. He was also exhausted, but there was a rumble in his belly. The tiny sea turtle left his drifting siblings to their rest, the urge to explore for food suddenly overwhelming.

"Hurry up!" the inner turtle voice now exclaimed. A little more than fifty years later, a great monster was hunting him once again.

The sea turtle was all too aware of the damage this kind of beast could do. It was even bigger than the one that had cracked open his shell while he'd been foraging for food near the coral reef. One minute the coast had been clear, and he'd ducked under the surface for the shrimp he'd cornered. Then the beast's great bow had struck him. The shrimp had escaped unharmed, while the sea turtle was left bobbing semi-conscious in his blood cloud.

That's the day he'd first met the little human girl whose voice had made his pain bearable. Before his injury, the turtle had watched her work from out over the reef. She spent her days on the beach moving from spot to spot like a feeding bird, busily gathering what he assumed was nesting material.

After he was struck by the beast and left for dead, she'd come for him, pulled him into her strange home. And the girl had told him stories while his shell mended, his oversized head cupped in the warm embrace of her human touch. From deep inside, his turtle voice told him it was wrong to be on land, urged him to run away, but he fought the urge, struggled against his instinct. The human lay next to him inside the hull of a flooded skiff, in the shade of a puka tree. She cradled his powerful jaws, which could crack open a clam or mussel with little effort, in her small, soft hands. The turtle fell in love with her when she'd huddled next to him, making singing noises like the whales and dolphins out in the deep water. She was warm, as if she had her own tiny sun inside her body, radiating heat that allowed him to sleep despite the pain. The turtle had never met his mother, had never known any of his own hatchlings. Courtship and mating had always been unpleasant. The females were aloof and resistant, and there were battles with other males. For the past few seasons, the turtle hadn't bothered to leave his coral reef when prompted by the vague impulse to mate. Until he'd been struck by the beast and rescued by the girl, he'd wanted to be alone.

And now the girl needed him. She needed him to swim fast. Whether the beast was after him or the girl didn't matter; both their lives depended on him. Since she couldn't breathe under water, and land was nowhere in sight, their fates were entwined. It was up to him to save the girl who had nursed his wound, kept him from being food for the sharks and the bottom scavengers. The thought made him cringe, and he found another gear.

He paddled straight ahead, just as he'd done to escape the black monster on hatching night. He found a rhythm with his strokes, which also kept the girl from having to struggle to hold on.

An hour passed. It was filled with the constant noise of the beast and the horrible reek of burning air. The monster's exhales were thick and black, poisonous. They fouled the air around the sea turtle, perhaps the evil creature's method of stunning its prey.

The sea turtle paddled and paddled, but his energy was flagging, his inner turtle becoming weaker. "When you stop, the beast will eat you." It no longer spoke with any sense of urgency. Its words were now presented as statements of facts. "It will swallow you whole and then turn on the kind human girl. The pain is growing inside you, devouring your last bit of strength."

"I have to save her," the sea turtle told the voice, but there was a throbbing pain deep within his shell that seemed to build with each stroke of his yellow and white dappled paddles.

"Do you feel that?" the inner turtle voice asked, as the pain began to bloom like a field of algae in a warm sea. "Your time is almost done and you are about to die."

"I have to save her." The turtle again searched the sky for signs of approaching night. The great beast still raged. The girl held on. The sea turtle could sense the water being pushed forward just behind him, as if reaching, hungering for them.

And then the darkness the sea turtle had hoped would descend on them, giving them an opportunity to hide, did seem to come. Its silent blackness enveloped everything in his world, and for just an instant, he was back in his egg, buried deep in the warm sand. The sea turtle's final heartbeat echoed quietly through his gnarled shell, mended not long ago by the loving hands of the girl still clinging to his back.

One final message came from his inner turtle voice: "Time to go home."

And the brave old sea turtle slowly and quietly sank to the floor of the ocean, down among the bottom feeders.

CHAPTER 9

Captain Jesus Dobby was not a cruel man. Not entirely, anyway. Long ago, in fact, his mother had gone to great lengths to make certain her son did not grow up to be a womanizing, alcohol swilling, no-good louse like his father. Dobby—born on Christmas Day, a bit more than a half-century earlier—had managed to avoid two of those traps.

Dobby owned the rust-coated Gypsy Dancer. He would troll the islands and vast open waters of the South Pacific for salvage, occasionally encountering day trippers who ran out of gas and needed a tow. He'd set the price according to how much cash they had in their wallets. Business was business. If they wanted a better deal, they were more than welcome to continue floundering; maybe they'd get lucky, maybe not.

Dobby figured his mother would be happy to see him gainfully employed. He could also more or less claim he never hit a woman—unless it was the last resort and all other options had been explored, including locking them in a closet or tying them to the bed posts. And those times were rare; the only women he associated with were prostitutes who had a financial stake in tolerating his more unsavory requests.

Dobby owned homes on three different islands, little more than fold-up cots under tin walls and thatched roofs. In exchange for some flotsam booty upon his return, neighbors would use hand-made brooms once a month to whisk the spiders and spook out the fox bats.

Although born in Amarillo, Texas, Dobby was a citizen of Tokelau, of British Pitcairn, and the famous whale-watching island of Niue. The majority of his nights were spent under the stars, though, on a bedroll tucked against the gunwale of the Gypsy Dancer's main deck. If the air was still, he'd drape a mosquito net from the winch above. Dobby slept much better rocked by the sea, which also offered ease and proximity for the late night pissing and vomiting resulting from his love affair with locally bottled hooch. Staring up at the swaying stars, Dobby drunkenly whistled one half of the duet from the second act of a Verdi opera, a tune of revenge after poor Rigoletto received a severe ass-beating upon trying to save his daughter from the Duke. A cherished memory, a magical night his mother had snuck them downtown to a summer stock production. She'd held his hand through all three acts just like a grown up date, and he never once fell asleep.

By now keeping pace with the turtle-girl barely required cutting a wake. Dobby knew it was just a matter of time before she surrendered. The creature was clearly unable to submerge, and despite the relentless strokes of its front flippers, her head lolled back and forth. Dobby knew the thing was more valuable alive than dead, and he was worried about swimming it to death or running it over. Now, in the growing shadow of the Dancer's wheel house, Dobby fantasized about the bidding war for this exotic critter, maybe among the big shot heavies at the Starkist Tuna plant on Pago Pago. *A thousand dollars! Ten thousand dollars! Do I hear twenty-thousand for this fantastic, one of a kind aberration from the darkest depths? I have thirty-thousand from the wealthy gentleman in the first row! Do I hear forty?*

The chase lasted into the third bottle of rum, when the turtle-girl surprised Dobby by dipping under the surface of the nearly calm sea. Dobby hit the engine's kill switch and fell off his bar stool, cracking his forehead on a hard plastic Easter Island moai head he'd long ago pulled from the ocean and kept as a silent companion. Dobby stumbled out of the wheel house and down the bridge ladder, snatching the throwing net as he climbed over the H-bitt to peer down into the shadowy water.

Nothing. Just deep blue sea and the sound of trickling water from the automatic bilge pump and the ticking twin diesel engines. Dobby cupped both hands around his eyes, but the alcohol made surrendering his hand-holds dangerous as he leaned out over the bow.

A few large bubbles broke the surface directly below, and Dobby decided the grappling hook was his only chance to at least haul in a carcass. Better alive than dead, but better dead than nothing, he drunkenly reasoned. He climbed back over the H-bitt to retrieve the ominous, four-pronged hook and line from its home on top of the capstan.

The captain worked quickly and methodically, as is only possible for the most seasoned drunks. He dropped the heavy hook over the bow, then worked it from port to starboard, jigging deeper and deeper until the round bottom knob struck what had to be the turtle-girl under fifteen feet of water. He pulled in a foot of rope, then dropped under the target and jerked the hook back up, snagging his prey. He brought her up hand over hand, careful not to mangle his trophy too badly, although if he did, there was always that saltwater fish taxidermist on Tokelau he drank with—the one who could work absolute wonders.

When the creature broke the surface, Dobby's heart sank like a thousand-pound anchor. Fortunately the prong of the grappling hook had snared a thin belt around the turtle-girl's naked waist and hadn't torn up her flesh. But the shell had come off, leaving what looked like a regular human kid. The thing began coughing up foaming water, as her nearly weightless body dangled a few feet over the sea, slowly rotating.

Dobby considered throwing the frigging thing back, just letting the hook drop and being done with this sorry bullshit. How much fuel had he burned? It would be fine if the hook dislodged from the girl's woven belt, and screw it if it didn't. Let the sea have the entire goddamn mess. Minutes ago, he'd been on the verge of the payday he'd hunted for thirty years. This thing would have a boatload of trouble attached to it.

"It's a turtle-girl that lost its goddamn turtle parts." Captain Dobby spit a huge wad of phlegm skyward, and then reeled her on board.

CHAPTER 10

The exotic television island invaded Dante's dreams with textures and smells, the cries of hidden birds, and constant motion. The images collected from his nightly visions filled the void left by whatever had brought him to this bed. They became his reality, his past and what he more and more frequently hoped would be his future.

It was the motion that triggered the most longing. Every swaying palm frond contrasted with his immobility. While his legs and arms were frozen and still, the liquid rolling of the sea teemed with life and possibility.

Shortly before each sunset Dante walked the narrow pathway to the leeward side of the island and stepped carefully into the calmer water, keeping an eye out for stonefish and prickly urchins. Waist deep, he'd lunge forward and begin taking long freestyle strokes, as the coral and rock bottom fell away. He'd grab quick breaths every few strokes, making short kicks, while keeping a heading due east, directly away from shore.

Most evenings Dante would glide perhaps a thousand yards before the island disappeared behind the chop of the sea, at which point he would stop swimming and tread water. He reveled in the lingering sense of danger. If he lost his bearings, he'd have only one chance to get back to dry land. But being out in the middle of the vast undulating water put his strong, athletic body to the test. He felt he could tread in this spot for hours, if not days. Every muscle was working, it seemed, warm and burning fuel slowly, like the well-oiled parts of an efficient machine.

As the first stars appeared in the eastern sky, Dante turned and began swimming away from them, back to the island in the direction of the setting sun. Just past the reef, which circled the entire island a few feet beneath the surface of the water, Dante heard the cries of a child. It was the voice of a young girl, who between sobs was calling out names that made no sense to Dante. They seemed to be the names of famous politicians and authors. This portion of Dante's dream distressed him, setting off far away beeps and alarms and switching on bright lights in places that were better left dark.

And when things made no sense to Dante's injured brain, it did its best to simply shut off for a while.

"Wheeler, Dante, here in bed four, sports related traumatic brain injury," a god-like voice boomed from above. Dante was no longer submerged in dark water, but was lying helpless and prone in a brightly lit room. He listened to the complicated, supposedly important words coming from this god: "biochemical cascades that occur in the days following … free radical overload … excessive release of neurotransmitter glutamate … dysfunction of mitochondria … pass me a banana … injured axon in the brain's white matter …"

Dante wished the god would shut up, head back for the door and cut the lights, allow him his peace.

"The prognosis for survival was maybe two percent at the outset," the god said. "Although prior physical condition was a strong contributing factor."

"How long since the incident?" This was a softer female voice, perhaps one of the god's angels.

"Incident?" wondered Dante. "Two percent of what?"

"Thirty-two weeks," said the god. "CT shows epidural hematoma, and there were epidural bleeds in the spinal column. Brain activity is strong, which is hard to explain. Moderate to extensive atrophy has occurred."

The god seemed to be shuffling papers. "Any questions?"

With the middle finger of his right hand, Dante began tapping frantically, his spastic version of Morse code. He certainly had questions.

"What is that?" asked the angel, and Dante opened his eyes, strained to catch a glimpse of the gentle spirit. He slowed the pace of his tapping.

"I'm lost," Dante tried pleading with his eyes and his middle finger. "I'm lost and I want to go home."

The god loomed over Dante's bed, slowly peeling back the thin blanket to expose his waggling digit, exhausted from tapping and the recent ocean swim.

"It sounds like he's trying to communicate." The angel's voice was hesitant, so Dante again increased the pace, tapping as hard and emphatically as he could. "Listen. Do you hear the pattern? Dash. Then dot, dot, dot, dash. Could it be Morse code?"

The god scoffed at his assistant's suggestion. "Ridiculous," he proclaimed. "The young man is, for all practical purposes, a one hundred-sixty pound prairie turnip."

"But with strong brain activity, right?" Clearly the angel wanted to believe, reaching down to hold Dante's right wrist, feeling his busy tendons with her light touch. "Isn't it possible this is a conscious effort?"

"Simple reflex." The god scribbled in Dante's chart, which he then returned to its hook at the foot of his bed.

Had the god been a Boy Scout—or even if he'd just happened to catch the same television biography of Samuel Morse that Dante had watched two nights ago—he might have recognized the simple request in Dante's feverish message. Some file in the damaged brain of the gravely injured ski racer had saved a bit of information it deemed might be useful later on. The dash, then dot, dot, dot, dash he was tapping combined to form two letters which, together, would have solved all of Dante Wheeler's crushing problems of the moment. His brain was one hundred percent certain the letters were his ticket away from this sterile, colorless world. His link to what his life had been.

Dante's eyes finally found the beautiful, round face of the angel, who was now peeking over the shoulder of the god. The angel's hair was pulled back from her face, exposing cherubic cheeks and the dark frames of thick, heavy glasses.

Dash, then dot, dot, dot, dash, he repeated to the angel, forming the letters T and V. Dante's body might have been reduced to a turnip state, but his mind pleaded for the television, absolutely certain his real life was on the tiny speck of an island in the South Pacific featured on channel sixty-three.

"East Pukapuka," he tried to tell the angel with his eyes. "Help me get home."

CHAPTER 11

Butter wondered if her journey to Happa Now had begun. Her body rotated slowly. She was waking from a nightmare, expecting comfort from familiar things, her mother's soft touch and calming voice. They would go together to meet her father, who'd hug her tight, then grab her under her armpits and throw her high in the air.

Butter's body jerked hard, and then jerked again, but it wasn't from her father's strong hands. A terrible voice boomed nasty curses. "Damn it all! God fugging damn this shit!"

Her belt was too tight on her hips and something hard was digging at her lower back. She was jerked twice more, saw the rusty bow of a big metal boat.

The grunting voice bellowed more curses as she spilled onto a wood deck like a fish from a net. "Too damn old to sell as a baby and too young for that Viti Levu whoremaster. Just fugg me and be done, for Christ's sake." Most of the words were her language, but they made no sense.

The man scooped her off the hard floor and carried her across the boat, gently settling her on a musky bedroll. He put a hand to her forehead and shook his head, making clicking sounds with his tongue. "Something bit you real good." He held out her swollen right hand, examining the bite marks. He crowded next to her, blurry behind her drooping eyelids, just a shadowy silhouette stinking of wapa juice. He examined her arms for more bites. "Must be what gave you this fever. Tsunamis make animals do queer things, gets them real ornery. Their homes get wrecked and they ain't got food, so they start actin' all crazy. You got rabies, girl?"

The captain had no idea how terrible the startled Habu viper had felt for striking out at the girl from his jumbled nest. He'd immediately withdrawn his fangs, done his best to retract any poison. She had been so kind, had tended to his burning wound after a village boy had chopped him in two for no reason. He'd been sunning himself on a smooth rock, sleepily enjoying the feeling of a half-digested frog in his belly. Then wham, out of nowhere, the machete sliced down through the air and left him writhing in searing pain, staring at his own twitching, bisected tail.

"What's wrong with boys?" Butter had asked her mother, refusing to leave the snake's side after stitching the wound closed. Her bare belly was still smeared with gore from cradling the mutilated creature and sharing her body's warmth as she rushed it back to her makeshift hospital. "How could they do this to a living thing?"

"Men and boys are the same, Butter." Her mother had brought her a warm bowl of mahi-mahi, boiled with ginger root and mirin, but she ignored the food. How could she eat? Her mama brushed matted hair from her forehead, away from tear-streaked cheeks. "Men and boys do things without thinking. It's their nature."

"Like spear fishing when sharks are in the water?" She was always saddest about losing her father when forced to witness the life and death struggle of an innocent animal. It was unfair that so much weight was piled on her fatigued shoulders.

"Yes, like swimming with sharks, honey."

Butter knew the Habu might be the offspring of the pregnant snake she and her father had returned to the east side of the island when she was three. Habus were an endangered species on East Pukapuka because their bite was so deadly. Anyone spotting one would run for a machete.

Kneeling over her naked body, the captain squeezed fresh water from a dirty rag onto Butter's parched lips. Her eyes fluttered open, but just barely, and she still couldn't focus.

"You been in the water a long time." The captain put the cool rag to her steaming forehead. "You got a bad fever, little one. You're on fire."

Butter watched his wide, hovering shadow, eyed his great hairy halo. She was terribly cold, could feel her teeth begin to chatter. "Where am I?" she wanted to ask, but the fever had dropped a heavy cloud. "Cold," she tried to say. "I'm very, very cold."

"Which one of these islands you get washed from?" The captain loomed closer, and it didn't seem like he was questioning her, just talking out loud to himself while inspecting her face. "Nothin' unusual in them cheekbones, just another mutt savage. I suspect everybody else that didn't have a goddamn turtle to hold onto drowned."

"My turtle," Butter mouthed. Where was her turtle? She tried turning her head to look, but white flashes of lightning erupted and made her give up. "My turtle," she said, pleading to the shadowy man.

"Jesus Dobby." The man thumped his open hand to his hairy chest. "Me Jesus," he loudly repeated, as if she was hard of hearing instead of feverish and nearly drowned.

"Jesus," she tried saying, her lips forming the word. Butter's fevered mind forgot the missing turtle and searched for the reason the name was familiar. "Jesus," she tried to say again, but a liquid blackness rushed in and her eyes rolled back in her head. The deck of the boat went dark, but she could still hear the slap of waves and the distant cry of sea birds. There was a tapping sound—like a bird trying to dig bugs from tree bark—that she eventually recognized as the chattering of her own teeth.

"Yeah, that's right, girl." The man's knees popped as he leaned his weight and bad smell even closer, stroking her cheek with a rough, callused hand. "You just call me Jesus, or maybe Mister Jesus. Who knows, if all your people are dead, maybe I'll keep you on as a deckhand for a while. You can earn your keep 'til I can swap you as a house girl. Even the dumbest savage can learn to swab a floor."

To Butter, the booming voice of Jesus provided a thread of hope from her lost life. Her village elders had spoken of a man named Jesus, recounting stories from the flying soldier. Jesus was the son of a great god and possessed his own magical powers to heal, although this man smelled an awful lot like the toilet pit after a heavy rain. Butter recalled the thick book written about him that her mother guarded. It was the fattest of them all, which meant it was the most important. But it would have washed away in the big wave, as lost and dead as her injured animals and everything else that had been her life.

Butter was overwhelmed by all the sad thoughts. She gave in to the darkness, the heat, and the cold. She had no fight left, no will to think, or even to live. And all the pain and mourning thankfully lifted, leaving her completely hollow. She slept, dreamless, for a week.

CHAPTER 12

The fifteen-meter Julius Caesar had been working as a small commercial fishing boat until it was hijacked by two drunken small-time Fijian crooks. The keys had been left in the ignition, so it was just a matter of untying a few knots, throwing her into reverse. A new scourge of the South Pacific was born.

Ratu and Jope were now valiant pirates, hard at work lugging their spoils, having recently pillaged the JetPoint Supacentre—one of Fiji's largest supermarkets—after a cleaning lady had grabbed a smoke and left the loading dock door ajar. This bit of fortune occurred when they'd cut through a back alley after selling two bags of crank for gas money for the boat. They had lingered behind the Supacentre when Jope noticed one of the rooms in the cat house didn't have a curtain pulled all the way down. Some cash, a quick glimpse of naked boobies, and they were all but invited inside a closed store filled with every imaginable item.

Luck seemed to be popping up everywhere for the twenty year old bandits. Forgotten keys and unlocked doors every which way they turned.

In near pitch dark, Ratu and Jope piled their ill-gotten gains onto the deck of the moored Julius Caesar, an eerie glow emanating from the tiny dials of some three hundred Timex Indiglo watches. An orange tint reflected from the dozens of bags of shanghaied Cheetos, sustenance for their upcoming high-seas enterprise. They had moved the fully equipped charter fishing boat to a public dock on the shadier side of town, making sure not to leave the keys in it while continuing their crime spree.

What better next step than to parley their fortune on the wide-open eastern waters, out where the luxury yachts floated exposed and unprotected. It had been Ratu's idea, copycatted from recent newspaper stories warning high-end yacht owners of a rash of strong-armed robberies by moonlight raiding parties.

"Read the middle part again," begged Jope, a young man who—while suffering through his early childhood years being beaten by his father and selling five dollar bags of dope to backpacking tourists—had never picked up the art of reading.

"Okay, Jope, lemme see," Ratu said as he crouched over the wrinkled newspaper article on the bare wood floor of their shithole, one-room efficiency. " 'The pirates came aboard as we slept and I woke to a heavy blade pressed across my throat by a large black male. I've never been so frightened in my life,' fifty-seven year old Stuart Bendellman, a retired venture capitalist now living in New Caledonia, told police."

"Yeah, man!" cheered Jope. "Adventure communist gotta be some dumbass white guy, don't ya think, Ratu? I bet he never wanna see another brother long as he lives! You think the heavy blade was a sword? I bet it was a big sword with a curve in it. The pirate coulda gone chop, chop, and that white guy woulda been hamburger. I'm hungry."

"And there's lots more big yachts out there, Jope," Ratu said to his best friend. "All of them sitting ducks, beggin' to be plucked."

"Read it again, Ratu!" Jope was so excited that he peed himself a little as he reached into his cut off jeans for another small bag of crank. It was tough to get ahead in the world when you snorted most of your product. "Read the middle part again."

Out at the dock on their heisted boat, Ratu battened down the watches and stowed the Cheetos, then climbed up to the pilot house to start the engine. Jope was in the seat to his right. They headed due north before realizing the navigational map was upside down.

"Easier if we had one of them maps that says 'you are here,' with a big red arrow." Jope was holding the map sideways, trying to make sense of the legend. "Look, it says we're like ten centimeters from where you wanna go. We could take my dick, just walk on it like it was a gangplank!"

"You doin' too much crank. Fuckin' up your head."

"I couldn't find the Cheetos." Jope turned the map over, examining the blank side closely.

"What are you looking for?"

"Maybe it's a treasure map."

"It's just a regular map." Ratu steered the pirate ship away from the Suva city lights, avoiding other boat traffic.

"I won a gift certificate for CDs on a Cap'n Crunch treasure map. I took the box to the store, but they said it was real old, no good anymore."

"That doesn't sound fair."

"It's okay, I don't got a CD player, anyway. But then the store manager says 'Hey, I know you. You was in here shoplifting two days ago.' I said, 'No way, man, it was a guy looked just like me.' Big dude starts coming around the counter, saying 'You stay right there,' just like he said two days ago."

"Did you get anything good?"

"Couple of CDs, but I don't got a CD player."

It was a three-hour, teeth-rattling trek over choppy seas to Makutu, then another sixty kilometers southeast to where luxury yachts were often seen adrift at night, following their long days of pure sailing in the wide-open waters. Paths bisected by lowly fishing vessels, the multi-million dollar jewels tacked slowly, artfully, then came about in tight, impatient arcs, sails gorging with the weight of the wind as they began to run full-out, slicing the sea with abandon.

The pirates approached an enormous main-topsail schooner, its elegant eastern pine and red oak hull gleaming in starlight. The newbie buccaneers snuck up as stealthily as they could, despite the diesel engine that blatted from cheap fuel and the lack of any recent tuning.

"Now! Kill it now!" Ratu called up to his partner and turned back to the closing ship.

Jope killed the engine, let momentum carry the Julius Caesar the final quiet meters, as Ratu leaned out over the bow railing and absorbed the impact of the exquisite hull with both hands.

"Yeah, yeah," Jope hissed, practically diving feet first down the ladder from the pilot house.

By boarding the sleepy yacht so brazenly, with no plan and no idea of how many armed bodyguards the wealthy owner might have in his employ, the pair was riding their recent luck. As they jumped over the side railing and onto the shadowy foredeck, the pirates brandished the matching track and field starter pistols they'd snatched from the JetPoint Supacentre sporting goods aisle. Both, dressed in old denim cut-offs, were shirtless and bare-footed, moving quickly for cover behind the large, double capstan, the drum-like machine used to wind in ropes. Their black skin helped them blend into the dark horizon beyond.

"Everybody's sound asleep," Ratu guessed, as they huddled at eye level in the wheelhouse of the tethered Julius Caesar.

"How many you think?"

"Could be none or could be forty, who knows? We just gotta take charge, tell them we'll shoot anyone right between the eyes if they don't do what we say."

"My gun ain't real." Jope turned the realistic looking pistol over in his hands. "I think it only shoots caps. Did you bring any caps? Mine got all wet."

"We don't need real guns. We don't want nobody getting shot."

"If they have guns, we'll get shot."

"Nah, no real guns on a big boat like this. These are rich white people. They maybe got a spear gun with their scuba gear, and a couple of flare guns."

"I seen a guy who got shot with a flare gun." Jope nearly dropped the gun; his fingers seemed to have taken on a jittery life of their own. The drugs had left him a paranoid, nervous wreck. Committing his first act of piracy on the open sea had pushed him right to the edge. "It was worse than a real gun, Ratu. He caught fire. I don't ever wanna catch fire like that."

"Stop worrying about everything. This is a piece of cake."

"His woman ran off with a big, fat bastard from Labasa," Jope continued, the pair still hunkering behind the double capstan. "Got drunk down at Timi's place and pulled the damn thing out of his pants. Was waving it around, saying he gonna kill that fucker who stole his woman. Went off by accident, ricocheted off the bar and hit him in the guts."

"Oh, yeah, I heard about that."

"Place burned right to the ground." Jope shook his head. "Poor guy looked like a burned up marshmallow."

"Okay, so no problem." Ratu gently patted his friend on the back. "Listen, you see a flare gun, you leave it alone, okay?"

"Spear gun no good, too. I once heard about this guy …"

"Look, there aren't any guns on this boat, okay?" Ratu tried to calm his shaking partner. The longer they waited, the greater the risk of someone wandering up on deck for some night air. "These rich white people have butlers and nannies, not guards. They got maybe one or two babysitters taking turns making sure no birds start building a nest anywhere. Nothin' to worry about."

"You promise, Ratu?"

"C'mon, Jope, we gotta find the companionway down to the quarters." Ratu rose to his feet, his starter pistol again held out in the lead. "It's time for us to get rich, Jope. No guns to worry about. Follow me and stick real close."

The Fijian pirates' run of good luck was about to be seriously tested. The fore hatch clicked open three meters ahead, its well-lubricated hinges perfectly silent. One of the two highly-trained babysitters on board was lifting it from beneath with the top of his head. Both of the man's hands were busy steadying the AK-47 that took aim squarely in the middle of the first pirate's chest.

The babysitter squeezed the trigger.

CHAPTER 13

Dicky Miller's mood had swung a hundred-eighty degrees since opening his mail at lunchtime. The article he'd submitted to *Publications of the Astronomical Society of the Pacific*, a prestigious monthly scientific journal, had once again been rejected, this time with a brief handwritten note saying: "Please stop submitting this. Thanks!"

Miller's article claimed something fishy was going on inside Earth's moon. The amateur astronomer's article broke the news that the shadowy Whipple crater, the second closest crater to the moon's North Pole, was actually a 15.7 kilometer hatchway to a hollow storage area. Miller's paranoid schizophrenia—medicated only by an occasional Bayer Aspirin—had fueled the belief that Pakistani leaders were in cahoots with an alien race of cosmic collectors. The aliens were hoarding items from Earth, and the Pakistani government was the enabler, allowing the remote mountains of the Hunza Valley to be used as a staging area for stealthy raids on Earth's treasures. Missing were entire Japanese skyscrapers, natural monuments from North Africa, and whole herds of Australian beef cattle. In his article Miller conceded he'd only just begun to tap the depth of the conspiracy, but he had thousands of slightly blurred photographs taken with his Meade LX90 telescope showing the comings and goings from the lunar portal.

Miller didn't help his chances for publication by writing the twenty-seven thousand word article backwards, aided by his bathroom mirror, entirely in red pencil (aliens have a hard time seeing the color red), lest it be intercepted and fall into the wrong hands.

Miller was standing over his telescope's tripod in the backyard of his one bedroom rental home in Borroloola, Australia, a remote fishing village in the Northern Territory. His mood of bleak rejection had shifted to elation when one of the other phenomena he'd been observing came zooming across the night sky in all its infinite glory. He watched the first flares of what he had christened in a letter to The Astronomical Society of the Pacific as the Camel Meteor Shower.

Miller had named the event for the Camelopardalis, or Giraffe constellation, whose nearest star, GJ 445, is seventeen and a half light years from Earth, off at the far edge of the Milky Way. As a middle school student he'd learned that meteoroids burning up in Earth's atmosphere don't really come from distant constellations but are named for the general direction from which they initially appeared. It would take our fastest rocket ship about a quarter-million years to reach GJ 445, so nobody would be heading there any time soon, Miller's sixth grade science teacher had long ago explained.

Dicky Miller had plotted a small comet's trajectory, calculated to the very minute when Earth would intersect its debris field. And the Camel Meteor Shower was right on time, precisely as forecast. Everything had unfolded perfectly for Miller for what may have been the first time in his life. Except that three weeks earlier he'd forgotten to mail the letter documenting his prediction. The stamped envelope meticulously documenting his astronomic event sat under the sugar bowl in his sparse kitchen. It would remain undiscovered for days or maybe weeks—until he ran out of sweetener and took the bowl for a refill.

Across the South Pacific, stories would be passed down through generations about how the night sky had gone brighter than any mid-summer day, forever blinding those islanders unlucky enough to be looking up when one particularly speedy piece of meteor ignited in Earth's atmosphere.

On the small coral island of Tarluga-Ben, a woman gave birth at the very instant the kilometers-long meteor trail was at its brightest. The duteous native islanders deemed the baby their future king, a special-delivery from the Celestial Gods to be waited on hand and foot. Up until his thirteenth birthday, the revered King-in-Waiting was given any of the other island children's toys he showed so much as a fleeting interest in, was never criticized or corrected, and was bathed in constant praise. A week shy of coronation, and with a National Geographic reporter and photographer recently arrived, the horribly spoiled, mollycoddled adolescent brat set fire to the community toilets during a petulant fit over the temperature of his coconut milk. The stinking destruction occasioned a meeting of the elders, who reassessed the true meaning of the supernatural flash in the sky. "It was the sun which had fallen from the sky, and the little bastard's birth was mere coincidence," proclaimed the oldest. No one bothered to point out that the sun had seemed just fine that next morning, and every day of the subsequent thirteen years. The prospect of a sixty or seventy year reign under the evil little reprobate who hadn't thought twice about torching the village johns trumped astral superstition, hands down.

On the deck of the shadow-filled luxury schooner, the pirates' luck held out, despite their being tremendously outgunned. Their cap gun starter pistols would only really be considered weapons if they were tossed with exceptional force, and even then only if they hit someone in the eye. On the other hand, the schooner's armed babysitters' AK-47 rounds traveled at a much deadlier sixty-seven hundred meters per second. The three meters separating them would have taken almost no time at all, and the damage would have been significant and permanent—the pirate's chest being much softer than the bullet about to be fired.

But eighty kilometers above the open ocean something smaller than the AK-47 bullet, traveling a hundred times faster, was about to cause a major hullabaloo all over the South Pacific. There were thousands of pieces of space dust in this debris field, but one burned hundreds of times brighter than all the rest. This speck of dust was roughly the size of a dragon fruit seed, but with a meteorite, it wasn't size that mattered, it was speed.

The tiny rock that hurtled through the vacuum of space at seventy kilometers per second, making for an incredibly bright display as it burned in the friction of Earth's atmosphere, was a complete surprise to the luxury schooner's heavily armed babysitters, who knew nothing about astronomy and couldn't care less.

The pirates' good fortune held, for the brilliant flash of the meteor simultaneously burned the retinas of both armed schooner babysitters, the second one having assumed the flank position, also leveling an AK-47 at the first pirate. Whether their blindness was permanent or temporary quickly became immaterial, because both highly trained killing machines stumbled overboard and sank from the weight of their bullet proof vests.

"What just happened?" Ratu said. He thought he might have seen a pair of ninjas jump overboard without resurfacing. Rich white folk were indeed strange creatures.

"I think something blew up in the sky." Jope searched the stars above. It had all happened behind their backs, causing the schooner deck to be filled momentarily with frightening, disconcerting shadows. "Maybe a UFO?"

"No, I mean what just jumped off the boat?"

"I didn't see nothing."

"C'mon." Ratu waved the starter pistol and Jope followed. "Hoist the Jolly Roger. Time to do some serious pillaging, Matey!"

"What's a Jolly Roger?" Carefully stepping over a coil of furling line, Jope let Ratu lead him into the darkness.

"You're a shitty pirate," Ratu said to his friend, without any real malice, as the pair climbed down the nearest hatch and into the belly of the deserted yacht.

CHAPTER 14

The fifteen-meter Julius Caesar was loosely moored to the swanky, forty-two meter schooner and doing one helluva job on its expensive hull. Each swell caused rough kisses, nicks and dents that would be an absolute bear for the owners to have buffed out.

"What was that?" Jope screeched at the noise of the bumping boats. He lunged into Ratu, who was scrambling to find a light switch.

"Must be goblins." Ratu was all too familiar with his friend's crippling fear of the dark. He'd also had to contend with Jope's fear of heights, cats, loud noises and open spaces. It was a lot of fear to overcome for any pirate worth his salt.

Coincidentally, it was Julius Caesar himself, Emperor of Rome, who was credited with coining the phrase "worth his salt," since his soldiers were paid, in part, with rations of salt. If a soldier was not up to snuff, he was said to be not worth his salt.

Ratu and Jope knew a little about this, having once snuck into a matinee of Marlon Brando's version of xx*Julius Caesar,* each packing two fat joints, their own two-liter bottles of beer, but no popcorn.

"How come everything is black and white?" Jope had asked twenty minutes into the movie, the first joint and half the beer gone.

"They didn't have color back then."

Jope had pondered this for a minute. "How'd they know when the light turned green?"

It was Jope's shaking hand that found the light switch first, after a second and third loud bump in the night shook the walls and floor of the big schooner. A moan escaped the skinny black pirate, and if his starter pistol had been a real gun, he most definitely would have shot off a few of his own toes.

"Okay, good," Ratu said of Jope's light switch discovery. "Hey, what you make of them packages?"

The oversized forward stateroom was nearly three-quarters filled with neatly stacked brown, brick-shaped bundles. As small-time crooks and occasional drug salesmen—mostly to island-hopping backpackers—Ratu and Jope had a pretty good idea of what was wrapped up in the bricks. And they'd seen enough cop videos of drug smuggling busts, always a little bummed because it meant the prices would be going up and their profit margins going down.

"Can't be." Jope's eyes were wide.

"No way, man." Ratu's eyes were even wider.

They stood side-by-side, starter pistols hanging limp in right hands, trying to decide whether this was the greatest thing ever, or if they maybe should slowly back out the door and scurry back onto the Julius Caesar and forget what they'd just found. Both knew this was some big time shit.

"That's gotta be a billion dollars worth of coke, Ratu."

"Not a billion. A billion would sink dis big boat. Maybe half a billion."

Ratu stepped forward, away from the door, and plucked a package from the top of the thick wall it formed. He felt its heft and then used the sight knob on the barrel of his starter pistol to rip through the brown paper and plastic inner wrapping. A thick white powder spewed from the wound; both men greedily jabbed index fingers and rubbed their gums.

"That's blow, yeah?" Jope asked, and Ratu shook his head in agreement.

Jope bent over the bag, closed one nostril with his cocaine-coated index finger and snorted what would be a year's worth of wages had he'd ever held a legitimate job back home. Ratu used his own index finger to do the same thing.

"I can't feel my tongue," Ratu tried to say. His entire mouth had gone completely numb from the nearly pure cocaine. The black chests of both pirates looked like chocolate doughnuts sprinkled with powdered sugar. Their noses were as white as their eyes.

Then Jope's own oral paralysis took hold with pins and needles as the pair stood looking at each other, unable to communicate.

"They'll kill us," Jope tried saying. "Please, let's leave this shit and get out of here fast."

"Yeah, let's grab as much as we can," Ratu attempted to say, but he sounded an awful lot like the old drunk guy from Ono who'd fallen off the Suva peer and hadn't been pulled up from the bottom of the harbor for a good ten minutes. The poor old guy sat on the curb of the main drag these days, occasionally making motor boat sounds.

Before Jope could reach the door, Ratu had scooped an armload full of bricks and was making motor boat sounds for Jope to come help. The high quality cocaine allowed the fearful pirate to overcome his clamoring inner voice.

"They gonna chop you up and use you for chum," Jope's inner voice warned.

"I can't hear you," Jope answered, sticking one finger in his ear and humming, while Ratu pulled down bricks to cart another load out to their boat.

"I didn't say nothing," Ratu said.

"They gonna chop him up, too," said the inner voice. "Chop, chop, chop!"

Forty minutes later, the planet's newest millionaire drug king-pins were pushing off in the Julius Caesar, heading out into the deepest waters. Paranoid and sweating freely from doses of cocaine of such high quality that it would have killed men with weaker hearts, the pirate duo stood on the pilot deck and began singing the only pirate song they knew. It was from another old black and white movie.

> Fifteen men on a dead man's chest
> Yo ho ho and a bottle of rum.

Because of their numb mouths, the song came out sounding like a couple of motor boats badly in need of tune-ups.

CHAPTER 15

When the meteor blasted across the sky, Butter was awake on the Gypsy Dancer's weathered main deck, gazing up at the stars. Wherever Jesus was taking them, it was sure different from her island, she thought, rubbing her eyes and trying to blink away the ghost images. The sky over her home never caught fire like this at night.

She worried about her old sea turtle, but was afraid to ask Jesus if he'd seen him or knew where he'd gone. She hoped his shell stayed strong and that he'd find a good home near a safe reef. While she didn't think the kindest man who'd ever walked Earth—as Jesus had been described in the flying soldier's stories—would have caught and cooked him up, she didn't feel capable of handling any more horrible news right now. A pair of older teenage boys had teased her when she'd first lugged the bleeding turtle out of the sea and up the beach to her hospital. Stopping in front of her row of cages under the big puka tree, they'd pretended to sharpen their machetes, licking their lips and comically rubbing their stomachs in big round circles. Not so funny when the sharp piece of coral bounced off the forehead of one of the boys.

"If your father wasn't stupid enough to swim with sharks, he'd beat you senseless for that." Blood poured from the small cut. Butter knew head wounds bled like crazy. Didn't matter if you were human, bird, or lizard. She wished her mama, the Keeper of the Books, had a book about medicines and how things worked inside different animals. Learning through trial and error often had sad results. She kept notes in a blank-paged book named xx*Diary*, which had arrived on the big aid ship that also brought the heavy bags of food. Butter took great pride in making her own book, hoping it might one day be part of her mama's important collection. Reading and writing had become a small part of her mother's daily lessons. The supply ship delivered plenty of pencils, but the books had blue lines and no words. Letters had disappeared from her people's alphabet and nobody seemed to care enough to rediscover them. When Butter was at a loss for a word or phrase, she drew a picture in her book of animal healing.

The sadness came flooding back as she realized her book was gone, along with most all of her patients and the hospital that she'd spent so many months wiring and nailing together.

The flying soldier had explained the healing powers Jesus possessed, which were far greater than Butter's. Maybe Jesus had the power to heal her island, to make everything the way it was before the big wave. The flying soldier had told how Jesus had parted an entire red ocean, made a pathway right at the bottom of it for pairs of animals who couldn't swim. And Jesus had healed a baby cut in half like her papa, had scared little miniature devils from inside the bodies of terrified villagers. Jesus turned mud puddles into little brown birds called sparrows. The stories were called miracles and Jesus had performed hundreds of them, according to the soldier. Each miracle was documented in the fat book called xx*Holy Bible*, although no miracle had saved it from becoming just as waterlogged and melded together as the fifteen other books in Mama's care.

Jesus was described as the Son of God. That would surely make him a full-fledged god, only younger, right? Sort of like the Wapa Juice Maker's son.

If Jesus could move an entire ocean, divide it right in half, couldn't he fix one puny island? Or would there be rivalry between the flying soldier's god and the sea gods? Would there be the same heated, drunken arguments that erupted between Old Deepop and Old Lampu, the two main family elders charged with most decision making on Butter's island? If you wanted to build a new hut, you went to Old Deepop for permission. If you needed to clear brush—cutting down a tree was a crime worse than murder on East Pukapuka—you sought Old Lampu's blessing. A civil war might erupt over who had authority, especially if the issue came up after the wapa juice had been flowing.

Maybe Jesus could bring her village back to life. He could turn water into wapa and evil women into pillars of salt, so would it be so difficult to make her island whole again? It was a little gross to imagine a god making the first woman from a bone he ripped out of the first man, but the story of their home being in a lush garden, surrounded by birds and snakes, was far better than Butter's image of Happa Now. In her people's version of the next life snakes and birds weren't welcome—a horrible reality. The Happa Now that Jesus' people called Heaven was so much better, so much fairer. What would eternity be like if you couldn't lie on a sandy beach with a chirping gecko sunning himself on your belly, licking his eye membranes and trying to change his color to look just like you?

That there was a burning fiery jail at the bottom of the ocean where bad people were sent made no sense. That story was surely impossible. The ocean would have extinguished it long ago. And in the days and nights she'd tossed and turned on the smelly bedroll while her fever ran its course, her sleep often interrupted by dreams of the big wave, Butter struggled with the idea of this ship captain god named Jesus.

Jesus did some ungodlike things in front of a little girl he thought was sleeping. The constant scratching and then sniffing of supposedly divine fingers seemed too mortal, too much like the men and boys from her island. And there was all the picking of his hallowed nose. Would a god really eat his own boogers? Would the holy man the flying soldier shared reverent stories about pee off the side of his boat as great booming farts growled from his wide rump and he nearly fell overboard from all the wapa juice he'd guzzled? The front of his pants were stinky and wet. Wouldn't a true god know not to aim into the wind?

Maybe a god would do all of these things. Butter wanted to believe in Jesus so badly for the sake of her animals. And maybe if she could get him to like her, he would put her father back in one piece here on this world. He would make him alive again and aware of how to get out of the water when the big sharks were near the good fishing spot.

Butter, who missed her papa, longed to be tossed into the blue sky again, screaming with laughter, as Mama stood close by with eyebrows scrunched. Maybe it was the lack of a living father that produced so much of the distrust she felt toward men and boys. The village men treated her widowed mama differently from the married women. Butter saw the long looks that struck her as some sort of attempt at conveying a secret message. It was the same look she saw them give the last piece of coconut pie. What was the message? Butter suspected it had to do with sex, since an adult female of any species was always courted at some time of the year. The nasty wet kisses they blew at Mama, and the way they held out both hands and pretended to squeeze boobies, thrusting their hips to flap their weenies. It had to be a mating ritual, like the crested iguana who could change its colors, or the smaller iguana who bobbed its head in a dance to impress a possible mate. Her mother told her it was nothing for a little girl to know about, but Butter wasn't upset by these ceremonies. She just wished her mama had a better selection, should she decide to choose another mate.

Island children learned about human sex at a very early age, with glimpses of copulating adults in dark shadows resulting from the fact that huts didn't have doors. And rooms partitioned by thin, wafting cloth provided only the slightest privacy.

The coupling was sometimes interrupted by fits of mad giggles coming from children huddled in their bedrolls. It was one thing for men to walk around with their thingies swinging in the breeze, but when papa tried to tickle your mama with it after bedtime, it seemed like some form of funny torture.

Butter had also seen the dark side of mating. The poor little banana slug male, who was about the length of a grownup person's longest finger, had a male part as long as his body. Sometimes the female slug would allow him to put it in her, but sometimes she'd change her mind and chew it off. There were stories of this happening among mating humans on the island. More than one of the younger children had reported witnessing the awful act, although none of the men ever appeared to be missing any parts. Did they grow back?

Many questions about sex remained unanswered, but the notion of gods and the afterlife was a thousand times more befuddling—and pressing—to a lost ten-year-old island girl whose home was nowhere on the horizon.

Butter decided that a real god might well wear filthy, grease stained pants, but wouldn't he know he'd left the vent open?

CHAPTER 16

The meteor shower that might have made amateur astronomer Dicky Miller famous was not visible in the sky over the Lake Mohawk Care Center in the rolling hills of Northern New Jersey, although it did make the television news. Nobody in New Jersey saw it live because it occurred in the middle of the afternoon in that part of the world, streaking across the heavens roughly eight thousand miles away.

The population of the South Pacific was just as oblivious to the jet-ski accident that occurred simultaneously out in the middle of Lake Mohawk, some two hundred yards beyond Dante Wheeler's closed window. The mishap made the news right before the weather as a fifteen second segment during the roundup of local stories. But it wasn't a fiery collision that caused the ensuing ruckus back at the Care Center. The accident went unnoticed by everyone but those involved out on the water. While being pulled behind a jet-ski on a rubber tube, the victim got a tow line entangled around his wrist. One unfortunately timed burst of acceleration had severed the man's hand, sending his beer can flying. It was a coincidence that the victim's girlfriend was a nurse's aide at the adjacent Care

Center, but she wouldn't hear about the accident until long after the paramedics had loaded her man into an ambulance and taken him away. It was a phone call to her from the police that set off the commotion.

On the five o'clock news, a Fish and Game Officer told an interviewer that they were continuing to search for the hand, not because there was any hope of reattachment—that shipped had sailed—but because nobody wanted a stray hand floating around their picturesque lake. While there was no cash reward, bathers were asked to keep an eye out.

The commotion might never have transpired if the cop calling to notify the nurse's aide—listed as the emergency contact on the victim's insurance card—had spoken a little more slowly. Having arrived from El Salvador two months earlier and equipped with only broken English, the victim's girlfriend was confused about exactly what had been cut off.

Nurse Derrick, Dante's most enthusiastic sponge-bather, put down the small hand mirror and stainless steel tweezers he'd been using to pluck his eyebrows and answered the phone at the nurses' station. He called down the hall for the little Salvadoran aide to come answer the call, then resumed plucking, his eyes watering like crazy.

"Miss Gonzalez?" A stern, cop-like voice boomed into the receiver that Dante could clearly hear from his squeaky chair. "Miss Miriam Gonzalez?"

"Si?" She waved for Derrick's help, tilting the handset to share. "Por favor?" she said. Derrick nodded, dropped the tweezers, and leaned in against her small shoulder.

"This is Patrolman Klein from the New Jersey State Police. I understand you are an acquaintance of Hector Ruiz?"

"Si?" Derrick watched her eyes go wide. "Es mi novio."

"Right, well, I'm afraid I have some bad news." Derrick felt the woman's weight push against him. "There was an accident out on Lake Mohawk and Mr. Ruiz was transported to Saint Clare's Hospital after suffering a severed hand."

Derrick glanced toward the large picture window, where overgrown hedges mostly obscured the view.

"Ah, mi Dios, his head?" Mirriam held the receiver away from her face, and Derrick stuttered, began telling her no, not his head. "Mi novio está muerto," she said flatly, her hand with the phone dropping to her side.

Nurse Derrick, who knew a little Spanish from high school classes and the many aides and cleaning people, caught the word "muerto," which meant "dead." The little Salvadoran woman began to shake violently. The mirror shattered on the floor as he reached for the hand with the phone and brought it back up to both their ears.

"I'm very sorry," said the officer. "They are holding out some hope of finding and reattaching it."

"Ah, mi Dios." Oh, my God. Miriam swooned, her legs buckled, and Derrick caught her before she went down. He had the phone in his left hand, cradling the small woman with his right.

"No, no, sweetheart, it's not that bad," Derrick tried telling her, holding the phone toward her, but she recoiled. "Please listen to him. The officer said it was his xx*hand*."

"Mi Dios," Miriam said, and began to whimper. "My Hector! They took his head!"

"Mr. Ruiz is in the intensive care unit and would like to see you." The officer paused, probably waiting for questions about the hospital, the room number, and the man's current condition.

"La cabeza es ida." Miriam voice became a hiss, and Derrick could see she was now clearly in shock. "La cabeza es ida," she repeated. His head is missing.

"Yes, ma'am, he's doing fine. I saw him for a few minutes and can tell he's a real fighter. They'd appreciate if you'd head over to the hospital for some paper work and spend some time with him."

Miriam Gonzalez abruptly stood and pulled away from

Derrick's hairy hands, broken glass crunching under their feet. She turned and sprinted down the long empty hallway, the only sound coming from her chirping rubber-soled shoes. If she'd been screaming, the orderly wheeling the television from the audio-video storage closet would have had plenty of time to stop and let her pass. Instead, the force of the diminutive Salvadoran nurse's aide was enough to topple the top-heavy television cart, the glass tube impacting the tile floor like a bomb, exploding into countless fragments and a gray puff of smoke.

The building's emergency system automatically relayed a call to the fire department, also triggering the sprinklers that began showering every square inch of the wing in cool water droplets. Derrick grabbed an umbrella from the lost and found box.

A startled Dante Wheeler sprang bolt upright in his bed, very much awake and alert for the first time since dying for a little while among the snow encrusted pine trees. His muscles were terribly atrophied despite all the nightly swims, his once perfectly defined six-pack abdomen now quaking from surprise mobilization.

Dante's eighty-year-old roommate, the retired teacher from Florida, pulled the covers over his head to shield himself from the howling alarms and chilly spray. "This place is going all to hell," he grumbled, and then chanced a quick peek over the white linen to see if the pretty boy might be drowning in his bed. "Oh, for Christ's freaking sake," the teacher mumbled at the sight of the young bastard sitting up, looking as if he might be deciding what to order for supper. As good as dead for months and still handsome—a face like Cary Frigging Grant's, with a little notch in the chin, a baby's ass crack that turned the whole staff into giggling imbeciles.

The old man had watched the young prick getting dozens of warm sponge baths and being endlessly doted over, while he lay there like an invisible, stinking lump. His bitterness surged as his hip throbbed from the cold, pooling water, and his feet swelled into fat sausages.

The water pitter-pattered off the skinny bastard's face and head, the scene backlit by the large window beyond, transforming the cold, sterile room into what looked like a television commercial for fancy shampoo and conditioner. Goddamn, if only he had his trusty old rock hammer; giving that pretty boy a few good knocks on the head would sure feel good.

"Yeah, well, don't it all just figure," the old teacher snarled, resigned to his fate of bad smells and now soggy bedding. He rolled away from the brutal unfairness. "Welcome back to the world of the living, turnip boy."

Dante Wheeler didn't seem to hear any of the griping from his roommate, didn't appear to notice the bawling alarm, or feel the cascading water from the emergency sprinkler system. In a voice cracked from months of disuse, throat parched despite water everywhere, Dante finally managed to speak just loud enough for his roommate to hear over the racket.

"I have to get home to my island."

The retired school teacher cocked his head at the far wall, wondering if he'd heard the turnip correctly. An island was exactly where he'd planned to spend these last years, down in the Keys, a far cry from this lousy joint two miles from his son and daughter-in-law's family. Never smoked a cigarette in his life and God gives him lung cancer, all wrapped up and tied with a bow last Christmas. Fa-la-fucking-la.

"I'll call you a cab, turnip boy," the retired school teacher said to the wall.

CHAPTER 17

"**Y**ou're goin' too fucking fast!" Jope's pencil nub bounced around the scrap of paper on the console of the Julius Caesar, its sharp graphite point sure to break from his wild jabbing. The pirates each sat in a helm seat, high up in the pilot house, pouring sweat despite the relatively cool air rushing at them from over the low windscreen. Running full-out, the fishing boat turned scurvy galleon bounded from white-cap to white-cap at thirty knots.

As anyone who'd snuck into a theater for a pirate movie would know, a ship's speed was more important than its weaponry. That was fortunate, for this ship was equipped with nothing but starter pistols.

As often happens with someone who has recently snorted a death-defying amount of high-grade cocaine, each pirate had become obsessed with his own individual mission. Jope needed to know how much all the cocaine they'd stolen was worth. Although the task was complicated by the fact that he'd never learned multiplication, extensive street corner drug dealing did provide a solid starting point.

"How much does a kilo go for?" Jope asked.

"A lot. A kilo is a lot." Ratu concentrated on the choppy sea below the bucking prow, his right hand cramped from gripping the helm too tightly. Ratu's cocaine obsession manifested itself in a need for more speed. As much godforsaken speed as he could squeeze out of their stolen charter fishing boat. Both throttle levers of the control box for the twin diesel engines were jammed forward, and Ratu continued to push with all his might, trying to get one more knot out of the straining engines.

"No, I mean how much money." Jope was trying to sharpen the broken pencil point by rubbing it back and forth on its side. "If you was gonna buy a kilo of coke, how much money would it cost?"

"We don't need to buy coke, stupid." Ratu's left hand was cramping from squeezing the hard shifter knobs. "We got like a hundred kilos, you dumb fuck."

"Don't call me a dumb fuck, Ratu." Jope, whose feelings were hurt whenever his friend called him names, was especially sensitive to words like *dumb* and *stupid*. "How much money would we get for selling a kilo?"

"I don't know, maybe five or ten thousand? Shit, Jope, it feels like we're slowing down." Ratu searched the various knobs and buttons for some sort of overdrive, some faster gear. "Don't it feel like we're slowing down?" Ratu considered the plausibility of getting a foot up on the gear box to force the throttle forward even harder. Sweat was dripping into his eyes, burning his vision. "Fuck, it's hot. We're going too slow!"

"Ten thousand? You mean ten thousand Fiji dollars?"

"Jesus, what's ten thousand Fiji dollars? What the hell are you asking me?" Ratu was annoyed by this interruption in his quest for acceleration.

"How many zeros do I make?"

"Go down and see what you can throw overboard!" Ratu squeezed the helm with both hands, his left foot up on the console in order to force both throttle sticks as far forward as they'd go. He appeared to be frozen in mid karate kick.

"A hundred is two zeros." Jope squinted down at the slip of paper, trying to navigate the pencil in a circular motion, but the bounding boat turned both zeros into lopsided figure eights.

"Jope!" Ratu yelled at his pirate partner. "We need to get rid of extra weight. Go down on the main deck and look for anything heavy we don't need and throw it overboard. We swimmin' like a big fat woman, too damn heavy. We gotta go faster!"

"Stop yelling at me." Jope abandoned his pencil, which immediately bounced to the floor and rolled away. He sat in the helm seat staring down longingly, making one brief attempt to do the math in his head, but the zeros looked liked lopsided figure eights in there as well. "Fuck it," he finally said, feeling a dip in his energy-filled high. His body countered by sending out a flourish of tiny electrical impulses demanding he replenish all these wonderful new chemicals.

"C'mon, hurry up, Jope!" Ratu's voice was straining from the muscle cramps, which had moved from his hands into his crotch. It seemed this position had stabilized the loss of speed, but he now had to contend with his wildly vibrating testicles. The coke had first made his balls crawl up and feel like they'd disappeared, but now they were back, looking to cool off, trying to escape his overheated body. "My balls really hurt."

"I'm going." Jope got up and turned toward the jostling ladder. It would be useless asking Ratu to slow down so he didn't break his neck climbing down to the main deck.

"Hurry!"

Jope's sweat-slick hands grabbed hold of the aluminum railing as he backed down to the main deck. He was motivated more by the need for another big snort than by Ratu's badgering and name-calling. Ratu acted like the boss only because he was taller by maybe one finger. And that was only from having bushier hair. People sometimes mixed up their names because they looked alike, especially if they hadn't showered and their hair had become greasy and flat. What had Ratu yelled at him about? Going faster? How was he supposed to make the boat go faster? Jope had forgotten what Ratu had sent him off to do. Ratu sometimes acted too crazy, like when he'd slapped a beer bottle out of the biker's hand at the Riki Tik for no reason. With a queer smile on his face, Ratu had just walked up to the huge monster looking dude, looked him in the eye and slapped the bottle into the air. It fizzed all over the tables and floor and white foam dripped from the guy's leather jacket and shaggy beard. The big biker had grabbed Ratu with two hands, one at his throat and the other at his crotch, lifted him over his head and thrown him through the big glass window of the bar. Ratu had landed in a groaning heap on the sidewalk, the same loony smile still on his face.

"Oh, yeah!" Jope remembered that he was supposed to find things to throw overboard.

CHAPTER 18

Jope was tossed from wall to wall of the kitchenette directly below where Ratu was kicking at the throttle sticks with his bare left foot, allowing the hard plastic steering wheel to jerk right and then left.

"Throw shit overboard." Jope repeated the order in his head, trying to memorize the task he fully intended to complete right after renewing his cocaine buzz.

"Go, you dumb bastard!" Jope flinched at Ratu's voice from the other side of the fiberglass ceiling. He wasn't sure whether his friend was cursing him or the controls, which didn't seem to be cooperating. The boat was going crazy, shifting one way and then back the other. The overworked engines smelled a lot like his old neighborhood after he and his friends had piled up old tires, lit them on fire and run like hell. They had targeted several intersections, creating smoky mazes of flaming piles of rubber. The taxi drivers would have to navigate these dead ends, often giving up and backing out.

The hundred or so one-kilogram bricks of cocaine were scattered in the galley and forward stateroom. The pirates had begun their transfer carefully enough, stowing bricks in the oven, cabinets, refrigerator, and even in the microwave. But they ended by piling armload after armload on and around the pull-out couch and coffee table, paranoia growing with each trip back onto the abandoned luxury yacht. The crazy, bounding action of the ride had spilled most of them across the floor, and Jope lurched around the bucking room, searching for the open brick they'd already sampled.

"The bread box!" Jope spun to the wooden container where he suddenly remembered stashing the brick. He kicked a dozen of the carefully wrapped packages aside as he lunged across the room and grabbed the bread box with big cherries painted on the front. He snatched the brick of cocaine from within and tossed the box to the jostling floor. Flopping onto the couch, he clasped the bag between his thighs and, steadying himself with his left hand on the wooden arm, scooped out a palm-full of cocaine.

The powder coated his sweaty hands and wrists, and he barely noticed how badly he was shaking. Jope's heart was slamming inside his chest to the beat of a heavy-metal rock band. AC/DC's "Back in Black" screamed inside his head, and he involuntarily bobbed and swayed to the blaring phantom music that didn't exist outside his brain. Jope assumed Ratu had left the radio on.

The boat crashed through a big wave as the Fijian pirate threw his hand to his face in a white puff of nearly pure cocaine. Inhaling with both nostrils, Jope hungrily snorted the mound. Every neuro-receptor in his body seemed to fire simultaneously in wild, crackling response.

Jope's coated hand slowly dropped to his lap, the torn bag falling to his feet. The boat stopped its insane rocking and the music went suddenly dead, giving him a very clear look at the god standing before him, smiling down with a thousand or so razor-sharp teeth.

Jope never dared mention religion to Ratu, who believed any sort of god was an excuse for white missionary wankers to trek around small island slums, knocking up twelve-year-old prostitutes with half-breed bastards. Ratu had made his religious feelings perfectly clear in regular rants back in the Riki Tik, especially after a dozen glasses of beer. Ratu's own father had been a white Christian missionary who claimed to be from some country called Chicago. Ratu assumed this detail was another of his stinking lies.

"Fucker didn't even have the decency to plant the right color jizz in Mama to make me look white." Ratu's tenth glass of beer had left him feeling blue. "Damn half-breeds get all the best resort jobs, ya know? I coulda been a towel boy, gettin' big tips for rubbing lotion on rich fat broads. Instead, Mama's crack habit got so bad she dumped me at the orphan house. It was a bad place, man, a real, real bad place."

Jope had longed to tell Ratu about his religion, which had been passed down through the men in his family. His grandpa had been an important elder on Benau Island, located opposite to the Somosomo Strait. The venerable artisan had been in charge of carving the figurines of Dakuwaqa, the half-man, half-shark god of seafaring and fishing communities. The coral and wooden figurines he made were mostly purchased by a rich Suva businessman who exported them all over the world.

It was said that one of these figurines, a muscular Fijian man with the upper torso of a great shark, sat on the desk of the President of the United States of America to give him guidance for directing his warriors in a land called Vietnam.

Jope was disappointed by many of the shark-god stories, which usually put him on the losing end of epic battles. The worst was when Dakuwaqa traveled inland to conquer Kadavu; an octopus-god had defeated the shark-god after a mighty struggle. It made no sense to Jope that an octopus-god could ever come close to kicking the ass of a shark-god. It was sacrilege to consider the possibility of an ink-filled, boneless bag of slime vanquishing his mighty shark-god.

But having a shark-god to worship did have some really cool

benefits. The dopey pale tourist women, willing to risk life and limb to experience real Fijian culture by visiting dive bars in Suva, couldn't get enough of the shark-god stories. In Jope's version of these tales, Dakuwaqa always came away the victor, not some shitwad octopus. Nope, not a chance Jope would spread those rotten lies. He delivered these revised endings with great pride.

"Wanna come up and see my little Dakuwaqa?" Jope would eventually ask the drunken white girl, who was more often than not wearing a cheap, polyester knock-off suluvakatoga. The traditional garment looked even better balled up at the foot of his twin bed, beneath the set of ominous, hand-drawn Dakuwaqa posters thumb tacked to the wall of his one room efficiency. That was, until Ratu moved in and taped all his Kiss posters on top of them.

The Dakuwaqa t-shirts were also cool, as were the big Dakuwaqa beach umbrellas protecting the light-skinned tourists.

Ratu would have said Dakuwaqa looked like a tuna fish with chicken legs, so Jope shut up about him. He kept the remaining evidence of his religion in the front pocket of his filthy cut-offs—a one-inch-tall Dakuwaqa figure his grandpa had carved out of white coral. Ratu sometimes teased Jope that he should stop playing with his nuts, when he was really just surreptitiously fondling his shark-god.

Jope looked up at the fantastic half-shark, half-man looming over him in the kitchenette.

"You're in some deep shit, son," the shark-god bellowed, his great, razor-sharp teeth gnashing wetly as his jaws moved to form the grim message. His horrible teeth were triangular and stained bright orange, with serrated edges to tear flesh.

"You can speak?" Jope's voice was weak. He was practically hypnotized by all the lethal orange teeth looming over him.

"I'm a god," said Dakuwaqa, thrusting his arm out in a dismissive gesture and spilling half the remaining bag of

Cheetos. "Of course I can speak. Listen, dummy, you and your loser buddy really stepped in it this time."

Jope's feelings were hurt again. Now his god was calling him names.

"You two heisted all this nose candy off some badass characters, with some even more badass friends." The shark-god's muscular human arms swept out across the kitchenette, indicating the bricks of cocaine. "This stuff is bigger trouble than you could ever imagine."

"We're pirates." Jope's voice was tiny and not at all pirate-like.

"Pirates, Schmirates!" the shark-god mocked, inhaling the rest of the Cheetos and balling up the bag. "The owners of this blow have sicced dudes from Malakula on your pirate asses. And you wanna know who the Malakula are?"

"No." Jope was near tears. "Please don't tell me."

"Cannibals!" Dakuwaqa roared, gnashing his thousands of teeth again for effect. "Big bad cannibals sent to eat you up!"

"No!" Jope slid off the couch and dropped to his knees at the human feet of the shark-god, his flesh burning from the rough indoor-outdoor carpeting. "Please, you're my god. You have to protect me! It's part of the rules!"

"Nah," said Dakuwaqa. "I'm just a hallucination from all the coke you snorted."

"And the cannibals?" Jope looked up hopefully, blinking through tears at his mighty shark-god.

"Sorry, dumbass, but they're real." Dakuwaqa licked his orange fingers, clapped his hands together, and vanished in a billowing white puff that might have been cocaine, leaving the terrorized pirate on his knees, whimpering.

CHAPTER 19

A thin line of black smoke rose from the baby, weaving upward in the dead air like a charmed cobra. Sweat poured from the warriors as they gyrated in the steaming jungle. Ten men in full paint spoke to the gods through dance and grunts, preparing to accept the infant's life energy. They kept rhythm to a steady drumbeat, circling the crackling driftwood fire, their motion creating a vortex to channel ancient spirits. Carved skulls wearing vicious grins topped a dozen giant totems that rose from the white sand.

Albino Paul's charcoal black feet kicked at the sand. His wooden spear jabbed invisible enemies, his nose crinkled from the smell of the singed infant, the stench of burning plastic mixing with fruity cologne and sour body odor. Two more loops around the smoldering feast and the procession in ragged loincloths and feather headpieces halted. They continued dancing in place, pulsating veins crisscrossing shiny, tight muscles. Albino Paul was the most ferocious looking member of the hunting party because he'd filed an incisor and one eyetooth to sharp points. More filing would be done once the toothpaste for extra sensitive teeth started working.

"Accept this blood," Albino Paul cried out in his ancestral language, scooping up a small bowl with his free hand and raising it toward the opening in the jungle canopy above. "And allow us the flesh so we may be stronger."

Just as the tinny music coming from cheap speakers stashed among the palm fronds cut out, someone sneezed, which was met with a "Bless you," from beyond the sacrificial altar. Albino Paul was distracted by the flourish of a bright yellow handkerchief against the dark green vegetation. A spectator blew his nose, sounding like a broken tuba.

"I hate white people," Albino Paul hissed in his forefather's language, wishing he'd remembered to slip a few Tums into his crotch pocket; his stomach was sour from an over-cooked hamburger lunch. Oh, what he'd give to break from the troupe, scream his throat raw with a death call, and see how these fat tourists would react to something a little more authentic.

"Shut up and finish," the tribe elder snapped, his face paint running together into a pattern that looked more like a hockey mask than a death's head.

They began the finale, turning to face the fire, but were suddenly pitched to their knees when the sand jolted beneath their bare feet. Albino Paul caught himself with both hands, spilling the fake blood to avoid splaying face first into the fire.

"What the hell?" one of the newer guys said. A flock of gulls took flight in a gray and white flourish, causing them all to cover their heads. From above the ring of tourists, the dozens of fox bats that dangled upside down and mostly yawned and slept through the spectacle beneath them let loose long streams of milky guano.

The next jolt freed large batches of coconuts, finally sending the tourists into a panic. A middle-aged trio in matching Bermuda shorts and guano-coated Hawaiian shirts bolted toward the warriors, shouting in what might have been German, perhaps demanding an immediate refund. The quaking ground took their feet from under them, and they fell into a moaning pile, six flip-flops surrounding their writhing bodies like dead fish. Another couple screamed about grandchildren and how horrible things like this never happened in Florida. An elderly woman in a floral print bikini top and Speedo bottoms bounded into the jungle, flailing hands tearing at hanging vines, flabby rear end quaking more than the ground. The group's lone tour guide followed right on her heels, attempting to reassure her as the duo was engulfed by swaying thick greenery.

From the speakers came the recorded message required by an insurance company to be played weekly, normally late at night when nobody was around to hear. "Please move to the nearest exit in an orderly manner. This is a test of the emergency management system. This is only a test."

Albino Paul slipped away from the mayhem to check on his boat. The Cannibal Culture Spree had taken a hit since the first big shake had opened a zigzag crater in the airport runway in Norsup. For two weeks they'd sat around swatting bugs, supposedly being kept busy on clean-up detail. If tourists didn't want to see wads of gum and cigarette butts in the sand, then maybe they shouldn't be such pigs in the first place. Today would be the third evacuation since the first big shake. It was bad for business, but a good sign that the gods were still watching.

Another small tremor made the rickety dock sway, as Albino Paul stepped down onto the sleek fiberglass hull. He grabbed a soft rag and polished out a few smudges in the chrome, but everything was safe and sound. The cell phone on the steering console lit up and a Gloria Estefan ring tone played from miniature speakers.

"Hello? Hello?" The cannibal shouted into the phone. Reception was lousy in these back lagoons. Albino Paul climbed onto the seat of his six-hundred horsepower Fountain 42 Lightning speed boat, getting as close to the satellite orbiting above as possible, straining to catch as much of the crackling assignment as he could.

"Pirates? Did you say two pirates?" Albino Paul tossed the rag over his shoulder. "Okay … Julius Caesar and it's a fishing charter? How many kilos? And it's the standard deal, right?"

Albino Paul flipped his phone closed. He stepped carefully down from the seat to scribble the encoded number of the GPS tracking signal he'd use to locate the two pirate scumbags who'd ripped off the shipment. He'd be able to link through the drug lord's command center, which was in Bogota, Columbia, or maybe La Paz, Bolivia. The drug lords never missed a trick, installing tracking devices in a few bricks of every cocaine shipment as insurance against this exact sort of thing. Still humming the Estefan ring tone, Albino Paul hunted for a pencil, his ceremonial human finger bone necklace clicking and clacking all the while.

Albino Paul loved the Miami Sound Machine, whose lead singer was an absolute Goddess. He'd read in *Tiger Beat* magazine that she was born in Cuba, which was also an island. He imagined Cubans tasted peppery, hot and spicy. On those rainy, blue Mondays spent lounging in his cramped hut, he would fantasize about coming across a lost Gloria Estefan stumbling through the Malakula forest—having made a wrong turn from the beach.

"Hello, Miss Estefan, I'm your biggest fan!"

Albino Paul would devour her slowly and with love, ruminating over every last morsel. He would honor the spirit of the peppery Cuban Goddess to the tune of "Can't Stay Away From You" and "Bad Boy." Albino Paul dabbed at the corners of his mouth with the rag on his shoulder.

The thirty-year-old Malakulan was named after Pope John Paul I, who was born Albino Luciano, serving just thirty-three days as Pontiff. The nursemaid who tended Albino Paul's mother had handed the squirming baby to his mother wrapped in newspaper whose front page featured a photo of the recently deceased Holy Father, lovingly nicknamed The Smiling Pope. Albino Paul's mother had wanted her son to be as blessed and kind as the man in the picture.

"He will grow to become a great man," the brand new mother had told the nursemaid, stroking the infant boy's crusty cheek and thick mat of coarse black hair. "He will be the bravest of the brave and do things few men have ever had the courage to do." The teary-eyed mother kissed the world's newest bloodthirsty cannibal on his chocolate forehead.

That her son turned out a bloodthirsty cannibal was perfectly fine in her book. Just as long as he enjoyed what he did in life, which was performing the traditional ceremonies for tourists when not tracking down and eating drug thieves for videos he posted online. The videos, which had tens of thousands of views, were the brainchild of his bosses. They were graphic warnings to anyone stupid enough to try ripping them off.

Albino Paul's mood had greatly improved following the aftershocks and a lousy morning dealing with the Vanuatu tourism flunky—Malakula being one of eighty-two islands forming the Republic of Vanuatu—who threatened to fire his ass for not wearing his namba during the tribal dances. The penis gourd gave him a nasty rash in the worst places. Albino Paul would love to have stepped it up and given the tourists on the Cannibal Culture Spree a rare treat. Maybe tie the flunky to the preparation tree and tenderize the little prick. Maintaining authenticity, he'd fillet the meaty parts to dip in laplap batter.

Talk about giving them their money's worth! Just one loud-mouthed office lackey would easily feed ten hungry Australian insurance brokers.

Albino Paul tolerated his steady day job, in which he and nine other Malakulans performed tribal dances then led guided snorkeling tours of the polluted and mostly dead Lana Loo Reef. One minute the village men were posing as human flesh eating demons, the next they were measuring and fitting snorkel masks and swim fins.

Albino Paul accepted the bad with the good. He refused to feel degraded at having to wear a smiley face nametag while struggling to fit tight rubber flippers onto bloated pink feet. He was simply buying time until he'd finished raising the cash to complete the master plan that would change the course of his people's history.

His calling came deep within in the form of the long dead voices of his forefathers, the true bloodthirsty cannibals. And although nobody on Malakula had been eating people on any of the nearby islands since before World War Two—except, of course, when they double-crossed the drug traffickers— Albino Paul refused to give up hope.

An embarrassment to recent generations, the rich history of Malakula—the former People-Eating Capital of the World— was a source of great pride to Albino Paul. If tradition was preserved, he believed, Malakula would rise again. And when it did, his people would surely change the name of their homeland, which translated to "Pain in the Ass" in French. A slap in the face moniker that mocked the fierce cannibal culture the outsiders had initially encountered on these shores. Imagine if a Vanuatu explorer had landed on the northern coast of New Zealand and christened it Saggy White Breasts?

Albino Paul punched the coordinates he'd received from the drug kingpins into his GPS device, making a mental note to tell his old tribal leader he'd be indisposed for a few days. His leader was more than okay with the occasional absences, since Albino Paul always brought him back a few fingers. Albino Paul was, after all, a very thoughtful bloodthirsty cannibal.

CHAPTER 20

The little savage Captain Jesus Dobby had snagged with the grappling hook had not woken any cannibalistic instincts. His ancestors were best known for drinking beer and brewing a blinding grain alcohol bootlegged from Albuquerque to Oklahoma City. There were a few cases of incest, a half-dozen murders, the usual number of arsonists, but nobody had ever been known to eat human flesh. Dobby would definitely have stewed up the damn turtle half of the girl if it hadn't sunk so quickly—separate from the girl, it would have been worthless anyway. He absolutely loved Chinese turtle soup.

In the days after pulling the sickly turtle-girl on board, Dobby had been sulking, despite the bounty of tsunami trash he'd harvested while navigating his tugboat in the remote waters southeast of the Cook Islands. A Scooby Doo lunch box in mint-condition, an infant car seat, and a matching set of brand-name wheeled luggage just weren't compensation enough for failing to land a bona fide turtle-girl.

"You speak any English?" Dobby had caught her watching him from the bedroll she'd converted into a nest. She'd folded it over and gathered some old sail material and the mosquito net to lie on. He was seated across the main deck, sifting through the day's catch. Every muscle and bone in the captain's body was sore from trying to sleep on a vinyl beach chair meant for someone with a much smaller bum. And speaking of bums, he'd carefully adjusted one of his old handkerchiefs over the little native girl's brown one, since she seemed only to sleep on her belly with her knees drawn up. The girl was only a youngster, but allowing any sort of bare ass to smile up at the clouds wasn't right.

"I can speak. And I've read books Mama's in charge of."

"Books? What, you people got some kinda library?"

"What's a library?"

"I dunno, it's just a place for books. Like a store, but you ain't gotta pay for nothin." Dobby pushed his belly forward to stretch his aching back in the flimsy chair.

The girl was silent for a moment, considering. "Yes, my mama is a library. She's a very big one with fifteen books."

"What sorta books did your people have?"

"Fat ones," said the little girl. "Great big fat ones from the flying soldier. They were written by Thomas Wolfe, Adolph Hitler, and Aldous Huxley. And there was one by Franklin Roosevelt, too. He's our best tree climber."

"I heard of Hitler."

The little girl's eyes filled with tears. "They're all dead now, aren't they?"

"How the hell do I know?" Dobby snapped, but felt a little bad when the kid flinched, cringing back into her nest. "I been out on the water a long time. You got a name?"

"Butter."

"You look hungrier than a stray dog. I suppose we oughta get something real in that belly besides water."

Butter lifted up to her elbows, testing her muscles. She rubbed at the bite. The swelling had gone down since she'd been pulled onto the rusty boat. A few times the captain had put alcohol from an old medical kit on it, trying to keep any new infections from setting in. Butter was shivering out here on the open water, goose bumps everywhere except under the dirty handkerchief covering her rear end. It was breezy and the sun was hidden behind the boat's pilot house.

Dobby let out a mighty groan as he rose from his chair to fetch grub. He saw her eyeing the one-armed baby doll mixed in with the pile of colorful trash he'd been examining at his feet. She seemed to be checking the broken pink infant for any sign of movement, probably deciding if it was dead or some type of carving. Dobby had a dog that did the same thing, back when he was a kid. Damn thing got spooked by Teddy bears and GI Joes. Queer how his dog was smart enough to recognize they were supposed to represent living creatures, but too stupid to know they were made out of plastic and pillow stuffing.

When Dobby returned from the galley with three bananas and a chunk of white coconut meat, the little girl was on her side, facing away from the captain, rocking the doll in her arms. The way her body shook, he figured she was cryin' about something.

Dobby mustered his softest voice. "I'll leave 'em right here for ya." Crying females were something Dobby never understood and did his best to avoid. His mother had spent most of his boyhood crying, often with bruised-up eyes and a split lip. A crying woman was never a good thing. It meant an evil storm wasn't far off. In his ma's case, the storm had been his boozed-up old man, turned all black from rage. Dobby had experienced the power of that rage, the flash of yellow from his daddy's wedding ring as the open hand came upside his face real hard. Goddamn if that ring didn't smart. It was like a streak of lightning, sometimes coming out of nowhere. And most of the time he hadn't done shit to deserve it. Dobby figured he was just the closest target for a wallop. There was perfect quiet and then a sudden whoosh, followed by the thunderous crack of leathery hand on a little boy's soft skin. Dobby would fall asleep to fantasies of sneaking one of his daddy's shotguns, loading it with the big red shells, and then waking the son of a bitch up with his own blast of thunder. Kaboom, kaboom, both barrels, you mean old bastard!

"I ain't gonna hurt you, girl." Dobby wanted very much to go crack open another bottle of rum but was unsure about leaving the whimpering kid. He'd feel like dirt if she up and jumped overboard. Did kids this age do things like that when they were upset? "You can keep that there doll, honey. It ain't your color, but it needs someone to look after it just the same."

"Can you really do magic?" Butter asked, the tears and snot making awful gurgling sounds. She was still facing away.

Shifting from foot to foot, Dobby looked down at the pile of junk, half expecting to see a box of magic tricks or something. He was, in fact, pretty handy with magic, having spent so many hours perched on bar stools, whiling away long days making quarters disappear and torn dollar bills whole again. If a couple of new suckers walked in and grabbed a stool, Dobby could manage to get most of his drinks paid for. And sometimes his ass beaten and tossed in the back alley.

"Well, yeah, I suppose I can." Dobby was relieved the tears had tapered off. "I can do pretty good magic. But you eat a little first while I batten things down for the night, okay?"

While Dobby tried remembering where he'd left the rum bottle that would get him through another night, Butter split the skin of a red banana and offered her new baby the first bite.

"Don't cry, little pink baby." Butter cooed to her doll, who was the same shade as the coral at the north end of her island, then crammed the entire banana into her own mouth. It was ripe and sweet, and she sat up and quickly tore open the other two. The doll lay across Butter's lap, watching her with strange blue eyes. Despite spending her entire life on a tiny, isolated island in a remote corner of the South Pacific, Butter had always been able to see land. Dozens of times she'd gone along on fishing trips in the outrigger-canoes, including the big one with a sail. But superstition prevented even the bravest fishermen from exploring beyond sight of the tall palms and thick puka trees. The villagers believed a person's vision worked as a tether. Losing sight of the island would sever the tether, and a reckless fishing party would be swept off into the horizon, lost forever. They repeated this warning to children who snuck off to swim far out into the calm, deep waters on the leeward side. Wander too far and the sea gods would pull you under and give your carcass to the bottom feeders.

Rocking the baby, Butter understood how scary this must be, even for a child not made out of real skin. The world was so big and it made you feel so very small, like you didn't matter one bit. The ocean seemed to go on forever and ever, in all directions.

"Jesus has magic powers to make everything better." Butter lifted the doll to her shoulder and gently patted its back. "He's going to fix my home and make everything the way it was before the big wave. You'll get to meet Mama and all the animals in the hospital I built. And I'll introduce you to my turtle."

Butter sang her new baby to sleep, while Jesus Dobby drank himself unconscious up in the pilot house. Night once again fell over the swaying Gypsy Dancer.

CHAPTER 21

Dante Wheeler peered through the scratched acrylic airplane window, searching the vast expanse of black water for lights, any sign of civilization. The surrounding cabin was also dark, filled with sleeping passengers. He was headed home, to a faraway place he'd never seen in person.

Dante had sensed a lack of commitment when his coaches argued for him to stay. He was, after all, done racing forever, according to the doctors. What was in it for the coaches if he stuck around? Before the crash, he'd been just another reckless kid with flashes of talent, able to hold his own on the second tier Europa Cup. But his career was all about potential and he still had no results in any of the big time events during intermittent call-ups. And now that potential had been irrevocably extinguished in a small grove of pine trees, in a blood-spattered crater in the snow.

Just one jolt to his brain, the doctors had explained, could end his life instantly. No reason existed for why he'd regained consciousness to begin with; it had just been some fluke of nature. Apparently Dante Wheeler wasn't a being worthy of miracles. No, his resurrection was simply a fluke, especially since he had no real memories of life before being startled awake in that sterile bed.

An occupational therapist who stopped in every Tuesday and Friday had brought Dante a handful of magazines each visit, everything from *Sports Illustrated* to *Popular Science.* "You know what a two-percenter is, Dante?" the therapist said. He shuffled through the magazines and pulled one out called *MENSA Bulletin.* "It's what these people call each other, the people with IQs in the top two percent of the population."

"Reading still gives me a headache. I look at the pictures."

"Your chance of survival was less than two percent. Your chance of a full recovery was more like two percent of two percent."

"It was a miracle, huh?"

"No, nothing like a miracle." Sitting at the foot of Dante's bed, the therapist had removed his wire-rimmed glasses, rubbed his gray beard. "The word 'miracle' implies divine intervention, or perhaps an extraordinary effort by your doctors. I think your recovery was just a matter of luck."

"I'm a fluke."

"Well, yes, I suppose that's accurate enough. The important thing now is to look forward. Maybe find something in these magazines that sparks your interest, makes you want to chase after it, like you did with your skiing."

"I wouldn't mind some travel magazines."

"You have to let that go, young man. Look at the color of your skin. You aren't anything close to Polynesian, although I understand it's a comforting dream. But a dream is still just a dream. There's no tropical ocean out that window, just a busy little lake."

At least once a session Dante had pressed the therapist for magazine articles on the South Pacific. Islands, people, fishing trips, it didn't matter, anything to help fill the void between dreams and the travel channel. From down the hall, Dante had heard the opening music for *Jeopardy*, right before Johnny's introduction of today's three contestants, and Alex Trebek's entrance onto the stage.

Dante imitated Johnny's voice: "An unemployed ski racing fluke from East Pukapuka, Dante Wheeler."

"And you were never on *Jeopardy*."

"I'd really suck at it now, wouldn't I?"

"If you're not going to focus on moving forward, I can't help you. And I'm not sure if I'm the first to tell you, but your insurance company is about to pull the plug on all this good fun."

No family had visited during his recovery. The doctors and nurses were purposely vague with details about a father living in Florida and a sister somewhere in California. Had Dante chased them out his life?

Late one Friday afternoon, a woman who claimed to have been one of Dante's ski team strength trainers had taken a turn sitting at the foot of his bed. She had worn tight-fitting Nike sweats that showed off her strong biceps and tiny waist. A fidgety, bored-looking group of six former teammates he didn't remember had cleared out of his room a half hour earlier. His trainer told him they'd made a special trip east, taking time away from a dry-land training session in Park City.

"That's not me." Dante pointed his strong right middle finger at the photo album she'd spread across his lap. "I mean, I don't remember any of this. Wouldn't something look familiar?"

"What do you remember?"

"I live on an island in the South Pacific."

"Dante, you have an apartment in Rutland, Vermont." The attractive woman sat Indian-style, looking at the photos upside down. "Your coach asked me to make sure your rent was paid while you were getting better."

"It's not possible," he said, more frustrated than argumentative. "I hate the cold."

"You've been a ski racer since you were four years old. You love the cold and you've made your life on the snow."

"I didn't even know what a ski was until you showed me these pictures."

"You went helmet first into the trees at sixty miles per hour, Dante," she said. "Things have changed."

"I'd be dead," Dante said, without conviction. "I mean I'd still be dead."

"It's all on video, from at least three angles."

"Jesus."

"It was the Lauberhorn."

"I don't know what that means."

"It's a famous ski race," the woman said, as she'd reached forward under his cotton blanket to stroke his bare shin. "Millions of people watched the crash live, and then it was replayed over and over again on the sports highlights."

"Jesus." Did he believe in God? Was "Jesus" just an expression?

"Sort of an agony of defeat moment," she added, careful to smile only a little. "You rode off in a helicopter."

"And you were my trainer?"

"I'm one of them." She leaned even farther forward to find Dante's cold right hand and rub it softly. "We were kind of boyfriend and girlfriend for a while, too."

"I don't remember." Dante shook his head. "I don't remember you, and I don't remember anything in these pictures. You used past tense to mean we'd broken up? I don't even know your name."

"Yeah, it didn't end so well," she said, even though her smile grew wider. "I should have known from your reputation."

"Jesus." There was that word again.

"Yeah, well, you're pretty well known in about a half dozen countries as sort of a 'player.' And my name is Jennifer. I introduced myself when I came into your room."

"You didn't introduce yourself," Dante said. The continued frustration was putting him in a dark mood. He didn't know why he was upset, just felt the anger coming on like a bad headache. Dante snatched his hand away.

"It's not a big deal." Jennifer's hand retreated to her lap.

"Bullshit!" Dante leaned back against the soft headboard. He reached across the metal gate that was supposed to keep him from falling out of bed and grabbed a small container of applesauce from his lunch tray. He read the words on the foil lid, but only half of them made any sense. It wasn't his first experience with the crazy new language surrounding him, but he'd tried to ignore it up until then. Dante had read the words on the container's lid out loud, but they remained gibberish. "This is all a big fucking deal!" he shouted and flung the applesauce against the far wall. It bounced, but didn't open.

"We were friends, too."

"I don't believe you," Dante said, and immediately felt like a jackass. Of course she wasn't lying. He was the one in a fucking hospital bed having to be told his own name.

"Have you noticed the small scar on the right side of your penis?" Jennifer asked. "It's about halfway down."

Dante begrudgingly lifted the thin cotton blanket with his left hand, hiking up the hospital gown to expose his scarred penis. "Jesus," he said once again.

"Bite mark," she'd said, matter-of-factly. "You told me the story. That's a pretty good example of how things ended between you and your regular cast of girls. I liked you, though. No biting between us."

"I'm sorry." Dante pushed the blanket back down. "I just want to go home."

"You have more tests and more rehab." Jennifer unfolded her legs and slid off the end of the bed. "They have a counselor to help you prepare for your regular life again. Checkbooks and disability forms. You suffered a traumatic brain injury, Dante. You were in a coma for a long time. They started thinking you were never going to wake up."

"I've been swimming in the ocean every day." Dante closed his eyes, shutting out the pretty woman he'd apparently had a brief, unpleasant affair with. He wished he was on the pathway to the leeward side of his island, about to step off into the calm water, leaving this room and this woman far behind.

"It was a dream," she said.

Dante opened his bright blue eyes, fixing them on the woman whose name had once again slipped his mind. He was certain he'd never met her. "I'm going to need your help."

"I'll do what I can."

"First, I need you to please stop telling me about ski racing, snow, and the women pissed off enough to bite me. Good so far?"

"You're right, I'm sorry. I didn't mean to upset you. They told me specifically not to upset you."

"Do I have money? Is a world-class ski racer rich?"

"Um, you have about eight thousand dollars in your checking account," she told him. "Like I said, they put me in charge of your bills."

"Do I own anything of value?"

"I really don't know, but I can find out. Why?"

"I need you to sell everything I own. I'm serious. *Everything,* as soon as you possibly can. Will you do that for me?"

"I don't understand."

"I have to go home," Dante told the pretty woman.

That had been weeks earlier.

As he looked out the small oval window of the quiet airplane, he saw that the moon was just a tiny sliver over the South Pacific, not big enough to reflect on the surface of the black water.

"I have to go home, and it's really far away."

CHAPTER 22

Ratu didn't understand the flashing lights on the boat's seventy-two kilometer color radar system any better than he did the GPS plotter. And he was too strung out on nearly pure Bolivian cocaine to make sense of the fuel gauge now solidly pinned to the left of the big red letter "E."

When the twin diesel engines died of thirst, Ratu tapped the fish finder with his knuckles and let out a string of jumbled oaths. When he turned and looked back to where Jope had paused at the top of the ladder, returning to reclaim his spot on the bridge, Ratu's eyes were huge white orbs, his pupils black specks. Blood was flowing freely from his nostrils, dripping off erect nipples and raining onto the indoor-outdoor carpet. His oily hair jutted in pointed spikes from his black scalp.

"You ain't looking so good." Jope's voice was hoarse and unsteady. Jesus, first the shark-god and now Ratu was looking like he'd been taken over by a demon. And not just some totally cool demon like you'd sometimes see at the free outdoor heavy metal concerts. His friend looked big-time possessed. He looked scary movie possessed. Jope wavered at the top of the bridge ladder, eyeing the set of comfortable pilot chairs. He'd planned on sitting back down next to Ratu and maybe telling him about the cannibals on their trail.

"I think we stopped." Ratu stared back, all bug-eyed, at his friend. Despite the overwhelming quiet, his words were difficult to understand because his parched tongue lolled from the corner of his mouth. The phrase sounded more like, "I ink we opt."

"Maybe you wanna go lie down, Ratu." Jope fought the urge to flee back down the ladder. Fear of having to deal with the shark-god again, not to mention the cannibals, kept him hanging onto the upright metal pole behind the bridge seats.

"We outta gash," Ratu said, making quick, jerky motions with his head toward the fish finder. "I ink we fugged."

Each of his friend's spastic movements made Jope flinch. His own mobility was shot to hell, his arms and legs twitchy and convulsive from all the cocaine. The two pirates stood face to face, each doing a bad zombie dance and totally freaking the other out.

"Shark-god say we in a lot of trouble," Jope finally blurted, trying to control a brand-new facial tick that was making him dizzy. He looked back down the ladder and gripped the rungs tighter. "We gotta give the coke back or real bad shit gonna happen. I can't take no more bad shit."

"We ant!" Ratu's hands seemed to be swatting at imaginary flies. "Gash ank empy, you dipship!"

"The shark-god said cannibals are coming to eat us!" Afraid of falling back down the slippery ladder, Jope stepped onto the blood-stained carpet. His free hands began to involuntarily mimic Ratu's, swatting at the same imaginary flies buzzing around between them. He couldn't help himself.

"Fut the sharp-gob," Ratu said. His flailing arms splashed blood from his nose across Jope's face and chest. As Jope lurched away from the terrible mess, the hull of the drifting Julius Caesar slammed into something big and hard, the explosion of wood and glass sounding like a bomb. The pirates were thrown into the helm, collapsing in a gory pile as Jope's nose began to gush with thick, dark blood.

"Please, please, I don't wanna die!" Jope was pinned under Ratu's wet, jerking body.

Ratu moaned as the boat pitched to the starboard side. The sound of snapping wood was like small caliber gunshots in the night.

"My wibs! Yew ewbow iz in my wibs!" Ratu's voice was a screech as he tried pushing Jope off his ribcage. "We hip sumphin."

"It's the cannibals!" Jope screamed, digging his elbow deeper into Ratu's ribs. Ratu tried to free himself from the weight of his friend, while Jope clambered to hug him for safety. Both were too slick from blood, sweat, and tears to be successful. The fifteen-meter pirate ship pitched farther to its side, setting off more small-caliber gunshots. "The cannibals are shooting at us!"

"Nod cannibaws. Daz da boat bwaking." Ratu struggled for breath under Jope's slimy weight. "We muzda hit a weef."

"Hold me!" Jope wailed, crying and bleeding, unable to get any sort of grip on his friend.

The next wave tipped the Julius Caesar on its side, directly over the western reef of the recently devastated island of East Pukapuka. Wood splintered, fiberglass cracked, and metal twisted and groaned, as the ocean began to disassemble the pirate ship with each small but powerful nudge. The walls collapsed around the trapped pirates. Glass domes covering navigational instruments exploded like firecrackers. The small amount of gas that remained trapped between air bubbles in the fuel line splashed over the still searing hot engine and caught fire.

"Diz ot good," Ratu whimpered. The pirates bloody faces were pinned cheek to cheek, salt water spraying them from splintered walls. Ratu was still unable to dislodge Jope's sharp left elbow from a soft spot between his ribs. "At urts bad!"

Jope squeezed the lower half of his right arm free and worked his shaking hand into the pocket of his shorts to find the tiny coral Dakuwaqa carving. He rubbed the figurine as hard and fast as he could, praying to his scary shark-god in mumbled sobs.

"Op ubbing your alls!" Ratu begged his blubbering friend, now pinned tighter than ever in the fractured, flooding pilot house of the doomed Julius Caesar.

The mighty shark-god was on his knees in the sand, his back to the water. The sinewy muscles all across Dakuwaqa's broad shoulders rippled and flexed in the pale moonlight. His strong hands plied at the sand as he whistled a tune between thousands of razor-sharp teeth. Behind him, dozens of small brown wrapped packages floated free from the wrecked boat's galley, bobbing in the black water. The stolen fishing charter continued to break up from the unrelenting waves. Even Dakuwaqa couldn't smell the cocaine—it was too pure—but he could smell the recycled paper it was wrapped in, which had once been used to ship coffee. Between whistles he sniffed the sweet scent, longing for a latte as he continued to shape the sand beneath him.

Dakuwaqa finished scooping a deep circular moat, then scanned the immediate area for bits of driftwood to add to his sandcastle. He settled on slivers of broken conch, carefully sticking them into the tower nearest the main gate. On one of the towers his country's flag would wave; the heads of his imaginary enemies would be impaled on the others.

Over the crackle of fire and rumble of breakers—and his own whistling—Dakuwaqa first mistook the strange sound carried on the slight wind as the call of a New Caledonia kagu, or even the throaty cry of an Eclectus Parrot. Being an ocean god, he didn't have much interest in birds, one way or the other. He ate his fair share, but crashing up from the depths to gnash his mighty teeth on a bobbing pelican was more for show than anything else. He'd take a plate of nachos over a bag of feather and bone every time. But when water finally extinguished the orange blaze and sent a trail of thick black smoke up over his head toward the twinkling stars, the plaintive wail became unambiguously human.

"Please come back, shark-god!" shouted a terribly frightened voice in the night. "The cannibals are trying to eat us!"

Dakuwaqa brushed sand from his big hands, sat back on his muscular rump, and smiled down at his work.

CHAPTER 23

Dante stood on the wet concrete between the Rarotonga International Airport terminal and the plane he'd just disembarked. The heaviest rain clouds had pushed off in the morning breeze, and if there was ever a moment for the former ski racer to experience déjà vu, this was it. The jagged Ikurangi Peak just to the east would have caught the eye of any of the regular European racers. This time of day, it was a twin of the pyramid-like Matterhorn, tinted pink with the same morning alpenglow.

Dante had raced in the shadow of the Matterhorn at least a dozen times, on the Zermatt race slopes in the Europa Cup competitions. The Europa Cups were where young racers lowered their points with the hope of promotion within their country's team, making the next step onto the World Cup stage. In fact, the race that had killed Dante for about five minutes was a mere sixty kilometers from the iconic Swiss peak. Had he been conscious, he would have enjoyed a marvelous view from the medevac helicopter whisking him to the trauma center.

"Welcome to the Cook Islands!" read a giant canvas sign spread across the glass walls of the terminal building. Dante shouldered his two stuffed backpacks and followed a sleepy group of red-eye travelers toward the doors marked for arrivals. His long legs were shaky from being crammed behind three subsequent airplane seats for nearly nineteen hours. Despite having emerged from a vegetative state just a few weeks earlier, Dante had rebuilt a good deal of his coordination and a fair amount of muscle. Still wobbly, he dealt with chronic headaches and felt winded and nauseated after basic physical activity. But his strength would come back, the doctors said. Not all of it, since he was forbidden to engage in stressful or high-impact workouts, but enough to lose the constant sense of frailty.

"You might live to be a hundred, or you could die tomorrow from one solid jolt to your brain," his twice weekly therapist told him. "Setting off on such a long trip away from medical care is suicidal. I'm half temped to commit you to the psych ward just to give you an opportunity to understand that this is fantasy. This obsession is a leftover dream your damaged brain has accepted as reality."

"I'm leaving tomorrow," he'd said.

Jennifer had delivered his backpacks stuffed with clothes, along with his passport and a receipt for electronic plane tickets. One of the backpacks contained plastic bags filled with fifty dollar bills, which she'd warned might raise eyebrows at airport security. Dante figured the truth would be enough. He would just explain that he was taking everything he owned with him.

"Yes, I know you're leaving." The therapist had expressed his frustration and disapproval with a great exhale of exasperation. He wore a name tag containing many letters jumbled in a way that may or may not have been another symptom of Dante's confusing new language difficulties. It was also possible that the brown-skinned doctor really did have a difficult foreign name. Dante was reasonably certain his brain was capable of masking or altering voices, since he'd recently listened to a television news anchor who sounded exactly like a young girl.

Curiosity finally got the better of him. "How do you say that?" Dante asked, pointing at the name tag.

"How do you say what?"

"How do you say your name?" Dante pointed again at the pin on the man's white lab coat. "How is it pronounced?"

"Are you serious?" he'd asked, and then realized the former ski racer was deadly serious. "It reads 'Alex Jones, DPT.' The DPT stands for Doctor of Physical Therapy. But that's not how you're seeing it, is it?"

"Jesus." Dante buried his face in his hands.

"And it is my professional opinion, based on years of experience with traumatic brain injuries, that you will be killing yourself should you pursue this wild goose chase."

"Everyone tells me I've been a ski racer since I was a little kid, Doc." Dante sat in a chair next to his bed, getting used to the feeling of jeans and a button down shirt. The last place he wanted to be was in that damned bed. It had come to feel like a coffin, smelled like death. He'd spent the last two nights sleeping in the old vinyl visitors' chair, despite how stiff it left him in the morning. "Not exactly an option to go back to, huh?"

"No it isn't, but you have plenty of other options. You have access to an occupational therapist and there's a very nice community college not far from where you live."

"I moved out. My stuff is all sold and my lease is broken."

"Nevertheless, running off is the worst possible decision." The therapist stood over him, chart open, reminding Dante of a cop on a reality show he'd watched with the other residents. The officer had explained that standing over a suspect reinforced the image of authority.

"It was explained to me that I have a tenth grade education." Dante felt the warm flush of anger returning. "And that doesn't mean shit because of how much was erased. I ask to pass the salt and they look at me like I'm from outer space. The salt, I say, pass the fucking salt! And then they all get up from the table, move away from the crazy fucker who's screaming about rabid cats. And there I am, some babbling moron sitting alone, staring across the table at a salt shaker. Yeah, great life, Doc, exactly how I imagined it would be."

"Your story isn't uncommon. Time and proper therapy may alleviate symptoms of the damage and help you recognize and deal with situations where you lose words. I understand your frustration, but running away is certainly not the answer."

"I'm going home."

"No you're not," the therapist said flatly. "You are a young man with his entire life ahead of him. You've been told the difficulties that lie ahead, as well as the potential dangers. And you've likely chosen to kill yourself."

"Okay, well, I appreciate your honesty. But I could die here, just the same, right? There's no guarantee I won't stumble into a bathroom door and drop dead."

The therapist sighed. "Again, with long-term physical therapy you will stumble less. You will run into fewer bathroom doors, or kitchen or bedroom doors."

"Your recommendation that I accept a new life of being taught how not to stumble into doors is duly noted."

"You pointed to a picture of an elephant when I asked you to show me the hamburger."

"I was kidding."

"If you were kidding, then that too is a manifestation of a serious psychological condition," he'd said, once again sighing long and hard for effect. "Okay, I have other patients I am seriously neglecting." He held out a long-fingered, delicate brown hand to Dante.

Dante took the hand. "I knew it was an elephant."

And now, contrary to all recommendations, here he was in the Rarotonga International Airport.

A smiling woman in a flower-patterned dress, whose skin was as black as any he'd seen, ushered Dante through customs with a friendly wave. He walked straight through the building and back out into the humid air on the other side of the terminal, stopping to consider his next move. Still some four hundred miles from "home"—easily the toughest segment of the journey since it meant going across open ocean waters—Dante decided to join the nearest line of waiting people. Let fate move things along for a while, he thought, as he stood next to the twenty tourists and locals who were lined up in an orderly fashion at the roadside curb. The quiet collection of people moved as one, looking first right and then left, prompted by the distant approach of each noisy vehicle.

When the first bus pulled up, Dante noticed that the big marquee over the windshield simply read, "Clockwise."

"Clockwise sounds good," Dante whispered as he climbed the stairs, brimming backpacks slung over each shoulder. "Maybe we'll stop for a nice elephant burger."

With a hard jolt, the bus pulled away.

CHAPTER 24

Dante sat at one of three picnic tables under a corrugated plastic awning of a burger stand midway between the airport and Avarua, Cook Islands' national capital. Trusting fate seemed to be working out so far. According to a local woman on the clockwise traveling bus, the capital would be the best place to hire a one-way boat ride to East Pukapuka. When he'd asked about the clockwise bus, she'd explained there was another bus somewhere out on the same highway, called the anti-clockwise bus. It made the same ninety kilometer loop around the island perimeter, traveling in the opposite direction.

Written across the four dollar, one-way ticket Dante held folded in his hand were the words, "Please smile."

The driver announced "breakfast time" and pulled the bus to a stop along the Ara Tapu, the unnamed main road circling the island. The milling travelers either waited in line for food or sat watching the light morning traffic zoom by. Noisy motor scooters and small cars raced along the paved Polynesian highway, chased by low clouds trapped by the hills and then pushed parallel to the coast.

"First time to Raro?" one of the passengers sitting across the picnic table from Dante asked.

"I think so." Dante was starving but tired. His leg muscles were burning from all the standing around. The line to the burger window wasn't moving, so he decided his stomach could wait. The unbearable humidity had plastered his polo shirt and khaki pants to his skin. From the center of the table, Dante snatched a few paper napkins being held down with a rock. As he swept the napkin across his forehead, fat drops of sweat caught in his eyelashes, stinging his eyes.

"Here for a holiday?" a woman asked. A small child wearing only a diaper—perhaps her granddaughter?—lay curled on her wide lap. She stroked the long black hair of the two-or-three-year-old who nuzzled into the blue checkerboard pattern of her dress.

"I'm passing through, heading back home."

"Where's home for you?"

"Do you know East Pukapuka?"

"You don't look like anyone I've ever seen from East Pukapuka." The woman raised her eyebrows. "Only brown people lived on East Pukapuka."

"Lived?"

"Yes, the big wave." The woman looked down and wrinkled her nose, lifting the diaper waistband to check for the source of the odor.

"What do you mean by *big wave*?"

"The big wave washed everything away." The woman again stroked the child's hair, having apparently found nothing in the diaper. "Everybody knows about the big wave. Lots of pictures in the newspapers, but maybe not back where you're comin' from, right?"

"No, wait, there was a tsunami?" Dante tried not to panic. He'd watched an hour-long show on channel sixty-three about the devastation of tsunamis. Entire cultures were wiped out, and once-bustling villages were left looking like trash dumps.

"You're certain it hit East Pukapuka?"

"Yes, of course I'm certain. Rescuers had nothing to do but bury the dead that were left. Fishing boat found one body way, way out at sea beyond the island, maybe forty kilometers. It was a terrible thing." The woman shook her head. "It was a really big wave."

"Everyone is dead? The entire village was killed?" Dante pictured the travel channel images of children's faces, of the handsome men and women who populated his dreams. But now they were dead? Dante tried to recall the voice of the sobbing girl he'd heard as he'd climbed from the dark water on the leeward side of the island following each night's swim. He knew she was lost and calling out a person's name, but the name was nonsense, another piece of gibberish from his screwed up brain. The dream always ended before he had a chance to look for the girl and help her search.

"No worries, everybody's okay," the woman said, but her eyes were filled with tears. "They've all gone on to Happa Now. It's okay to miss them, but the people are in a good, good place."

"When did this happen?" Dante knew the woman meant the people had gone to some form of Heaven. His stomach had begun to churn at the smell of onions and frying meat. He wasn't sure how to react, how news of this catastrophe should make him feel. It was as if a long lost twin had died in a car crash while coming to meet him for the first time. Dante watched the cars zip past, feeling guilty that the entire event was beginning to seem less horrible. After all, there were no other people on East Pukapuka he'd come to know; they were nothing but images from a collection of snapshots or exotic postcards. Complete strangers, except for the unseen child whose plaintive voice called out the name of a long-dead writer from thousands of miles away.

"It's been maybe a couple weeks, now. You had people there? East Pukapuka was really your home?"

Dante struggled to answer the Raro woman, just as he had

struggled to respond to his therapist. At the care center he'd been pressed again and again, until his brain physically hurt. To be absolutely certain something was true when faced with indisputable evidence it was not caused actual physical pain.

"Leave me alone," had been the answer he had given his therapist when confronted with facts refuting what he knew to be true. But that surely wasn't an acceptable answer for this woman holding a baby in her lap at a roadside food stand. Dante was forced to respond honestly by the innocence of the woman's question and the fact that he'd come into her life by boarding her clockwise traveling bus. Dante decided to keep trusting in fate.

"I had an accident." Dante looked directly into the woman's brown eyes. "They told me I suffered a traumatic brain injury that put me into a long coma. Now I'm here, trying to get home to a place I've never been. I know it's crazy."

"I'm sorry for your injury." The woman paused, stroking the baby's hair. "But maybe it's not crazier than a sea god who sends a wave to kill a hundred people."

"My memory was erased. Everything was gone except for this path I kept following each evening, just before sunset. It led to the edge of the water. I'd swim far out, until I could barely see the tree tops."

"This path was on East Pukapuka?" the woman asked in a hushed voice, turning the baby over in her lap to rub small circles on its naked back.

"Yes, my home."

"The people are all gone from the island," she said in a gentle voice. "They moved on, far away to Happa Now. No comin' back."

"I'd hear a little girl's voice when I climbed back out of the water. She was crying and calling out for someone, trying to find her family, I suppose."

"So you dreamed a girl survived the big wave?"

"My therapist insisted it was a dream." Dante paused,

watching the traffic. "But I know it couldn't have been a dream. I felt the coral scrape my knees when I swam across the reef, and the texture of the thick mat of seaweed I had to push out of my way closer to the shore. It all happened, night after night. I tasted the salt water, felt the broken shells on my palms. The little girl's voice …"

"She was calling out somebody's name?" The woman's eyes narrowed. "What name did she call?"

Dante hesitated, embarrassed by how nonsensical this memory was, how his mind mocked him, turning language and chunks of words into gibberish. The name he'd clearly heard, night after night, had to be a mistake, a misfiring of his wounded, jumbled brain function. What he heard were the cries of a brokenhearted little girl on a South Pacific island, the sole survivor of a disastrous tsunami. Dante knew she had suffered the loss of her entire family, her home, and was now crying out for a famous English biologist—dead for more than a century and featured regularly on cable channel science and travel shows.

"She was sobbing," Dante finally said, once again feeling like the dimwitted fool unable to convey a simple request for a salt shaker, "and she was crying out for Charles Darwin."

The woman's eyes widened as she scooped the sleeping child up in her arms and hugged her tightly. "Charles Darwin was a very, very nice lady. She was my cousin on your island."

CHAPTER 25

In his dream Captain Dobby took a swig and sang an old pirate song about rum, his legs twitching and jigging to the tune. His dream-knees were like new—didn't make popping and crackling noises, never threatened to give out. His actual bottle of rum lay empty on the tugboat's pilot house floor. Propelled by the undulating sea, it turned slow revolutions on its side, as if ghosts were playing spin the bottle.

Dobby lay slumped across a salvaged wicker loveseat that left the skin of his half-naked body dented and creased—a sight that always scared the hell out of him upon first waking. For the love of Christ, what miserable disease this time?

In his dream Dobby stood on the bridge of a luxury yacht breathing in a spicy fragrance. The glorious and familiar scent flicked on the switch to his salivary glands. Spittle meandered between gray chest hairs, finally pooling in his belly button, which was already half full with filthy lint.

Dobby's drool was produced by the heavy herbal smell of Chinese turtle soup. How long had it been since his last taste? Back before he'd left Pitcairn three months ago, give or take an alcohol-clouded week. It had been at the tavern with the oily

skinned brown girls who offered dollar lap-dances to the same
bar stool regulars. The ones with wives who would strangle
them bare-handed if they were ever caught straddled by one of
these bimbos. Polynesia was a man's world, but a place where
the quiet wrath of a woman should never be underestimated.
There were sharp knives absolutely everywhere.

Dobby had sat on a tall stool of the Little Bible Beer and
Grub, a favorite haunt for locals around Adamstown. It was
an easy hike from the shack he kept on a rocky bluff, which
offered a wide view of the yam plantations. The drunken
stumble home was fraught with danger, however; one bad step
meant a sixty-foot plunge into a jagged lava rock patch.

At the rickety wood table Dobby hunched over the steaming
bowl of turtle soup, spoon to his nose, eyes watching the
chunky bimbos making their lazy rounds. The spices cleared
the crusted sea salt from his sinuses, overran the musky taste
of locally brewed beer, and took him back through the years
to when his mother stood over the huge simmering pot every
Thanksgiving. As usual, his dream wandered through time,
took him to a place where he was maybe eight years old and
the smell of turtle soup evoked love and fear.

In Texas his mother had served snapping turtle instead
of turkey on important holidays. Normally dinnertime was
peaceful; it would take a few hours for enough Old Grandad
bourbon to combine with the beer and turn his father all
black and ornery. Dobby knew this was the reason his mother
stretched out the meals as long as she could. She brought out
each course real slow, fussing over his father. It was her way of
buying time before the hitting started. His father was probably
even in on her game, but he sure seemed to relish being treated
like the king of his own single wide. He was Texas royalty,
lording over the end of the table, a stained napkin jammed
into his shirt collar.

While his mother got to work on the dishes, Dobby was
outside throwing stones at the old TV next to the dog pen.

He'd heard his father go on and on in a bragging tone to his buddies from down at the slaughterhouse, while they drank Lone Star longnecks and made half-assed attempts to split wood out back of the trailer. The boy didn't know the meaning of most of the words his father used to describe his mother to them, but they were all preceded by "stupid" or "dumb." He sure knew what those words meant.

"Go gemme another cold one, ya little dumb fuck, and wipe that stupid look off yer face, for Christ's sake."

Turtle soup was the good smell of his mother when she came into his room after midnight. She'd be wearing her old torn pink robe, its sash cinched tightly in a knot at her waist, her hair a tumbled mess. She'd be sniffling back a mix of blood and snot, the little bit of makeup she was allowed to wear while serving the holiday meal smudged and giving her silly-looking raccoon eyes. Her cheeks were puffy and bruised. As she climbed into his warm bed, she picked at the knot of her threadbare robe, pulling it open and inviting him to snuggle right up against her cool bare skin. Her funny patch of scratchy hair down there tickled his legs, but he didn't mind one little bit. God, he loved her so much. Here in his mama's arms was the only safe place in his entire world. They lay huddled, wrapped in a thin pink cocoon, her occasional shudders making him squeeze closer. Her lovely fragrance of nail polish and turtle soup washed over them, as tiny tears escaped his clenched eyes. He wished he could build a jet airplane and fly them both away from the awful snoring coming from the next room. Or maybe build a boat and sail them into the dusty sunset.

And then the grown-up captain's dream shifted forward through the years, back to the bowl of turtle soup on the island of Pitcairn, where he closed his eyes and let the aroma waft up and cover his face like a shroud. It was a smell as complicated as being in love with your mother and wanting to murder your father.

When Dobby opened his eyes in the dream, he saw the half-naked bimbo grinding her big round bum against the crotch of a leathery old fisherman. Dimes and quarters bounced on the table each time her knees struck its low edge. It was a dream he'd had a thousand times and would have a thousand times more if he lived long enough. A tear for his long dead mother splashed into his steaming turtle soup, just as the sound of a blood-curdling scream wrenched him from the dream and sent him scrambling to find the little brown girl.

CHAPTER 26

The strong breeze tore small slivers of red and black paint loose from the chugging tugboat, swirling and fluttering in the air pocket behind the pilot house, reminding Butter of the dancing butterflies during their island to island migration. The butterflies were mostly black, with a white circle on each wing. The males had intense blue auras around their circles and the females had flecks of orange.

Franklin Roosevelt, the village's best tree climber, had tried to convince Butter that the butterflies were the confused souls of the recent dead trying to find the path to Happa Now.

"No they aren't. They're just butterflies." Butter stood in the shade of a tight grove of puka trees as Roosevelt expertly husked a young coconut with a machete and carved out the soft white meat.

"I see them when I am in the tall trees." Roosevelt pointed the machete at Butter, a square of meat on the end of the blade. "They fly around all crazy, looking for the path. I think the souls must be blind. The butterflies who venture farthest away from the pack, who climb up on the highest wind currents, get sucked into the tunnel to Happa Now."

Roosevelt made a popping sound with his long brown finger and cheek to mimic the sound of the lucky ones getting sucked into the tunnel.

"Only people can go to Happa Now," a skeptical Butter said, taking the piece of coconut from the blade and sucking the sweet milk.

"The souls ride on the wings; you see them as blue and orange spots. The souls are allowed in and the rest of the butterfly is spit back out." The tall, skinny man spit a chunk of coconut, showing the little girl how the afterlife worked.

Even though Roosevelt was held in high regard for his climbing skills and was married to the fattest and most beautiful village girl, he wasn't necessarily telling the truth. Butter knew that about grown-ups.

Grown-ups said things just to make sad children feel better, like when they would step on your favorite conch shell you'd spent days decorating with paints and gluing on tiny starfish and shiny tumbled rocks.

"Oops," they'd say. "I'll help you fix it tomorrow." That was a lie. No fixing was ever done the next day. Not by the grown-ups, at least.

And Butter was five or so when all the magic of the Tooth Devil was spoiled. She'd done her best to stay awake in her bedroll—hours after the village had gone silent. Mama had placed her little white front tooth with its bloody flecks on the Devil Spoon, an item each household on the island possessed. The wooden spoon and child's tooth were to be left on the ground at the threshold of the home as an offering to the Tooth Devil. In exchange for the tooth, the Tooth Devil always left a fine black pearl, supposedly from the deepest part of the ocean where he lived.

Hours passed as Butter lay quietly waiting. Occasionally she heard footsteps pass her hut—human-sounding and accompanied by soft whispers—a distant coughing fit and a brief argument between a man and his wife; then silence fell over the village.

Sleep came for the tired little girl just as an alien sound pulled her from its grasp. Was it real, or a sound from behind the curtain of a dream she was approaching? The sound came again, and Butter's heart raced when she heard the odd rustling. Her eyes flew back open and searched the darkness. Right there in the open entryway of her home—maybe seven steps from where she lay curled in her soft blanket—stood the beast from a thousand meters under the ocean. It was hunched over the Devil Spoon, murmuring something in its devil language. The Tooth Devil had apparently dropped her tiny tooth in the darkness and was padding around the floor and front step searching in the scant light of the sliver of moon.

Butter was petrified. What if the Tooth Devil couldn't find it in the dark? What if it had dropped through a crack too small for its hand or horrible tongue? Might it not expect another as replacement? It was, after all, a long trip from his home in the deepest water.

"Damn it to hell," the Tooth Devil hissed in Butter's own language, and she shrank back even deeper into her covers, her own tongue frantically testing her remaining front tooth for any hint of a wiggle. There was none. It was still in there as solid as could be.

That's when the Tooth Devil turned on her and came for it. She had imagined it would hold her down, one devil hand on her forehead, the other on her chin, forcing open her mouth. The effort would require just a tiny portion of the strength it took to swim the thousand meters to and from its murky home. She had imagined its face would come down to hers, as if to kiss her open mouth, instead breathing in the intoxicating scent of the little kid teeth it lusted for.

"Please take only one," Butter would try to say, but her jaw would be locked open as the beast began to nibble at her gums.

Butter wanted to cry out for her mama and papa, but

was frozen in fear as the creature slowly crawled across the polished wood planks of her home's floor. The Tooth Devil's bulk blotted out any light from the moon, and the Devil Spoon clicked in its hands as it used all four limbs to scramble closer.

Butter clenched her eyes shut as tightly as she clenched her jaw, waiting for the prying to begin. She had somehow known the smell that would come—the stench of spoiled fish and rotten seaweed. The smell of dead crab in the hot sun would close her throat, keep her from screaming. But none of that happened. Instead of stink, instead of clawing and biting, she felt just a brush of rough lips on her damp forehead. She knew those rough chapped lips. They had kissed her goodnight ever since she was a little baby. When she dared open her eyes, she saw the Devil Spoon there on her bedroll, with a small speck of fine black pearl right where it was supposed to be.

The little girl felt relief, then confusion, then betrayal. As she watched her papa push aside the billowing silk screen that separated her bed from her parents', Butter reflected with some bitterness that she had been lied to. She reached out for the small black pearl, rolling it between her thumb and forefinger. It was hard, smooth, and cold. Not the least bit magical.

Now, as Butter stood on the main deck of the Gypsy Dancer watching the butterfly paint chips, she suddenly realized that everything the grown-ups told her had been a lie. Every word had been made up.

So she screamed as hard and loud as she could to drown out all the lies. Grown-ups only pretended to care about you, when they were really only worrying about themselves. They broke your things and smashed your heart all up. They did stupid things that got them sent to Happa Now while you still needed them. They deserted you. They went off to be happy and left you all by yourself. Birds and snakes didn't do that to their babies. Lizards didn't either. Nothing else did, just stupid human parents. Grown-ups could go on with their lives on Happa Now, while all her patients had nowhere to go. They simply died. And here she was on this stinking boat with the dirty rotten god who might have caused it all.

Butter's screaming made the hurt stop.

Chapter 27

"It's ... not ... fair!" Butter wailed between banshee-like shrieks and blood-curdling screams, some of which caught in her throat, interspersing her tantrum with coughing and gagging fits.

Butter lifted the pink doll in front of her face and squeezed it hard enough to make deep indentations in the plastic. "It doesn't hurt because you're fake, too!"

She clutched the doll against her ribs and with her left hand grabbed at its head, her neck muscles taut and straining as she pried under its chin where it was connected to the torso. When the round baby head finally popped off, Butter grunted with satisfaction. She turned and threw the head over the side of the boat with all her might, then lifted the body and slammed it down onto the deck. The doll bounced almost straight up.

Butter began to yell again, "Everything is dead! Dead, dead, dead!" Her feet were planted at shoulder width, her brown, compact body naked except for a narrow woven belt. Her arms were bent at the elbows, her hands clenched into white-knuckle fists, as if ready to challenge any comers. "Everything is lies and everything is dead!" Butter screamed, a high-pitched wail that turned into a dreadful approximation of a boatswain's pipe, the whistle that announced visiting dignitaries aboard ships.

The screaming went on and on, while a confused and winded Dobby stood at the base of the pilot house ladder on the twenty-by-forty foot deck—piled with salvage and other junk—fearing the girl's next move. She had no obvious wounds, was not dripping blood. There was nothing flopping around on the deck, no flying fish or dying birds. She'd apparently gone berserk, or maybe was possessed by a devil.

"What's wrong with—" Dobby began during what seemed like a lull, but the little girl's voice wound back up like an air raid siren.

"I took care of every hurt animal!" Butter shouted, spittle flying. "I was always good! I washed the bedding! I swept when I was told, and I piled the coconuts and I took trash to the fire pit! My mama and papa and everybody are dead and now I'm alone out in the middle of nowhere! No stupid god has any right to hurt people like that! Any dumb god who would do that shouldn't be a god in the first place! The god should be dead instead of all the people and animals! Dead!"

Another pause and Dobby took a step toward the girl with no idea what to do. The only blind fury he'd ever witnessed was his father's and the time some drunk in the bar had decided the guy sitting next to him was the one who made his wife run off.

"It's your fault!" Butter screamed at the captain, more spittle flying. "It's all your rotten fault!"

"What did I do?" Dobby retreated one step, surrendering the space he'd just ventured into.

Butter directed her white hot fury directly at Dobby. "Who kills little babies?" Her voice was gravelly, older.

"Babies?" Dobby's head ached from the hangover and all the screaming. He shifted from foot to foot, needing very much to pee over the gunwale. Little bits of black and red paint were raining down on him from the rusting smoke stack, as a strong breeze blew across the choppy water. "I swear I never kilt no baby."

Butter turned her full wrath on the captain. "You're a lazy, fat god, who eats his own boogers and sniffs his stinking armpits! I've seen you!"

Dobby was used to being alone and bad habits were easy to develop. He was instantly ashamed, but even now was fighting an overwhelming urge to turn his head and sniff his armpit. It was just awful how that worked. "I'm sorry."

"I never did anything wrong to you or any other stupid old god!" Butter shouted, her naked body glistening with sweat. She was pointing her right index finger at Dobby, stabbing at the air. She moved toward him, menacing, stepping over her decapitated baby doll.

Dobby was cowering, flinching at every screeched accusation. "Oh, please, girl …" he muttered, attempting to retreat. He had backed into the lower bridge door and was groping for the handle with his shaking hand. His dirty fingernails tapped against the rusty metal, finding rivets but no latch. Dobby's head and bladder were filled with a sick heat and he needed to get away. His stomach rolled over.

"You and your gods killed my snakes!" roared the little girl, jabbing her finger at him with each word. "You killed the birds with broken wings! Who would kill a bird that couldn't fly? You killed everything! You killed Franklin Roosevelt and Charles Darwin!"

"I'm sorry," Dobby moaned, regressing into the little boy his father had so often belittled. Worse, he'd promised his mother never to hurt a woman, and now here was a miniature version accusing him of killing her family, her pets, and a famous president. "I'm sorry. I have to pee," he said weakly.

"You have to fix everything right this minute!" Butter demanded, now just a few steps from the captain, who had given up finding the door latch behind his back. Instead, he covered his face with grimy hands. "I want to go home right now!" Butter howled and lunged at the captain, pummeling his bare arms and chest with tiny, balled-up fists.

It was Dobby's turn to begin sobbing like he often did in bars right around closing time. His mother had warned him about god and karma, even though they'd never once gone to church to experience them first hand. His father had forbidden church-going, didn't trust a word out of that lying preacher's pie hole. And Dobby now knew he was somehow responsible for everything that had happened to this little girl. The bad things he'd done, despite promises to his mother, couldn't be blamed on the booze. This epiphany slammed down on Dobby's shoulders like a two-ton anchor. He was guilty as charged, had gone ahead and let down another person instead of bein' any kind of hero.

Butter punched and slapped the defenseless captain, ripped handfuls of gray hair from his chest. She splashed Dobby with her sweat and tears, making small nicks and cuts in his arms with her jagged fingernails. Her long black hair whipped about her face. "You killed everything I care about! You did it! I hate your stupid guts!"

Dobby caught hold of the slick girl, who tried to wriggle away from his grasp like a trapped animal. "I'm sorry," he said again.

"Let me go!" But Dobby's rough, callused hands held tight. He scooped her up from the deck as she aimed a few final kicks into his thighs, delivering one glancing blow to the testicles. Dobby's kept his grip on her.

"It'll be okay," Dobby tried, but that only unleashed another struggling flourish, making his right testicle ache deep inside his stomach. Now he needed to pee *and* puke. "Oh god, please stop, girl."

"You're a rotten liar!" Butter shouted painfully into his left ear. She would have bitten it off if he hadn't immediately twisted his neck away, recoiling from her caterwauling. "You're a killer!"

"What can I do?" Dobby pleaded. "How can I help you? I'll do anything, just tell me. I never meant to hurt nobody."

Suddenly the fight drained out of Butter. It was there and then it was gone. Beyond exhaustion, she hung limply in the captain's arms. All the anger and hate that had flooded her body was now far away.

"Take me home," Butter whispered in the ear she'd just tried to bite off. "Make everything alive again."

"Oh, dear god." Dobby groaned at such a task, knowing he had no choice but to try. He'd promised his mother and knew he couldn't let her down again. Dobby hadn't been able to save his mother from his drunken father, who'd been taken over by that black rage. That's the way his father had described it to the sheriff's men who'd come and driven Dobby's father away in one car and Dobby in another. That awful black rage came out of nowhere, just took over his mind and there was nothin' anybody could do about it. It made him start slapping his wife, tearing the old pink robe off her body and throwing her down the steps onto the dusty ground out behind the trailer. And the slaps turned to punches because he needed her to know how mad she'd made him, how angry the black rage made him feel. A fist full of hair bunched up in his left hand and his right knuckles pounding away like he was pumping the tire jack under his pickup truck.

After his father was done punching, Dobby had run to his mama. When the black rage lifted, his father was calm as could be, sorta like when a tornado came through, wrecked your barn and killed half your cows, then just blew away and disappeared. It got quiet, too, with no more shouting and no more crying. The little boy knew right away his mama wasn't going to be okay. Her face bones were all broken and sunken in and her lips were torn away from her face, just hanging by threads and showing her teeth like she was trying to smile. Dobby kissed her anyway. Knew he was kissing her goodbye.

Dobby looked down into the face of the little girl clinging to him.

"Where's my turtle?" Butter suddenly asked, as if realizing for the first time she wasn't still clinging to its shell. And the captain's heart sank again, maybe down to where dead turtles wind up.

CHAPTER 28

Eight-thousand miles from the Vermont apartment his ski team trainer claimed had been filled with his belongings, Dante hunched over a partially eaten burger. Those belongings had included four flat screen televisions, three water bongs, and five overflowing cartons of girl-on-girl porn videos that she'd sold or bagged for the trash while he suffered through daily rehab.

It began raining—noisy drops tapping at the corrugated plastic awning.

"My oldest daughter is a policeman here on Raro, a Senior Sergeant," the grandmother across the picnic table told Dante, while patting the child's bare back. A chilly new gust of wind cut through the humid air and stole a few napkins in a flutter. "She knows most of the rescuers who went to East Pukapuka after the big wave, and there was nobody left. They buried a few bodies, but most were washed away. They've all moved to the next life on Happa Now."

Dante pulled a nylon ski team jacket out of one backpack, scratched at the itchy beard taking over his pale face. He no more recognized the face he touched than the thin jacket with sponsor logos on the chest and shoulders. Oddly, he knew VISA was a credit card, but didn't know what an Alka Seltzer did. As for his face, he tried to make sense of what his former trainer had said. How he'd been able to seduce so many women, herself included. When he looked in the mirror, his blue eyes looked droopy and sad to him, almost pathetic, like the eyes of a beagle who's chewed up something irreplaceable and is about to face the music. The funny cleft chin that he pinched to make deeper. Did he inherit it from his father? From his mother?

Dante had plenty of scars on his legs, but most were older and not from the final crash. The damage that lingered from the recent accident was mostly on the inside. He had stood before the mirror in the care center bathroom clenching his teeth, flexing the big muscles at the hinge of his jaw, watching the unfamiliar face change. His brown hair was short and his jaw line sharp.

"Who are you?" But the face that looked back at him wore an oddly blank expression.

"I'm nobody."

"You're just a bunch of blurry pictures in photo albums." Dante grabbed both sides of the sink basin, his legs weak from standing on the hard tiles. "Almost funny, isn't it? You were such a great guy that the people who visit sit tapping their feet, wishing like hell the time was up so they can get the fuck away from you."

"There's no fixing it," the face said.

"Damn fucking straight there's no fixing it," Dante replied. "So what's next? I just get on a plane and go home? I just forget these people?"

"You're a joke, Dante. Who do you have to forget?"

"Okay, I get it. You're right."

"People have wanted to escape from you for longer than you want to know. One of the pictures they stuck under your nose was of your old man. I guess one of the docs wanted to see if something clicked inside your empty head. Bet you didn't see that guy's mug bringing you flowers and a box of chocolates. Any get well cards with a Florida return address? Hey, for that matter, exactly how many get well cards did you get?"

Dante looked away from the mirror, back toward his bed and the empty table next to it. "Enough, I'm done." His leg muscles burned.

"You wanna hear the last straw with dear old dad?"

"I know what happened."

"Guess who was sneaking out of the team hotel rooms in Europe while his mother was dying of cancer? They had to plant one of the ski tech guys in the lobby just to keep you from bars and whorehouses while Mom was wasting away from chemo."

"I remember."

"They put up with your bullshit because of your potential."

"I didn't even call her, did I?"

"Hey, you want to hear something else that's a real hoot? You picked up a few of those bar sluts by telling them about your sick mother. Nice, huh? You couldn't be bothered to pick up the phone and tell her you loved her, but you could use her cancer to get some of that fine pussy. Just between you and me, I'd say that pretty much makes you a royal asshole."

Dante's legs wobbled and he considered punching the glass, shattering this stranger's face just for the hell of it. He turned and went back to bed instead.

Back in Dante's present reality at the burger joint, the grandmother finally said, "You had a vision," and nodded her head. But Dante was still lost in thought, staring off at the misty hillside. "A vision from a place you've never been."

"The doctors said I had a dream."

"That's what a vision is, young man. You come tell my Ophelia your dream about the sad little girl and who she was looking for. My name is Mary."

Dante took her hand across the picnic table. "Dante," he said.

"That makes sense for you. The name Dante means 'to never

give up.' You aren't the kind of person to give up, are you?"

"Does Ophelia have a boat?"

"Hah, this is an island, Dante. Everybody has a boat," Mary teased, as the two watched the bus driver push aside his empty plate, rise, and walk to the edge of the awning to wait for a break in what was now a steady downpour. "Your vision is comforting news."

"My dream? What's comforting about it?"

"Yes, your dream is probably some kind of message from Happa Now." Mary paused and rolled the child over in her lap, adjusting the diaper. "It's very common for people to be homesick."

"You mean people who have died? Dead people get homesick?"

"People who have moved on, like my cousin Charles Darwin," Mary corrected. "When one person moves on, he may speak to his loved ones very quietly. Only they will hear his voice, like a whisper on the wind. But imagine the noise after a bus crash?"

"Or an entire village wiped out by a tsunami," Dante said. Even though he understood that he'd somehow been elected as a spiritual medium, he wasn't ready to buy into the whole concept. Had he believed in god before his accident? He should have asked his trainer if there were any bibles or crucifixes mixed in with the gigantic collection of girl-on-girl videos she'd made snide remarks about.

"Yes, that's right," said Mary. "An entire village of people not prepared to move on to Happa Now died too soon. Small children and strong, healthy adults, all with many years supposedly ahead of them, chosen by the gods to be sent on to their next lives."

"Or maybe it was just a dream."

"Like I said, dreams are visions. They all have meaning, even if you don't want to believe in them. But you come tell my Ophelia, okay? I want her to hear it from you."

Ninety minutes later, Dante was sitting in the great room of a Raro bungalow. It was so completely engulfed in thick vegetation it was difficult to decipher how big or small it really was. Ducking under low hanging palm fronds, Dante followed Mary up the flat stone pathway, through a wrought-iron gate, then up four steps behind her to the arched front doorway.

"Ophelia's still sleeping," Mary whispered over her shoulder, then hoisted her grandson, who was also still sleeping, over that same shoulder and led them inside. Mary whisked the child off to bed then reappeared to fuss with an ancient coffee percolator. "She's my youngest daughter's child. One of them is an important police officer; the other drinks in bars and sometimes doesn't come home for days."

"I'm sorry," Dante said.

"Life has a way of evening out. There's always bad with the good, nothing to be sorry about."

The rain had tapered off into a blowing mist beyond the large glass panes that took up most of one wall. With so many deep shades of green it was hard to imagine this part of the island ever getting hot. Dotting the garden landscape were tropical flowers in variations of orange and red, with bursts of yellow. A tall wooden fence, mostly hidden behind thick foliage, circled the entire perimeter of the property.

"It's really incredible here." Sitting on a thick cushioned couch, Dante searched the many dark nooks and crannies of the high-ceilinged room. It wasn't the home of a wealthy family—more like one handy with tools and woodworking. What would the tools that made these walls feel like in his hands? Would they be vaguely familiar? Had he ever used any sort of tools? Dante hoped so. He expected a fair amount of rebuilding awaited him on East Pukapuka. He'd anticipated paying for a place to stay, slipping right into a new life. The house meandered away from this one large room via three narrow hallways, almost cave-like tunnels that disappeared into shadows cast by windows covered in lush plants.

"How do you like it?" Mary asked from the kitchen, just as a brand new vision appeared at the mouth of one of the dark hallways. The vision was a tall female, arms crossed over a bright floral kimono robe. Her skin was pale white, highlighted by the few rays of light filtering in through the high window near her left shoulder.

Dante believed he was seeing a ghost.

"Sugar? Milk?" Mary popped her head out of the kitchen to see why she wasn't getting an answer. "Oh, good morning, Ophelia, I put Christian to bed a few minutes ago."

"She's still not home?" the blond vision asked. Her face was as long as a fashion model's, with high cheekbones and lovely full lips. "Where did you take him?"

"I left a note. I took him to the fruit stands in Nikao."

"There's fresh fruit?" asked the vision, who had apparently decided to ignore the strange white man sitting on her couch.

"Well, we stopped at the beach to watch the hermit crabs ..."

"So there's no fruit? You went all that way and you two ended up playing with hermit crabs?"

"This is Dante." Mary pointed at him. "We met at the burger stand on the trip home. He was on our bus."

Still ignoring Dante, the vision asked about coffee.

"Dante is going home to East Pukapuka," Mary said, measuring water for the percolator. "He's never been there, but his reasons are a bit complicated. He has a very interesting story I think you'll want to hear."

The glorious young woman was now glaring at Dante instead of ignoring him. She hadn't changed her stance in the hallway, as though protecting someone behind her. Dante realized it was the hallway Mary had dashed off to with the little boy. Dante recalled Mary saying her daughter was a police sergeant.

"My new friend Dante has had a vision, something he calls

a 'dream.' " Mary switched on the metal coffee pot, which immediately began making sucking sounds. "His vision was about a little girl still alive on East Pukapuka. Isn't that right, Dante?"

Dante sat quietly.

"The island you said he's never been to?" the exquisite woman asked, and even her accusing voice was angelic and lovely. Dante melted back into the couch, wanting to hide. The circumstances behind his story never seemed to translate well into words.

"I had an accident," he tried to explain, but the two women had gone back to ignoring him. "I was in a coma."

"He heard a little girl crying out for Charles Darwin." Mary set three cups side by side on the counter, grabbed a towel to wipe up stray coffee grounds.

"Mom, Charles Darwin has been dead a hundred years. That's not a vision. That's a footnote in a book."

"You have sick days." Mary located a clean spoon for the sugar bowl.

"I do not!"

"You have vacation days."

"He's brain-damaged!" the vision shouted and pointed at Dante, who was trying to blend into the couch's floral pattern. "Hit by a car? A train? What was your accident? Did you jump off a building?"

"Don't be cruel," Mary told her daughter. "It was just an accident. He doesn't want to talk about it."

"It's six hundred kilometers, Mom. I'm not taking him."

"Your Aunt Darwin is family," Mary said. "How would you like your coffee, Dante?"

"A little sugar, please." Dante tried not to stare at the beautiful blond policewoman in the kimono.

"There's no way I'm taking you." The vision stormed past him for her cup, then turned to head back down the hall. "You want to get there so badly, you're welcome to swim."

When she was out of sight, Mary spoke quietly. "You noticed Ophelia's skin is white?"

"Yes."

"Once she was also a lost little girl with no family," Mary said, setting Dante's cup in front of him. "You never leave a crying child alone in this world."

CHAPTER 29

"Help me, Ratu!" Jope called out in the dark, slapping the surface of the water with open hands as a wave picked up his skinny black body and tumbled him across the sharp coral reef. "Ouch! That hurts!" Jope screeched, trying to grab his new sore spots and still keep his chin above the roiling salt water.

"Ratu!" Jope called helplessly into the night, his nose and ears full of water, knowing one more wave would fill the rest of him. "I can't swim!"

Ten seconds later, a wave that had been gathering steam for some two thousand kilometers flipped Jope upside down and sent him headfirst toward the bottom of a deep spot between the reef and the island. "Ratu," Jope attempted to say again, but he painfully discovered that trying to talk while submerged was only good for filling your lungs with stinging sea water.

"Aaaaak!" Jope tried to say, but only topped off his lungs and slowly drifted toward the bottom, straight as a pencil, until his head bumped the sand. A big crab scuttled away. It was probably a good thing it was pitch black, for the crab would have literally scared the crap out of the pirate. Jope was deathly afraid of crabs, especially creepy talking and singing ones, like in the movie previews of *The Little Mermaid*.

Jope stayed in this position, upside down like a piece of sea grass, the current from the waves above shifting him to and fro. But just as Jope was beginning to enjoy the peaceful feeling—the tickling at his toes and the funny way his penis bobbed inside his cut-offs—Dakuwaqa the shark-god swam out of the blackness and sat down near his face, a glowing light-blue aura surrounding him.

"I can't talk," Jope told him. "I'm underwater."

"Uh, you are talking, dumbass." The shark-god pulled a fat cigar from a hidden pocket and struck a long match on the back of a starfish.

"I hate it when people call me names," Jope whimpered.

"Aw, now you're gonna cry?"

"Did you come to save me?" Jope fought back tears. "Saving people is what gods do."

"Boy, I don't think anyone could ever save you. Take a look around." The shark-god waved his cigar, its smoke forming a visible line like airplane contrails.

"Do I at least get one last wish?"

"Last wish?" The god cocked his head.

"You know, like before a firing squad shoots you. They have to give you whatever you want."

"Okay, sure, what the hell," said the shark-god, taking a big puff and sending a plume of gray smoke toward the surface. "You got one wish, kid."

"I wish that you'd save me!" Jope heard the pride in his own voice at his cleverness. It wasn't often he felt clever, especially not in front of a god.

"Yeah, sorry, that's not going to happen." The shark-god jammed the cigar back into the corner of his dangerous looking mouth.

"But you said you'd give me a last wish!" Jope was crestfallen.

"Well, I said I'd *give* you one." The shark-god casually flicked an ash into an open clam. The gesture occurred with a mild stutter, as though the underwater world worked a little slower than up in the air. "I didn't say I'd grant it."

"That's not fair." But Jope was used to these sorts of disappointments. He'd been enduring them his entire life. Why should dying be any different? "You aren't supposed to be an evil god. I made posters of you for my bedroom."

"All right, all right." The shark-god snickered and puffed gray swirling smoke. "How 'bout I give you three wishes? You wanna be rich? Have a giant wang?"

Jope kept his mouth shut. He wasn't falling for the same trick again. He just quietly wafted back and forth, upside-down in the gentle current.

"Ah, you ain't no fucking fun." The shark-god stubbed out his cigar in the sandy bottom. "Here you go, pal. Abra-fucking-cadabra!" Dakuwaqa used his deepest shark-god voice, theatrically crossing his muscular arms, nodding his head and blinking hard, like a Baghdad genie.

Jope continued to slowly waft, blinking back at the shark-god.

"Your skinny black ass is saved," the shark-god pronounced. "And you're welcome, dumbass!"

As the shark-god turned to swim off, Jope felt a tug on his right big toe. He immediately recoiled, fearing it might be a singing Disney crab, or maybe even one of those bloodthirsty cannibals from Malakula. Jesus, don't let it be one of those bastards! While some tribes didn't bother eating anybody unless they had the pleasure of killing and tenderizing him themselves, story had it that the Malakula tribe would eat week-old roadkill covered in flies and wriggling maggots. Jope swooned at the thought.

Whatever was after him had a solid grip around his ankle, and Jope had no leverage to fight. He caught a glimpse of the soles of the shark-god's feet kicking away, but everything else was murky. Up he went, pulled from above.

"Don't go! I'll take it!" Jope called after the shark-god. All the jerking and tugging made him feel like a rag doll in a dog's mouth. "You can leave me dead, but make me rich. Or give me a giant wang! Something … anything … please, please come back!" But the shark-god was long gone, not a bubble or hint of cheap cigar remaining.

Now that he was dead, Jope prayed that this was just some new god taking him toward the tunnel to Happa Now rather than the beginning of a lurid, cannibal-feeding-frenzy. He went with the flow, not that he had much choice. There was no sound as he broke the surface of the water. Tiny stars twinkled down as if in greeting.

"Hello," Jope said to the stars, as his flaccid body was dragged across the coarse sand. And then the stars disappeared, eclipsed by a round black object.

Jope liked this part of the journey to Happa Now very much. Back in Suva, the prostitutes charged three whole dollars and still wouldn't let you kiss them. Not on the mouth anyway. Here, the kiss was free and delivered under the beautiful twinkling stars of a tropical island. Wait, did this mean prostitutes on Happa Now gave away their services and kissed you on the lips? An afterlife with free hookers?

Jope's wang had not been made huge by the shark-god, but it stood proudly at attention as the kissing went on and on. If only Jope wasn't dead, he could maybe get the heavenly prostitute to move over a bit and climb aboard his modest pole of love. The tender embrace had created an almost impressive tent under his cut-off jeans.

Jope turned his head to spit up most of the salt water that had caused him to die in the first place. He hoped that wasn't too much of a turn-off for the hooker. With air filling his lungs, Jope was able to tell the angel whore what he usually told the prostitutes back home: "Please spank me."

Ratu spit out the water Jope had puked up during the mouth-to-mouth resuscitation. He grabbed his best friend in the whole world and hugged him tightly, frantically, not caring that Jope's boner was poking him in the stomach like one of the fatties they used to smoke together when business was good.

Chapter 30

The God of Time was a heavy sleeper. Fat chunks of decades often slipped away during his watch over Happa Now. That hadn't mattered much, except when he was late to a particularly critical meeting of the gods. The four had gathered to find a substitute for all the coral that couldn't make the trip to the next life. Aesthetically, the missing coral reef in the eternal version of East Pukapuka would be potentially upsetting to new residents, not to mention the reef's crucial protection as a wave break.

"Sorry," the God of Time said, taking his place among his fellow divine entities. They gave him the cold shoulder. A dozen hurricanes and a thousand tides had come and gone while they'd waited for him. They had continued on as if he wasn't there.

"Look, my job is the weather," the God of Weather said. "You try dealing with Aura God every day. She gets a hangnail and starts tossing around snowstorms and lightning bolts for laughs. Crazy bitch."

"Yeah, well I've been busy with the tides," the God of Tides countered. "Every six hours, day after day, year after year. I never get a friggin' break."

"For crying out loud you're all gods! What the hell did you think coral was?" The God of the Stars clapped his hands together. The three other gods flinched, expecting at least a moderate catastrophe, but nothing came.

"Look," the God of Weather said. "Your gig is to make sure stars don't start falling, am I right? How hard can that be? You shoulda been all over this."

"Guys!" the God of Tides shouted. "We aren't solving our problem with a bitch fest. We know only plants and humans can live on Happa Now. That's page one, paragraph one in the Laws of the Universe. But we need enough live coral to protect one lousy endless beach. Anybody? Anything?"

"I have an idea," said the God of Time.

It was partly cloudy and eighty-two degrees on Happa Now, just like most days, thanks to the God of Weather. The gentle breeze that came out of the southwest at seven kilometers per hour wouldn't have been strong enough to keep the sand flies from pestering anyone sunbathing or fishing on the beach. But there were no sand flies on Happa Now. No jiggers or bright yellow banana slugs, for that matter. And even if it was possible to fashion a fishing pole, there were no fish in the water or worms to bait hooks. No more trouble from Habu vipers.

To say that Happa Now was an especially happy place would be misleading. Although designed by the gods as the ultimate blissful sanctuary, the place had plenty of sadness to go around. Over the centuries, human beings had become too complex to be satisfied with nothing but warm sunny days, an absence of sand flies and the end of hunger. To the frustration of the gods, humans had come to define happiness more broadly to include cups of wapa juice in the evening and chicken eggs for breakfast. Not to mention the sheer joy of having a dog lick their faces after a long day. The four creators of Happa Now couldn't possibly understand the meaning of those licks. The gods relied on their own observations, which included all the other things dogs spent days licking.

Happa Now was—and is—an oxymoron. It is an island, of course, but an island that extends forever, whose seas are fathomless and whose sandy beaches are impossible to measure. There was a great dearth of theories concerning the creation of Happa Now, at least among the inhabitants of this part of the great island, because no theoretical physicists had "moved on" from this region of Polynesia. Had Albert Einstein fallen overboard while tuna fishing off Pago Pago, perhaps some of the mysteries of its origins could have been explained to its people.

Einstein might also have tapped into his Theory of Relativity to explain the lack of hostilities and the general sense of contentment bordering on malaise. Time slows down as an object's velocity increases, Einstein postulated. The God of Time had designed negative emotional responses on Happa Now to slow down in direct proportion to the amount of emotion expended. Accidentally kick someone who had fallen asleep lying across the path to the outhouses in the ribs, and the air might fill with clear molasses. Mention how thin someone's wife looked—a tremendous insult—and it might be three hours before the next person blinked.

Were there any Parisians or New Yorkers or Sudanese on Happa Now? That question was never asked by the people who had come from East Pukapuka and its surrounding regions. Impressionist Masters, Manhattan Bagels, and those long, tunic-like garments known as thawbs had no place in their Happa Now experience. And they wouldn't become part of the wonderful mystery until someone from the Sudan ate a bad plate of oysters in Hanga Roa while waiting to catch his plane back to Africa.

Happa Now was designed to make newcomers comfortable and at home. Since there was no discrimination, and the only requirement for entering Happa Now was that you had become dead, a lot of segregation was necessary. The original Malakula cannibals, for example, were isolated in the vast interior section, far away from the victims they'd already eaten once. Black people were kept far away from the New Caledonian slave traders, since the lingering hard feelings would be contrary to the overall goal of maintaining perpetual bliss. There was a village filled with abusive husbands and a colony composed entirely of women with low self-esteem. If not for the segregation, everything would slow down so badly that nobody would get a chance to enjoy this next life. They'd just stand around scowling, and that was surely no way to spend eternity.

Somewhere in the northwest corner of the great island that is Happa Now, the most recent arrivals were appearing one by one, each having taken slightly different and often chaotic paths on the wings of butterflies. They materialized on the beautiful sandy beaches with shaky knees and ruffled hair at the same moment their fluttering butterfly chariots were unceremoniously spit back out of Happa Now. The newcomers milled about, getting accustomed to their new yet somehow familiar surroundings. The puka trees were almost the same. The palm fronds brushing the old lava flows were nearly the right colors. The coral reef, a hundred meters off the beach, was the only obvious blemish to the near perfection. The God of Time had used a million liters of waterproof pastel paint on piled up rocks to replace the organisms that couldn't make the trip to Happa Now.

A middle-aged woman named Charles Darwin stood knee deep in a lagoon that looked amazingly similar to the one fifteen meters from the hut she'd been born in—the lagoon where she'd spent her entire life. Now that she was dead and reborn, everything was a little off. For one thing, there wasn't a single minnow swimming around her toes, sampling the tiny air bubbles clinging to her skin. There were no scuttling crabs, no clams, and none of the big pink conches whose insides tasted so wonderful fried up with a squirt of lemon juice. And she wasn't the least bit hungry, despite not being able to recall her last meal.

Charles Darwin tilted her chin to scan the sky that was equally void of life. There wasn't a single gull, tern, frigatebird, lapwing, heron, or egret. No chirps came from hidden spots among the coconut clusters. No hoots, and no cuckoos. It was pretty enough, but it was awfully weird. She was not a happy camper—as the saying goes—and her increasingly agitated emotions were slowing time down all around her. Wriggling her chubby toes in the not quite right sand, under the not quite right water, the naked godmother of a ten-year-old girl who had gotten lost on the trip to Happa Now was growing increasingly distraught.

Charles Darwin replayed their final moments at the edge of their island. The villagers clasped hands to form a great chain around the lagoon that was almost identical to the one in which she now stood. It had been a moment of perfect peace, of complete togetherness shared by her doomed people. Total bliss, right before the big wave crashed down on them, killing every last being. The gods had summoned them to their new lives with noisy voices.

So where was Butter? As godmother, Charles Darwin was fully responsible for the girl's spiritual development should her parents meet an untimely death, which they certainly had. Charles Darwin had looked under every bush, searched every tree, and called and called for the little girl to come out from wherever she might be hiding. She'd even tried the universal cry, the plaintive appeal every child recognized as the all-clear sign that it was safe to come home.

And here in water—which was either just a little too salty or maybe not quite salty enough—Charles Darwin cupped her slightly wrinkled brown hands around her mouth and took a deep breath.

"Olly, olly, oxen free!" Charles Darwin shouted into the vast green and blue expanse, which looked so much like the vast green and blue expanse of East Pukapuka's horizon. She cupped her hands behind her ears to catch any hint of an answer.

Except for the low murmur of the calm sea, there was only silence.

CHAPTER 31

Albino Paul gunned the six-hundred horsepower speed boat engines, welcomed the intense vibrations deep in his bones as if satisfying a physical hunger. The bloodthirsty cannibal from Malakula was bare-chested, sporting a brand new loin cloth and hundred dollar Nike Air Jordans. The human finger-bone necklace whipped in the air as the sleek black hull sliced through the light chop at one hundred-fifty kilometers per hour. At these breakneck speeds, fuel economy was lousy at just about two kilometers per liter, but sometimes it was all about the rush.

Albino Paul ran hard for a full hour before cutting back to cruising speed and punching the CD play button. The brass section of the Miami Sound Machine blasted full volume from eight top-of-the-line speakers, and the Cuban goddess Gloria Estefan sang along with Albino Paul about shaking your body, baby, and doing the conga!

The bloodthirsty cannibal waggled his booty in a stationary conga line. A long journey lay ahead. He was feeling good about this job, embracing his role as the boogeyman. After a couple of stagnant months of tourist performances, these road trips were invigorating, providing a lungful of fresh air out on the open sea. Albino Paul felt bulletproof to whatever might be unlucky enough to get in his way. After expenses, he'd clear another twenty grand easily, all of which would be wired to his Swiss bank account. Maybe another dozen assignments and he'd have enough to finally buy the entire island of Malakula and secede from the heavy-handed government of Vanuatu.

Albino Paul didn't want to be a king, he just wanted to be free. Free from the lard-ass bureaucrats who paid his people shit for posing less and less like an authentic cannibal tribe—which had at least offered some feeling of pride. Each year they were handed instructions demanding more dancing and less of what the tour operators considered humdrum traditional prayers. Once his people were free, those pricks might be the first to be tied to the tenderizing logs. The island would be renamed … how about "Mala Conga"? The rich heritage of his people would rise from the ashes left from tourist marshmallow roasts. Never again would his people kneel down before pale white men in flowered shorts to measure their chapped pink feet for swim fins.

A big-time drug lord on family vacation had taken the Cannibal Culture Spree with his wife and seven kids a few years earlier. He'd gotten the idea to harness some of the human flesh eating fear for his own business purposes. Cannibals would be used as deterrents for anyone considering ripping off one of his shipments. Thereafter the money had begun to flow fast and easy for Albino Paul. He was just the man for the job.

He'd been hooked after his first gig. Albino Paul had been offered a ridiculous sum of money to track down six Filipino thugs who'd ripped off a fishing boat loaded with a ton of Columbian Gold marijuana. Albino Paul caught up to them at a Chevron refueling station in Erromango, where one was working the self-service pump while the others sat around the thirty-foot outboard stoned off their asses.

Albino Paul cut his engines, coasting right up to the dock as if getting in line for gas. In full view of everyone—including several dozen curious tourists—he pulled a Peruvian teak box from the console and began applying traditional hunting paints made from roots and berries. Giant white teeth artwork made his face especially menacing. Albino Paul began the hunting dance on the glossy black bow of his expensive speed boat, not ten meters from the pumps. He waved a long sharpened spear like the baton of a marching band leader, quickly drawing a good-sized crowd of onlookers.

Tourists snapped picture after picture of the makeshift show, and even the stoned Filipinos relaxed and started enjoying the spectacle, jiving and grooving to the background music coming from the cannibal's awesome stereo system. The Filipino thugs were too stoned to protest when he leaped on board their boat and began dancing the conga on bales of carefully wrapped Columbian Gold. They were clapping along with the surrounding tourists, dopey wide grins and bobbing heads. One dropped a bong with a smoldering bowl, spilling smelly water across the deck. The stoned thug held in his hit as long as he could, then let go a burst of sweet blue smoke, smiling as though a couple of ice cold brews would really hit the spot about now.

"Yeah, yeah, shake your body, baby, do the conga!" Albino Paul had sung, and the five stoners struggled to their feet, wanting in on the dancing. Camera flashes went off in rapid fire and one little boy began drawing the scene with a crayon and paper his parents used to keep him busy. Albino Paul let out a haunting tribal scream as he turned on his conga line and began thrusting his spear into the belly of one Filipino after the other. Albino Paul performed the brutal, unrelenting slaughter for the benefit of the camera mounted above his boat's console, to be edited and used as a dramatic warning to any prospective drug thieves once it was uploaded to YouTube. Filipinos dramatically clutched at their stomach wounds, staggering like actors in an old silent reel before collapsing in shuddering heaps.

What a show it was.

Tourists cheered and clapped, and every moment of this wonderfully choreographed pageant was also recorded in at least a half dozen cell phone videos.

With five Filipinos down, Albino Paul turned to the one holding the gas pump nozzle, also stoned and now very much in shock. Albino Paul snatched the man by his wrist, pulled him close as if wanting to slow dance and plunged three of the thug's middle fingers into his painted mouth. Mothers covered the eyes of young children, worried about this awfully homoerotic scene. Fingers in other people's mouths? Mental notes were taken for nasty letters to be written later. The Filipino screamed bloody murder when his hand came free because his fingers had been bitten off.

The cheering and clapping stopped as the Filipino held his wounded hand out to the tourists, as if pleading for help, and then passed out cold. Albino Paul spit the severed fingers into his own hand and tucked them into his loin cloth for safe keeping. You could never have too many human fingers.

"Hey, I think he really bit off his fingers," exclaimed a dapper man with a New Zealand accent, who stood next to an attractive woman with a gaping mouth and twin boys cradled in each arm. And as if reacting to the report of a starter pistol, everybody except Albino Paul and the six Filipinos ran like hell, leaving the cannibal from Malakula to casually load the bales of marijuana onto his boat. Albino Paul topped off his tank, set the Filipino boat on fire, and got out of Dodge.

No, he didn't want to be a king, he just wanted his people to be free and his music to be loud. And, most of all, he longed to be a real bloodthirsty cannibal.

CHAPTER 32

Dobby rooted through a mound of salvaged clothes taller than the naked girl, tossing anything that might fit her into its own separate pile. His aching knees crackled and popped as he struggled back to his feet. He held out five tropical-print dresses, a Frederick's of Hollywood lace bustier he thought might be some kind of necessary underwear, and a bridal veil. Butter took one of the dresses.

"There's hundreds of islands in these waters, in every damn direction." Dobby's back was turned to the little girl as she slipped the dress over her head. "Ain't no island just called Home, girl. Not East Home, or West, South, or North Freakin' Home. Home ain't a name."

"A ship comes every full moon with rice and flour." Butter carefully inserted the buttons through their narrow holes. She could weave a fancy waist sash or even an intricate basket, but buttons were odd, clumsy things. They'd make wonderful jewelry—maybe hung from fine reeds—but when used to cinch cloth, they left gaps, making them a silly choice for this purpose.

"What island does the ship come from?"

"The big island." Butter's fingers lingered over the smooth round buttons and soft fabric of her dress. She was struck by how the dress kept the breeze away from her skin. It wasn't like being buried in sand, or swimming under water. And it wasn't like being held, either.

"Christ, girl, the only real place called Big Island is three thousand miles north of here and has hula dancers and high rise hotels. That don't sound familiar, does it?"

"I don't know what a high rise is." Butter felt exposed and vulnerable wrapped in so much material. Like when some of the boys used berry juice to draw a big bull's-eye on Adolph Hitler's back after he'd fallen asleep from too much wapa juice. For the next week, Adolph would suffer surprise attacks of hurled rice balls and chunks of coconut meat from behind, until one of the mothers tipped him off and ended the game. Having a dress covering her body made Butter feel like she was wearing a target.

"It doesn't matter. Does your island have any tall mountains, maybe a volcano sending up smoke signals?"

"No, but there's a flock of diving birds that feed every suppertime out where the sun goes down," she said hopefully.

"Any of them able to work a radio?"

"Huh?"

"Never mind." The captain flopped into an aluminum beach chair that sagged under his weight, one French fry away from collapsing. At his feet was the morning's haul, spread out as though on display in a soggy yard sale. There was an acoustic guitar with no strings, a deflated soccer ball, a pretty nice set of Rock'em Sock'em Robots, and a globe of the world that showed how much blue was really out there.

"Here." The captain tossed Butter a Purple Pizzazz Crayola Crayon from a waterlogged box of sixty-four, pointing to the least grease-stained spot on the crowded deck. "Draw a picture of what you know, the shape of the shoreline, any big rocks, whatever you can think of. If there's any of them tiny outer islands, even if they're just boulders in the water, draw them too."

Butter kneeled, her new, mostly yellow and white dress spread out around her, the crayon poised in her right hand. The afternoon sun cast long shadows of the captain and the little girl off to one side.

Dobby fell asleep while Butter wore the first purple crayon down to a nub. She eyed the big box of sixty four and the snoring captain, then crawled around her first outline and quietly slid the yellow and green container from underneath the straining chair. She carefully emptied the crayons into a pile at her knees, picked up the shocking pink, sniffed and nibbled the flat end. She did this more from curiosity rather than any expectation that it might taste as good as it looked. Most of the beautifully colored flowers on her island were also bitter and inedible.

Butter chose more colors and went to work depicting the sunset diving birds of her island home. She drew the birds in plain old black, silhouetted, wings tight to their long bodies. Some had just begun their descent, while others had broken the surface, sending up compact splashes of water that would have impressed the most finicky cliff-diving judge.

Butter chose silver to draw the shark that had bitten her father in half. She struggled with the white crayon to get the teeth big and sharp, but the raw umber she selected for her father's two halves worked great. The swirls of hot magenta blood left no doubt as to what was going on in her picture.

Above the simple island, frenetic shark attack, and the beautiful sunset, Butter traced the face of her mother. She drew her long, curly black hair as it swept down over her shoulders, and the chestnut eyes that were narrower than Butter's. They had been narrowed by the constant smile she wore to combat the sadness of losing her husband too soon. The Keeper of the Books believed in the power of a person's expression, and the impact it had on other living things.

"You scrunch up your face while tending to your hurt animals," her mother told her. "Give them softer eyes to look into. Give them a smile to know the hurting will stop soon. I promise it will work for the both of you."

And it had worked. When the little girl needed to pick shards of broken shell from the forehead of a diving bird, she did her best to smile reassuringly. The injured bird seemed to calm, its speeding heart and shallow, rapid breathing slowing down. The operation was a success and she devoted an entire chapter to the healing power of smiles in her Diary book.

Butter looked up at the strange god who was emitting thunderous snores and tried to smile at him. Were all gods just as imperfect? She had blamed this god for everything but knew deep down that a much more powerful god had killed her family and most of her animals. This god was weak and clumsy, and stank of wapa and rotten fish. Back home, she had listened raptly to the stories of what this god had endured. Having to build a big cross and then allowing himself to be nailed to it, the way the village fishermen spiked eel heads into a tree to peel back their skins.

Jesus had no bad scars on his hands or feet, but gods must heal differently. Plus, it had happened in early times, long, long ago. People honored the terrible suffering of Jesus by wearing little crosses around their necks. Butter thought the crosses must be a reminder of what Jesus had suffered. Or maybe it was some sort of warning. A symbol of what would happen to anyone doing something bad, like the heads the cannibals mounted on tall stakes to discourage trespassers.

For her last drawing Butter chose a crayon labeled Atomic Tangerine. The picture featured the sea turtle who had so bravely saved her, had used every bit of his might to keep swimming toward the surface of the violent, churning wave as Butter clung for dear life. She drew the picture as if looking down from Happa Now; it was from her mother's perspective. The great turtle was frozen in thick swipes of crayon, making valiant strokes away from all the sadness and death, while Butter hung on.

In the remaining daylight, as Dobby continued to snore, Butter abandoned her mural and crawled toward the pile of salvaged clothes. She ripped a decorative length of silk cord from the front of the bustier, then she located every item of clothing with buttons and bit them off, one by one, spitting them into a tin cup until it was nearly full of various sizes and shapes. Some were wood, but most were shiny plastic. She carefully threaded the silk cord through the buttons, making an effort to smile instead of scrunching her face.

Butter tore a long piece of material from the hem of a dress, measured it out, and then knotted it into a loop after attaching the cord and button crucifix she'd created.

As the sun began to dip into the sea to the west, Butter tiptoed back to where Dobby lay slumped in the metal beach chair, his snores replaced by incoherent murmurs. Butter gently took hold of a handful of hair and pulled his head forward. The captain grumbled in his sleep as Butter managed to get the gift over his head and ears. The cross of buttons nested in a mat of kinky gray chest hair

Jesus Dobby must have been dreaming that it was safe for everyone to go home, wherever that might be. "Olly, olly, oxen free," he whispered in his sleep.

CHAPTER 33

"Do you have a bigger boat?" Dante watched the long-legged Ophelia step down from the dock onto her twenty-six-foot Sea Ray. Her thick, honey-blond hair would often fall into her face as she worked her way around the small boat. The image that came to mind was an industrious Praying Mantis—graceful, delicate and possibly menacing.

"This was your idea, racer boy. It's a mighty long swim."

"Well, that's why I was asking about a bigger boat." Dante was shuffling his feet, reluctant to step on board the tidy white recreational craft that was not constructed for long, deep sea voyages. Just as well, Ophelia thought, since getting the boat ready for the trip was quicker without someone trying to help. Her mom, not wanting the neighbors to catch them out in the bay with streaked windows and mirrors, would bring cotton rags and a bottle of glass cleaner. She would even polish the throttle knobs.

"This is my only boat." Ophelia stowed a bag in a front hold, then scrambled back to open and close latches, checking tow ropes, the medical kit, and life-preservers. "And I intend on getting it there and back in one piece."

The Avatiu Harbour was filled with small wooden fishing boats painted the bright colors of exotic birds at one end, while enormous cargo ships were slowly unloaded at the other. Cranes plucked railroad-car-size containers from the spines of ships the length of football fields. Ophelia occasionally glanced up from her work, watching for friends who might be headed out fishing, but remembered this was a Tuesday morning and they were all at work, which was exactly where she should be. "I can't believe I'm doing this."

"We have enough life preservers, right?" Dante stood on the dock, holding his two stuffed backpacks as if they might serve that purpose.

"We have eight," she said over her shoulder.

"Maybe the boat just *seems* small from this angle." Dante was still not ready to commit to coming on board.

"Do you need help getting down?"

"And maybe because it's smaller than all these other boats." Dante looked out across the marina where dozens of bigger boats rocked in their slips.

"If the weather holds, we'll be fine."

"What's the forecast?" Dante took a half-step backward, away from the boat.

"We don't get a localized forecast for down in that region."

"There could be storms? We'd have heard if there was a hurricane coming, right?"

"I'm more worried about running out of gas."

"Wait, we could run out of gas? Can't we take more gas? Look, we could borrow the gas cans from this boat right here." Dante used his chin to indicate a much larger boat nearby with two red fuel containers lashed to its stern.

"I have extra cans. We'll be heavy from all the gas we're hauling. You don't smoke, do you?"

"No, absolutely not. What if we caught fire halfway there?"

"Are you seriously asking what would happen if we caught fire three hundred kilometers from land?"

"I think so."

"We radio a distress call with our coordinates and hope there's a fishing boat nearby."

"Are there a lot of fishermen in that part of the ocean?"

"I don't know," she said. She was done checking fuel and water levels and done with the rest of her pre-trip rituals. She was also done with this former ski racing superstar acting like a total pansy after he'd used her mother to pressure her into making this pointless trip. "None of us ever go fishing that far out. It's much too dangerous out there."

Ophelia steered them away from the Avarua marina, heading east and then southeast, keeping the Rarotonga shoreline off to the right as they traveled halfway around the island before heading out into the deep, open water. She wore long tan cargo shorts that came to the tops of her shins, pockets bulging here and there with energy bars, packages of fish hooks, and chewing gum. You could imagine her bulky fisherman sweater keeping Hemingway warm on a chilly night in Havana.

Dante tossed the thin hardcover copy of Hemingway's *The Old Man and the Sea* onto the cushion next to him. He scanned the horizon for any sign of land or giant marlin. In the book, it had taken the old man eighty-five days to finally head out into the deepest waters to try breaking his streak of bad luck. But it had been worth it when the giant fish took the bait. For three days, the old man battled the great fish, ending the epic struggle with a thrust from his harpoon. Dante had stopped reading at that point, wanting to keep it a win for the old guy. He didn't trust where the story would head, fearing that the big fish might mysteriously reanimate and eat the sad old Santiago.

The back of this little boat—or *stern*, as Ophelia called it— reminded him of the hot tub at the care center. Add a few hundred gallons of hot bubbling water to the soft semicircle of waterproof benches and he could almost imagine he was back in rehab. He recalled dozing off and almost drowning in the hot tub and wished he'd never had the thought.

"Are we there, yet?" Dante called to Ophelia, whose honey hair was whipping seductively behind her.

Ophelia turned away from the windscreen to actually flash him a smile. "Maybe ten more hours and you can start asking. You wanna drive for a while?"

Dante glanced down at his book, which lay on the seat vibrating from the powerful engine behind them. "Really?"

"You haven't spent much time on boats, have you?" Ophelia crouched over his right shoulder as he climbed into the helm seat.

"I don't know." Dante gripped the faux wood steering wheel in both hands. Despite the wind, he found himself basking in the clean, soapy smell of the woman over his shoulder. It was making him a little dizzy. Despite the innumerable sponge baths and hand jobs he'd received while comatose, this was the closest he could remember being to a woman. "I didn't see any boats in the photos they showed me. I'm not sure if I can swim, except in dreams."

"So what's it like to wake up and find that your entire life has been erased?"

"Not as great as it sounds."

"But think of all the things you get to try again for the first time. Every food and movie is new again."

"Yeah, well, one good jolt and I could die instantly."

Ophelia stood up to reach over his shoulder and pull back on the throttle. As the boat slowed, the noise of the engine dropped a pitch and the bow dipped slightly.

"Let's try to keep you alive a little longer, racer boy," Ophelia whispered. "At least until we get you back to this island you've never been to."

Dante wished she'd keep speaking in his ear.

CHAPTER 34

Ratu and Jope slept peacefully on the beach, tangled in a lovers' embrace. They were only occasionally disturbed by hermit crabs checking out various small crevasses in search of bigger and better homes to lug around on their backs. Shortly after sunrise, a hermit crab scurried into a pair of denim shorts and found a new home in Jope's butt crack. It was a high-pitched scream that began the day for the newly cocaine-addicted pirates on East Pukapuka.

"Look, Ratu." Jope groggily pointed toward the ocean with his right hand, his left hand digging at the back of his shorts. "Our new boat don't look so good."

Ratu's mouth was as dry as sand and he could feel just how bloodshot his eyes were. A red haze tinted what at first seemed like a picture-postcard world. He didn't give a rat's ass about the boat. He knew their heisted ride was done the minute they'd slammed into the damn reef. He scoffed at those fancy-pants white people running around the movie screen 'cause they bumped into a chunk of ice. Icebergs? Try running into a coral reef at twenty knots and see if you have time to gather your jewelry. They bitched about the water being cold, but warm it up and just see what kind of teeth are waiting for you.

Ratu had woken in a sour mood. It was morning on a tropical island and his brain was hollering something about it being coke time. As he scanned the shore line for brown packages of cocaine, he noticed for the first time that some heavy shit had gone down on this place. But, as with the ruined boat, his mind also didn't want to waste time worrying about how screwed up the island looked.

"Move your fucking leg." Ratu had spotted one of the bricks in a mass of seaweed on the beach. He rose on his skinny black legs, jogged along the water's edge and retrieved an armload of wet packages that must have come in on the tide.

"We're saved!" Ratu shouted to Jope, kneeling down to stack the carefully packaged bricks of cocaine in the warm sun.

"But the boat is in a whole bunch of pieces." Jope was rubbing his sore belly, which ached from all the salt water he'd swallowed. The constant beating of small waves on the stuck hull had broken the Julius Caesar into several thousand smaller pieces. Half submerged, the second-story pilot house had broken free and drifted a few hundred meters south. The motor was charred black, having caught fire before being doused by a wave. "Can you fix it?"

Ratu, his back to the shipwreck, carefully ripped a seam in the plastic inner wrapping and tapped a huge line of nearly pure cocaine into a bleached clam shell. He fumbled with the brown paper, tearing off small bits and then rolling the driest piece into a four-inch snorting tube.

A thousand dollars' worth of cocaine completely changed Ratu's foul mood. He sat back in the sand and smiled. "Jope!" he called, pinching at his right nostril while flexing his twitching muscles. The red haze had gone electric green and shocking blue. "Come have breakfast!"

"I'm not hungry." Jope was worried about the boat, and the shark-god had warned that the cannibals were on their way.

"Not food, you dumbass!" Ratu poured a clam shell portion

for his friend. "Come do some of the finest mojo this side of Mata-utu."

Jope looked glumly out at the wreck. Before grabbing the straw and bending over to inhale the thick line, he took a moment to observe all the havoc that had recently visited the island. "Look, Ratu, something really bad happened here. Maybe the cannibals did all this."

To Ratu, East Pukapuka appeared to have been run over by a gigantic truck. Then the truck had backed over the island and crushed things some more. The primitive buildings were all smashed up, and every single tree and bush was bent over. Some trees had sprung back up, minus most of their leaves and fronds, but some had snapped in the middle. All that was left of lush tropical foliage was dead brown leaves and a twisted mass of branches and undergrowth. On most of these lightly inhabited places you couldn't see more than twenty meters in from the beach; here you could catch peeks of the sky and ocean on the far side of the island, several hundred meters away.

"It looks like a big truck ran over the island," Jope said. He leaned forward and used the straw to make the little mound of cocaine disappear.

Ratu tapped out more and they took turns using their other nostrils.

"We gotta fix the boat," Jope said suddenly, now fully aware of the island's electric greens and blues.

"The boat's all mashed up." Ratu began nodding his head repeatedly, involuntarily. The coke was taking over his body, making his fingers tingle. He could feel his hair growing. No wonder rich people were willing to pay so much for good coke. This stuff made everything okay. Unlike with beer, you didn't have to pee all the time. His head still nodding, Ratu flexed his right bicep and squeezed the small knot of muscle with his left hand. "Just like Superman."

"We gotta find a place to hide," Jope said, nodding his head in rhythm with Ratu.

"Island's all squished down, Jope." Along with the nodding, Ratu began to blink his eyes rapidly. "Ain't no place to hide. Here, let's do one more line, then I wanna see if I can fly."

The former pirates were both nodding spastically. Other than each others' faces, everything they looked at was blurry.

"What do we gotta hide from?" Ratu was painfully and repeatedly jabbing the inside of his nose with the straw while snorting and spilling thousands of dollars' worth of coke.

"The shark-god said the cannibals are coming to eat us for stealing the blow." Jope was blinking rapidly, stabbing at his own nostrils.

"Nah, ain't no way cannibals could find us out here. We're just a little booger in a really big nostril." Ratu sniffed hard, wiped at his nose, and began talking quickly. "You ever swim in a pool, look down and see a little booger floatin' by? Even if you know it's a booger for sure, you don't wanna believe it. Who wants to know they been swimmin' in booger water? You tell yourself, 'No, that ain't no booger. That's somethin' else.' "

"I can't swim."

"Then a bathtub, Jope! We're a booger in a bathtub is what I'm trying to tell you. And there ain't even much of a boat left to spot. One more line and you climb on my back and we go fly up high in the sky. We a bird, we a plane, we Super-negroes!"

"Oh, God, Ratu, look!" Jope recoiled from the open brick of cocaine as if a snake had poked its head out from the powder.

Ratu tried to focus his blinking eyes on Jope's discovery, but the bobbing of his head was making that difficult.

"Shark-god knows his shit. We're in big trouble. Big, big, trouble." Suddenly despondent, Jope nodded his head, blinked, and picked the flashing GPS transmitter out of the open brick of cocaine. He dropped it in the sand as if it were burning hot. "I seen on cop shows how they find criminals with this kinda thing."

"Holy shit," Ratu said, nodding and blinking back. He picked the transmitter out of the sand, turning it over in his jittery hands. "I think your cannibals just found a couple of boogers."

CHAPTER 35

In one long, brutal weekend, Ratu and Jope had gone from small-time crooks, to high seas' pirates, to cocaine-addicted castaways. Knowing they were being hunted down by bloodthirsty cannibals took every last bit of fun out of their huge bounty of devil's dandruff, paradise white, ninety-nine percent pure uptown whiz bang.

Instead of skinny-dipping in the lagoon and cracking coconuts to toast away their thirst, the former pirates were on a frenzied mission to create a military beachhead to ward off the impending cannibal invasion.

"They'll come from that direction, following the GPS track. They'll come the same way we did." Ratu pointed a shaking finger out beyond their wrecked boat.

"Maybe they'll crash, too," Jope said.

"I don't think so, Jope. Cannibals are primitive and crazy, but they are also big-time clever. They get the scent of blood and they're like them dogs tracking escaped prisoners. Except these fuckers have GPS."

"It could happen, though, right? It's possible they could crash?"

"We gotta keep working," Ratu said. "Maybe just one more quick toot."

"What do they eat first?" Jope's heart could be clearly seen thumping inside his chest. Sand coated his sweaty black body after multiple trips to the water's edge to fetch heavy buckets of wet sand for the project that was to be their final stand.

"Probably parts that don't kill you right away." Ratu hefted his sloshing bucket. "Cannibals ain't got Frigidaires and they gotta keep your meat fresh."

The two men had gone on their own salvage mission, wading far enough out to collect a pair of bait buckets, some tangled fishing gear, and a broken pair of Ray Ban sunglasses. Then they began the tedious process of marking off their fortress foundation.

Jope looked down at his fingers, reached up with his free hand to touch his left ear. "Oh God, they eat fingers and ears first, don't they? They just bite them right off." Having just one lens in his new sunglasses added to the sense of impending doom. He tossed the Ray Bans in the sand.

"Measure twice and cut once," Ratu said under his breath, pacing off where the thickest wall would go, leaving marks in the sand with his heel. The constant nodding of heads had begun to slow as small muscles tired and started to give up. It made seeing much easier.

"What are we going to cut with, Ratu?" Jope asked, still worrying about his fingers. With all the places he'd stuck them, he couldn't imagine they'd taste very good.

"It's just a saying, Jope. We ain't gonna cut anything."

Over the next few hours they wore a path of damp, compacted sand from the wide white beach to the edge of the jungle destruction at the northwest point of the island. In this spot the land jutted the farthest out to sea, giving them a wide, panoramic view of the blue expanse. They dumped bucket after bucket, forming one shoulder-high wall and then the next. Their ambitious, cocaine-fueled construction was interrupted only by breaks to snort lines of Bolivian marching powder.

Having eaten nothing in nearly three days, the two men were beginning to look the worse for wear. When Jope's shorts dropped from his emaciated hips to his ankles, he simply walked out of them. The same thing happened to Ratu five minutes later. He just grunted and kept lugging his heavy bucket.

They fell into a steady, butt-naked rhythm, collecting beach sand and delivering load after load to the fortress, passing each other midway, usually at about the same spot.

The intense sun and subsequent dehydration was also beginning to cause hallucinations.

"Ratu, are you seeing them rabbits?" Jope didn't bother to stop as their paths crossed. Instead he jerked his head to indicate the line of smiling rabbits peering at them from the edge of the broken trees.

On the next pass, Ratu said, "Those ain't bunny rabbits, Jope. I think they're some kinda penguins, but they don't look dangerous."

The difficult work continued.

"Maybe we can make a cannon," Jope said, a few passes later, veins bulging on the arm lugging the bucket.

"We ain't got no cannon balls," Ratu told him on the next pass.

Jope was silent while he thought hard.

"Rocks!" Jope said at the next opportunity. The line of what he was sure were smiling rabbits were continuing to watch them work. "We could load the cannon with rocks. We just gotta find really hard rocks."

"Why you wanna shoot the penguins? They ain't bothering nobody. And look, they're all gettin' busy."

Jope waited to look until he had filled another bucket with wet sand and was headed back to the fortress. Sure enough, the smiling rabbits at the edge of the broken jungle had paired off and were mating. Jope thought about the last time he'd paired off with a girl—back before Ratu had moved in with him.

Jope had met the girl in line at an illegal fireworks stand by the airport along the Rewa River. He'd sold out his nickel bags of crank and had cash to burn. Roads leading away from the airport were a great spot to deal drugs, Jope had found, since it was harder and harder to smuggle your dope onto airplanes. There was an unofficial bus stop along the Rewa where back-packing travelers would beg the driver to pull off, then run down the steps and set upon the dealers for a fix. Jope had been one of the first of a small but growing group of crank dealers at these pull-off spots. By the time the drivers arrived at the bus depot at the end of their shift, the floors tinkled with empty glass vials.

Thirty-four dollars in his pocket, Jope anxiously awaited his turn in line at the tin roof shop, which had a sign advertising hour-long massages and putt putt golf. He was purchasing an armload of Roman candles and bottle rockets.

"I seen you dealing." The female voice came from behind him.

Jope recognized the young woman from another unofficial bus stop just up the road from his. Her stop had a thicket of low growing bushes the prostitutes used for turning quick tricks while the buses idled.

"Oh, yeah, I seen you turning tricks."

"It's been pretty slow," the prostitute said, holding out two packs of bottle rockets as if they showed how slow things had been.

"Hasn't been too slow for crank." Jope tilted his armload for her to get a look at all his bottle rockets. "You wanna come shoot some off with me?"

"Look, Jope, the penguins are all smoking cigarettes." Ratu interrupted Jope's memory as the two former pirates passed each other in the sand. "That just don't look right."

Jope saw the smoking rabbits on his return trip up the beach. The prostitute he'd met at the fireworks stand had used her cigarette to light his bottle rockets, which they'd launched at passing boats from under the old steel Rewa Road Bridge. She stuffed the long sticks into an old coke bottle and lit the fuses while Jope pushed up her dress and mounted her from behind. The prostitute angled the rockets to explode over fishermen heading back up river after a morning in Laucala Bay.

"I still think we oughta build a cannon," Jope said on the next pass. Despite all the cocaine in his system, his slender erection was now boldly pointing the way. The memory of shooting off the bottle rockets with the hooker had been good, even though she beat him up and stole his last five dollars. At least she'd let him finish.

CHAPTER 36

Ophelia had programmed her GPS unit with chart plots to her favorite fishing spots and coordinates for ship wrecks she planned to visit someday. She had entered the location of shallow reef formations and rocky hazards as well as tracking the long deepwater route to East Pukapuka.

"There's only one more can after this," Dante told Ophelia, who already knew how much gas they'd used and how much remained. Keeping a steady pace over flat seas caused them to burn much less fuel than expected, and she had plenty of gas for the return trip, whether racer boy came back with her or not.

Ophelia had learned to completely cut the engines to allow Dante to drain the spare cans into the main fuel tank. When she'd only gently throttled back for his first attempt, he'd doused himself. Carrying so much fuel on her small boat, especially out in the middle of nowhere, made her nervous. She'd helped tow in her fair share of boat fires and engine troubles over the years, all part of the job. Boaters were family and it was more common than not to have too many captains respond to a distress call. The severity of the call didn't matter. A dead motor, an empty gas tank, someone with a seizure, even just a tourist losing their bearings—all of these situations brought more help than was needed in the waters surrounding her island.

Ophelia had once delivered twins to a woman thirty kilometers out, as a dozen other boats stood by. She'd seen the glint from telephoto lenses, heard the pictures being snapped. The pregnant woman and three friends had decided to combine a baby shower and an afternoon pulling in some tasty wahoo and Spanish mackerel. The first contractions coincided with a ruptured fuel line to the twin 260 horsepower engines of the ten meter Windjammer. Ophelia delivered the babies two minutes apart, stabilized the mother and her three hysterical friends, then waited for the coast guard to shuttle their group back to Avarua Harbor. Ophelia had been buzzing on an endorphin high, feeling somewhere closer to understanding the meaning of the universe as she tied off lines and prepared to tow the floundering boat to port. Her white bikini top and light tan shorts were soaked in blood and afterbirth, making her quite a sight as she stepped back onto the dock and posed for a newspaper photographer.

It was the breathless, panicked cries from on board a burning boat that would send painful chills down her body. If you couldn't immediately extinguish the flames, you were taught to grab a life preserver and swim to a safe distance. It was incredible how many times the wrong decision had been made over a five-thousand or even five-hundred dollar piece of metal and fiberglass. The fire would often leave nothing but a charred disaster—unrecognizable as a boat. At other times, the explosion would blow out the fire, leaving one person with face and chest heavily singed. And there'd be another person—usually a wife or girlfriend—clutching two life preservers in their own dead hands. Their last seconds of life had been spent pleading that they should please, for the love of god, get off the boat.

No babies or fiery explosions today, which was exactly how Ophelia wanted it. Her plan was to make this trip as humdrum, business-like, and anticlimactic as humanly possible. Mama had gotten it into her head to help this relatively sweet nutcase, and she knew it was the proper Raro thing to do. He had come to their island with his own version of a distress call. And Mama had handed the phone to her.

The first seconds after Ophelia cut the engine were disconcerting. After hours of constant outboard engine noise and vibrations, of the continuous thwacking of wave on hull, the thick silence put them on pins and needles. Both worked their jaws to pop their ears. The heat of the late day sun baked skin that had previously been cooled by tepid wind and made them want to scratch various body parts.

The first sound to return was the slapping of water against the hull, followed by the light ticking of the cooling engine. Dante grunted as he lifted the heavy red can, unscrewed the lid and poured gas into an orange funnel. Without the wind, the glare seemed to intensify, maybe because of the building heat or because without the rushing air there was no need to squint. Dante ripped an arm's length of paper towels from its roll to wipe up the gas he'd spilled while pouring the last can into the boat's fuel tank.

"I have to pee," Dante called up to Ophelia, who had closed her eyes and tilted her head to the sky.

"Climb over the seat." Eyes closed, Ophelia allowed the sun to put its warm hands on her face. "There's a swim platform you can stand on. Don't fall in and don't pee on the motor."

"Why shouldn't I pee on the motor?"

"Jesus, because I don't want anyone peeing on my motor, racer boy."

"Oh." Dante climbed over the vinyl seat cushions to balance

on the swim platform at the very back of the boat. The boat rocked in all directions; he held onto a low aluminum bar to keep from falling in while accidentally peeing all over the hot motor.

"Do you hear that?" Dante strained to distinguish a distant buzzing over the slight hiss of steaming urine.

"Hear what?"

"A buzzing sound." Dante tucked himself back into his shorts with one hand. "Really far off."

"I don't hear anything." Ophelia yawned and stretched her arms out over her head.

"It sounds like bees," said Dante, who now sat on the stern, feet resting on the dive platform. "I swear, it sounds like a big swarm of bees. And I think it's getting louder."

"Can I trust you to take over for twenty minutes?" Ophelia asked, intending to close her eyes for real, but now she thought she might be hearing Dante's bees. "What is that?" She stood, stretched her long, stiff legs, and spider-walked across the cushions to sit next to Dante. Both squinted off behind the boat, just below where the sun had begun its slow descent into the sea.

"An airplane?" Ophelia guessed, as the swarming of bees grew tenfold. "I can't see anything."

Dante turned eastward to scan the rest of the almost cloudless sky, which had turned deep indigo. No birds, no bees, and no airplanes. Whatever was approaching was coming directly out of the west, the sun over its wings or shoulders. And it was coming fast.

"What could it be?" Ophelia cupped her hands around her eyes as the sun drew a shimmering path on the water toward the source of what had become an angry roar.

"Maybe a rocket?" Fear had pitched Dante's voice higher.

"Let's go!" Ophelia clambered over the cushion toward the wheel. "Fast!"

Dante had been hypnotized by the brightly glimmering ocean and whatever mechanical beast was bearing down on them. An image flashed across his injured brain, as a small sliver of memory returned for a split second. The image was big and dark, and turned out to be as hard as steel, at least compared to a ski helmet and a human skull. Dante could see the old grove of tall Swiss pine trees hurtling toward him at an incredible speed. He figured he was going to die and hoped it wouldn't hurt too badly, or at least for very long.

Dante heard a scream. He was reasonably certain it had been made by a female. He certainly hoped *he* wasn't capable of screaming like that, especially not with all the television cameras around. Imagine the snickers from the Germans crowded around their televisions watching replays of the hot-shit American downhiller, going headfirst into the woods screaming like a twelve-year-old girl!

The sleek black hull of the bloodthirsty dude careened off the side of the much smaller Sea Ray at eighty miles per hour. Dante was a little confused as to how and why some criminally insane looking shirtless guy with a bone necklace and big white teeth painted all over his face was driving the grove of pine trees from his dreams, or maybe his memories.

"What the heck?" Dante was suddenly upside down in the air again, this time over water. At least it wasn't frozen into snow and ice, which provided some consolation.

Despite the distinctive rhythm of funky Latin music, the screaming of one female, and the booming racket of a million horsepower speed boat engines, Dante could clearly hear a calm and hopeful voice coming from somewhere up above his tumbling body. It was quite comforting, actually, even though it didn't evoke any memories from his damaged gray matter— all childhood memories having been lost.

The plaintive call was repeated, perhaps coming from behind one of the few, almost-round puffs of clouds.

"Olly, olly, oxen free," the voice called, and then Dante splashed down, hard.

CHAPTER 37

Butter's mother and father, Anonymous and Clarence Darrow, were doing what an awful lot of couples had done after being separated on Earth and then reunited in the next life: they were going at it fast and furious.

"It was a really lovely funeral," Anonymous whispered huskily from underneath Clarence, as his wiry hips worked like greased pistons. "Everyone in the village came to sing and toast wapa."

"I missed you so much," Clarence moaned as he pushed his toes against the hut wall for better leverage.

"You looked almost good as new after the weaving group sewed you back together." Anonymous arched her back, grinding her hips to meet his lunatic thrusts. How many years had it been? Anonymous had put up with all the leers and tongue-wagging, all the disgusting mating dances and wiener-grabbing, biding her time until she could find her way back into Clarence's arms.

Clarence showed no signs of having been bitten in two by the mischievous shark—one of the truly great things about Happa Now. And his condition didn't go unnoticed, especially by family members of people who'd been surprised by ship propellers and bisected by big sharks.

"Oh, god, I'm getting close again." Clarence made his funny, strained face and whimpered.

The newly arrived villagers from East Pukapuka shuffled away from the amorous noises coming from inside the loving couple's home. One wiseass teenage boy grabbed a sharp stone and a piece of flat driftwood to begin writing a sign: "If this hut's a rockin' …"

"When they poured on the cooking oil and set you on fire, you glowed the color of a summer sunset," Anonymous crooned into her husband's ear. The long-lost voice of his recently deceased wife pushed Clarence closer to the edge of orgasm. It was all he'd imagined during those endless nights he'd lain awake and restless, waiting for his beloved wife to die.

"You … never … looked … more … beautiful," he struggled to say in short, one-word bursts. His eyes were closed as he briefly allowed himself a quick, guiltless image of the wonderfully fat wife of the village climber—that lucky bastard. Fantasizing about other women was a no-no among the people of East Pukapuka, but this was, after all, their second go-round in less than half an hour.

"I picked your teeth out of the ashes," Anonymous hummed into his ear. She was nearing the Promised Land—that old tingling sensation beginning in her feet and running past her knees, right up to her quivering brown thighs. "I kept them in a bowl with Butter's baby teeth."

"Aaaaahhhhh!" Clarence froze in painful ecstasy. Only his member continued moving. Couples were free to copulate without fear of pregnancy on Happa Now. No babies were ever born, because, like fleas and spiders, sperm and ova had been banished by the gods.

"Not yet!" cried Anonymous, trying to restart his hips as if attempting to get a stubborn donkey to 'giddy' up.

"I love you." Clarence's damp forehead collapsed between her heaving bosoms.

Inside the hut, suddenly still, the sweat-drenched couple lay folded in each other's arms. Anonymous was waiting to see if Clarence might be up for a third reunion when a terrifying notion crossed her mind. The rogue thought came out of nowhere, but instantly seemed the only thing she should have been thinking about since setting foot on Happa Now. It made her feel like the worst person in the world, dead or alive, at that very moment. Sure, she'd spent her first few postmortem hours enjoying the freedom from a nagging case of bellyworm that hadn't made the trip to hound her in the next life. Now guilt welled up and filled the space where the parasites had recently flourished. It was well within reason to be lost in the embrace of her long-dead husband, but some things surely were inexcusable no matter what the situation.

"Where's Butter?" Anonymous asked her husband, who had already begun to snore.

CHAPTER 38

The sight of testicles drawing up and disappearing into the body of a severely frightened person was familiar to Albino Paul—what with his side work involving tracking down and eating people. It was one of the human body's little magic tricks he always got a kick out of. That it was currently his own testicles playing hide-and-go-seek was not quite so awesome.

And it hurt a little.

Looking back over his shoulder, Albino Paul tried wrapping his mind around what had just occurred between his priceless machine and the little piece of crap boat he'd just swamped. His narcissism floated a thought toward the surface of his mind: he'd intended to do that. He'd come raging out of the blinding sun at a hundred thirty kilometers per hour, bearing down on the small, insignificant vessel in his path, cutting the wheel with perfect timing to deliver a sideswiping blow. What felt like a glancing nudge that hardly smudged the seventeen coats of deep lacquer paint on his thirteen meter speed boat was a bare-knuckle punch in the face to the little day cruiser. In truth, Albino Paul had fallen fast asleep at the helm, the warm sun on his back, the massaging rhythm of the almighty horsepower urging him into cozy cannibal dreams. Those bloodthirsty visions came easily, especially since he'd applied his hunter's paint at the last piss break.

There was a moment in every hunt that was especially meaningful to a cannibal. Consuming the flesh was show time, the big attraction to tourists and magazine writers. When *National Geographic* had come poking around, his grandpa described eating the victim's flesh as the high point, the money shot. But it was what they had wanted to hear, the idea that sold the most magazines. The real spiritual moment came from the look in the victim's eyes when they knew they were damned. In that instant the last flicker of hope escaped their grasp and they realized their terrible fate was sealed. There might be screaming, begging, or dead silence. It didn't matter. It was all about *the look*—knowing that the worst possible thing was about to happen to your body, some of it while you were still conscious.

A white Christian missionary from Chicago had given Albino Paul the greatest moment of his bloodthirsty cannibal career thus far. Tracking down and eating drug thieves was good, but they were often stoned and confused men, filled with panic instead of terror. Their lifestyle had also accustomed them to near-death situations. But the missionary had been different. He'd come sniffing around Malakula, figuring a little Bible thumping and cash would score him young island pussy. Albino Paul had taken the money and led the missionary to an empty hut in a remote spot on the island, even promising a choice between three of the youngest and purest girls.

"I'll be back," Albino Paul said, and the missionary agreed to wait. Twenty minutes later, the bloodthirsty cannibal returned in full hunting paint, spear in hand, penis gourd polished and proudly worn. At first the missionary appeared to be in complete denial, perhaps clinging to the hope that this was all part of the show for a sacrificial virgin. But there had been no virgins hiding behind the lunatic cannibal who stepped into the hut and slammed the handle of the spear across the top of his head.

When the missionary woke up, he began making all sorts of promises. Thousands of dollars, the cannibal's very own apartment in a nice neighborhood in Chicago, walking distance to Wrigley Field. Did he like baseball? Did he know about the Cubs? If he was a White Sox fan, the missionary was sure he could get great tickets behind the first base dugout. Was there any chance the cannibal could loosen the ropes? Being lashed to the fat tree trunk was horribly uncomfortable.

Albino Paul bent over the missionary as if to kiss him on the face, but went for his ear instead. Any hope of talking his way out of this mess had evaporated for the missionary, leaving Albino Paul the wonderful pleasure of looking into the eyes of a man who knew he was condemned to the most horrible of fates.

Albino Paul chewed the missionary's ear lobe as if it were a wad of Juicy Fruit gum, relishing the flavor and the moment.

Albino Paul, like a bat making use of echolocation, was startled awake by a sudden change in sound. The pitch of the engine was suddenly being returned by something closing fast. Eyelids flying open, he cut the wheel instinctively—at the last possible instant—creaming the little boat with a tremendous slap of water and fiberglass.

The cannibal also had a snapshot image of a large white man sitting at the back of the boat, head cocked like a curious dog, about to be ejected as if from a wounded fighter jet. The white man did in fact become airborne, still in the sitting position— an awful lot like Rodin's *Thinker*.

At the helm was a woman, also white and particularly large. In that brief moment, she appeared to be frantically trying to start the engine, apparently aware her boat was about to receive a mortal blow.

The strike from the sleek speed boat cracked the hull of the much less significant boat, splintering wood and fiberglass.

And although it threatened to roll, the full gas tank provided just enough counter ballast, which allowed it to rock back into an upright position. Water flooded the wound, swamping the boat in seconds, but by the time it was a mere speck on Albino Paul's aft horizon, the white peoples' little boat was still refusing to sink.

Heart pounding robustly and testicles still in absentia, Albino Paul checked his GPS, corrected the wheel slightly, and began surveying the location where East Pukapuka was about to appear.

Tempted to circle the island and get the lay of the land prior to commencing his attack, the cannibal could see he may have come all this way for nothing. It was immediately apparent why the scumbag coke thieves hadn't gone any farther. A mid-size fishing boat floundered capsized and decapitated on the shallow reef that appeared to encircle the archipelago.

Albino Paul approached the wreck and dropped anchor. He was pissed that he'd have to swim—his hunting paint would wash away—but any hopes for a hunt seemed to be dashed. If the bodies were recoverable and fish hadn't done too much damage, he could still stage a massacre. The very idea of eating cold meat turned his stomach, but he'd do what he'd have to in order to get paid. He grabbed his spear and jumped in. Propelled by one arm, he got enough of a foothold to swim up and over the reef to examine the ravaged hull. He prodded empty seats that would have held bodies and peered down into the single berth, but there were no drowned thieves still attached to the wreckage. There were just oscillating bits of the mangled fishing charter, and a dissipating ring of oil and gas that made the water slick and rank.

Albino Paul turned toward the island and lunged back into the deep water, swimming until his feet hit sandy bottom. The shoreline showed signs of some recent disaster—a tropical storm, or maybe even a tsunami. The palm and puka trees that hadn't snapped were beginning to right themselves, reaching back for the sun. He paused, waist deep, leaning against his spear, the gentle push of small waves from behind urging him forward. No signs of people—no smoke from cooking fires, no buildings. He stood sniffing the air, but being upwind only smelled the boat wreckage. At the closest jut of land, Albino Paul tried to make sense of a huge mound of sand. Piled up away from the beach, at the fringe of the decimated vegetation, it would have been completely out of place anywhere except at some touristy resort beach.

The huge sandcastle was protected by a moat and head-high walls. There were turrets and arrow slits, and the front entrance was a barbican where the encroaching enemy was to become confined and lose the ability to defend itself. Enthralled by the deadly weapons of the period, Albino Paul had read dozens of books on medieval castles but was completely confounded by the one facing him here in the South Pacific.

A flash of motion from the parapet followed by a heavy kerplunking sound in the water a few meters behind Albino Paul made him jump. Another blurry flash … This time the projectile struck the cannibal squarely in the forehead, knocking him off his feet, backwards and underwater. Coughing and rubbing at the angry knot sprouting from his sore head, Albino Paul saw that the small hairy coconut that had struck him now bobbed at his loin cloth.

"Son of a bitch!" Shifting into bloodthirsty cannibal hunting mode, he let out a tribal shriek and began plowing through the water amid rapid volleys of more small coconuts. Once out of the water, Albino Paul could see the castle defenders twenty meters dead ahead: two skinny black men on the parapet whose wide eyes expressed absolute terror. Like any good cannibal, Albino Paul could smell fear, and this close up the air was absolutely dripping with it. The fear turned him into an unstoppable killing machine. He let out another ancient tribal shriek to let everyone know resistance was futile. Coconuts bounded off his shoulders and chest; one clacked off his right knee and opened a nasty cut. But he charged on, breaking into a sprint as he pulled away from the deep sand. He leaped across the dry moat and scrambled up the side of the wall, making the same battle cries of the hunt—practiced over recent years in front of pasty-white tourists with video cameras and dumbstruck faces—that his grandfathers had made. As he breached the wall, Albino Paul pulled back his spear, intending to force these two thieves into surrender with sheer terror; then a new, unexpected weapon was introduced into this combat. A sliced-open brick of nearly pure cocaine slapped him across the eyes and nose, like a pie to the face, sending a miniature mushroom cloud all around his upper body, temporarily blinding him and filling his lungs with burning powder.

As he lay slumped over the sandcastle wall, clenching his eyes and gasping for breath, Albino Paul braced for the spears he expected to tear into his defenseless body. Instead, he heard retreating footsteps and the unmistakable sound of two grown men crying like frightened children as they escaped into the devastated jungle.

CHAPTER 39

"Ratu, you remember back when we stole all them watches?"

"That was last week."

"Them was the best days. I don't think we ever gonna have days like them again."

"Yeah, Jope, they were the best days."

The small-time Fijian crooks lay splayed out in the shade from the tallest wall of their sandcastle, hearts palpitating wildly from what should have been fatal doses of cocaine. They'd done their best to copy the castle design from the cover of one of Jope's comic books called *Dark Age Slut Princess from Narnia*. They panted like dogs, trying to cool themselves. They'd reached the point of terminal dehydration, as their bodies had become incapable of producing sweat.

"Did your shark-god say when the cannibals would get here?" Ratu panted, not the least bit surprised that the cloud formation above was in the shape of a Pit Bull Terrier lifting its leg to pee on a young boy. He had fond memories of his childhood dog, Killer. Ratu had been taken out of the orphanage three times. The first family had lasted almost an entire year. The man of that family had used Ratu for cleaning his shithole house and any other lousy chores he could think of. The man had beaten the dog for being a lousy fighter; he'd beaten Ratu just for the hell of it.

The instant Killer had been let off the leash for training, he'd torn down the back alley and disappeared for days at a time. He hadn't returned until nearly dying from scrounging putrid shellfish. Five-year-old Ratu would sneak Killer scraps he'd collected while the dog was missing, sneaking the food to the bony, cowering dog who'd come back because this was apparently as good as it was ever going to get for him. Killer would repay the little boy by turning sideways and lifting his leg, dousing young Ratu in warm dog piss to claim the child as his own. And the man of the family would take the dog back and beat him some more because this was the best dog he'd ever be able to afford. Ratu loved that dog and it broke his heart to be sent back to the orphanage, despite all the beatings. Having a dog love you was just about the best thing in the world. It was probably the reason Ratu appreciated Jope so much.

"He's not just my shark-god, Ratu. He's everybody's shark-god."

"Okay, so when did everybody's shark-god say they were coming?"

"They're coming real soon. The cannibals are right on our tail and we're in big-time shit." Jope wanted very much to crawl down to the cool water, but he knew how hot the white sand in between had become. The beach was on fire and the former pirates could feel the heat radiating all around them. Digging a shallow hole on the leeward side beach to bury the cocaine booty—all except one brick to keep their hearts beating—had sapped the very last of their energy. They walked, then crawled, back through the broken jungle, lunging across piles of brown palm fronds and downed pukas. There they found even more evidence of the bad things that had visited this island. On the narrow path Jope tripped over a rag doll, cursed hoarsely, but then picked up the little bundle and carried it for a while like an American football. He thought it would be nice to have some extra comfort, especially since Ratu's temper had gotten worse. When they absolutely had to take a break from their zombie-like march—they were down to about ten meters of progress each minute—the pair collapsed in broken shade.

"I have to name my new baby doll." Jope's head ached and his vision was blurry, but when he pulled the thin soiled blanket away from the baby's face, he saw it was a dead human child. He brushed a sticky slug away from its empty eye socket. It had kinky hair like his—after he'd slept outside on the sidewalk in the rain. He'd wake up in front of the bar window with hair just like this little baby's. Jope checked and saw it was a little boy.

"It already got a name," Ratu said quietly. A few minutes later, more tired than when they'd sat down to rest, the pirates trudged on, leaving the baby boy alone in the shade.

"We should keep lookout," Ratu said, head lolling on the top of his skinny neck. The tall walls of their castle were cool and comforting. "You go first."

"I'm so tired, Ratu." But Jope didn't argue. Instead, he rolled to his belly and shimmied up the side of the interior wall, careful not to spill the piles of small coconuts they'd collected for their arsenal. He squinted out into the glaring sun and was mildly surprised to see the awesome vision of a sleek speed boat swaying in the gentle surf, just beyond the reef. It wasn't quite as good as the vision he'd seen while trudging through the interior—of the noni plant that had mysteriously transformed into the big-melon stripper back at the Sticky Finger Bar in Lautoka. Jope would have had his way with the bush if Ratu hadn't socked him and called him a pervert for humping a bush.

"You gotta see this, Ratu," Jope crooned, staring out at the exotic hallucination. "I bet that Sticky Finger stripper would do me for free if I had one of them. I'd pull that up to the dock, tell her to come see my big black machine, yes sir."

"What you runnin' your mouth about, dumbass?" Ratu was too tired to share Jope's hallucination. And that Sticky Finger stripper was a hundred fifty kilos and had a big bald spot on the top of her head.

"It's a cool black racing boat, Ratu." Jope shaded his eyes, jealous of all the strippers and whores a boat like that would attract. "It got maybe ten-thousand horsepower and goes faster than a jet plane."

"That's good, Jope." Ratu closed his eyes to the sound of his friend's voice and began to drift off.

"It has color television and a water bed." Jope imagined lying in the water bed next to the Sticky Finger stripper, looking up at the mirror on the ceiling. He flashed himself a big thumbs-up sign in the mirror, and the stripper giggled, nudging closer. "You own that boat and everybody would know not to call you a dumbass no more. They know you could rev up that big engine and blow them right outta the ocean."

"It have a bar on it?" Ratu mumbled, nearly asleep.

"Hell, yeah, there's two bars on it! You gotta have two bars 'cause so many people wanna come party with the pimp king who got a badass boat."

"You take me for a long, fast ride, okay?" Ratu nestled his head in the sand.

"Hey, some crazy fucker is messin' around on my boat," Jope said, suddenly upset at the change to his awesome hallucination. "Looks like one of them Aborigine pricks always pickin' fights at the dive bar across the street from the Sticky Finger."

"That's good, Jope."

"Now he's poking around the wreck with a long spear, Ratu, like he's lookin' for something."

"Tell me when he finds it, Jope." Ratu yawned big and round, creating bottomless crevasses between the straining tendons of his neck.

"Hey, he's comin' this way." Jope was beginning to seriously doubt his hallucination.

"Let me know when it's my turn to drive."

"Ratu!" Jope cried out, his flailing arms knocking over the piles of stacked coconuts, a dozen of which rolled down and bounced off Ratu's head.

"What's the matter with you!"

"It's the cannibal!" Jope pointed out to the ocean with one hand while grabbing a handful of Ratu's hair and pulling with the other. "He's here to eat us!"

"Let go of my hair!"

"I don't want to be eaten!" Jope looked from side to side in panic. "He comin' to eat us!"

"Christ, who's here, Jope?" Ratu pulled away from his friend's grasp and hoisted himself to the top of the wall. "Oh, shit!"

"Don't let him eat us, Ratu!"

"Shut up and grab the coconuts," Ratu ordered. "Don't throw any 'til he gets close enough to really hurt." But Jope had already begun wildly heaving the small coconuts rapid-fire. The first two didn't make it out of the sandcastle, just slammed into the wall and created little craters.

Ratu got his footing and took aim with his own coconut. The bloodthirsty cannibal stood waist deep in water, a sitting duck despite the long distance. Ratu reached back and then heaved the coconut with all his might. It arced high over the nearly still water before delivering a direct hit to the middle of the cannibal's forehead. The bloodthirsty cannibal fell backward, disappearing under the water.

"You killed him!" Jope screamed with glee, reaching to hug his best friend in victory; then the cannibal rose from the dead and began hollering some lunatic, flesh-eating chant. Ratu and Jope began tossing the coconuts one after the other, blindly, as the cannibal bore down on their castle.

"Don't eat me!" Jope cried, as the cannibal easily hurdled the dry moat they'd spent hours digging and mounted the wall directly in front of their firing position. Their coconut arsenal spent, Jope reached for the brown brick of nearly pure cocaine they'd used to keep their spirits up. He slammed it into the hideous face of the human flesh-eater, just as the cannibal prepared to shish-kebob him on a sharp spear.

With the bloodthirsty cannibal surely chomping his razor-like teeth at their heels, Ratu and Jope made their inglorious retreat toward the interior of the brutalized island.

"Don't let him eat me!" Jope hollered, and as they ran, both cried like frightened children.

CHAPTER 40

Butter watched the red streak rise in the twilight and then drift like a bird gliding on a warm updraft. It floated in the distant sky, sparkling like a tiny, angry star. Maybe "angry" was the wrong word, thought Butter. Maybe it was a tiny, important star. The line and twinkling mass were mirrored in the water below. Had she really just witnessed the birth of a star? Were all stars born from the sea, climbing to their place in the night sky, a compressed broiling flare, full of mad energy?

Butter's mama hadn't known where stars came from, or what special purpose they served besides nighttime decoration. If the moon wasn't keeping them company, they didn't even offer enough light to keep you from tripping over your own feet. Maybe somewhere a book about the stars offered a full explanation. But they all seemed so far away and impossible to know. They were probably a mystery even to the owners of the supply ship and the flying soldier, who was now old enough to be young again on Happa Now. If the flying soldier had known, he'd certainly never shared any special knowledge with her people.

"A star," Butter said aloud, as if to announce its birth. "A beautiful baby star."

Dobby was on his knees under the light of a dangling bare bulb, hands coated in grease, trying to scrub tiny motor parts clean with gasoline and a toothbrush. Looking up into Butter's eyes brought him groaning to his feet and then scrambling up the ladder to the bridge. He reappeared with a metal tube thrust to his eye and aimed it toward the glowing spectacle, twisting and turning the object in his hands. The faulty god dashed back and forth, in and out of the pilot house, acting excited about this new life in the heavens.

"Do you think more will be born?" Butter called up to him, but he was too busy to answer.

Being a salvage man first, Dobby turned his short range radio to channel sixteen and listened without touching the microphone. Any transmission from his end might tip off other ships out of visual range of the flare, which could mean he'd have to bid for the tow job. And if the distressed boat was floundering, chatter on the radio could bring witnesses to any creative bargaining for rescuing the crew. Dobby was a mostly honorable mariner and never let a distress signal go unanswered. It didn't matter what your motivation was, as long as you were willing to step up to aid someone in trouble. Who did it hurt if you also made a buck or two? Everybody won when you came to the rescue and the rescued expressed their gratitude with a little something you could spend at the bar.

But the shorter range VHF emergency channel was dead silent, not even a click. It could mean nothing, or it could mean anything from an electrical problem to a fire. Dobby checked the compass and started the engine, sending a plume of black smoke into the purple sky.

The flare was no more than ten kilometers to the northwest, maybe forty minutes at a safe speed. Dobby had to ease the tugboat around what might be shallow waters—the Gypsy Dancer's depth-finder having been swiped by some lowlifes at the Suva docks. Stealing boats or navigation gear in these parts was akin to horse thievery back in North Texas. And if the police didn't catch the stinking thief, they might just find him swinging from a long stretch of rope.

"No boat should come within five hundred yards out here," Dobby told Butter, warning the little savage to keep an eye out for approaching boats while he was asleep or drunk. "You see a boat, you start hollering like there's no tomorrow."

"Where are the yards?"

"Christ, girl, *this* is a yard." Dobby had held his arms out the length of a yard, but the puzzled look remained on her face. "Come get me if you see any boats. That ain't too difficult, is it?"

"What if they're hungry?"

"Pirates don't want your food, they want your valuables. And you sure as hell don't wanna know what they do to a female they get their hands on, even a dirty little savage girl."

"My mama said pirates take misbehaving children away on their giant wood boats," Butter explained to Dobby. "They have blue beards and legs made out of the same wood as their boats. There's a book written about pirates."

"That's pretty darn close," Dobby said. "She tell you about the big old parrots they keep for pets? They sit right on the pirate captain's shoulder barking out orders."

"Parrots don't bark!" Butter said, giggling. Dobby smiled down at her. She hardly ever sounded or acted like a normal kid. Not that he knew much about normal kids. But this damn girl sure seemed to spend too much time brooding, crying, or complaining.

As Dobby cut the big rusty wheel, something warm leaned into his left hip.

"It's a new star," Butter told him. She'd snuck up the ladder to the bridge despite being warned to keep out of the pilot house because there were too many things she shouldn't be messing with in here. In truth, he just didn't want her to see the dog-eared girlie magazines stacked along the back wall of the cabin. Most of the photographs didn't reveal any more nakedness than what she'd described on her island. Dobby had been to more than a hundred inhabited islands. Quite a few had swinging boobs every which way you looked, but not one had been completely bottomless, too. And while the idea of all that exposed punani had a certain appeal, Dobby looked down at his own dimpled belly and figured he wouldn't be such an enchanting vision were he to hang his hat on the girl's island for a spell. If there was anything left of it, that is. And the very idea of sitting in the sand without britches was equally unappetizing.

"That ain't no star," Dobby said, as the girl pressed into him, her little head against the side of his belly. Cool air was blowing in through the broken windows, so Dobby took his left hand off the wheel and draped it about her shoulders. It was the first time he'd touched the girl since she'd pitched a fit over him killing babies and innocent animals.

"I saw it born." Butter's arms half circled his big round belly, which jiggled mightily as the snubbed bow of the tugboat plowed through the chop toward the wafting star. "Everything is born in the sea."

"That's what you people think, huh? I guess it ain't so wrong. Some of the savages in these parts believe airplanes brought people to Earth from outer space. Came here like they was riding on the Mayflower, just stepped off and started fishin' and havin' babies."

"No, people came from the sea." Butter shook her head against Dobby's belly. A new, cooler breeze had rushed in as Dobby rolled the wheel a quarter turn. "Even you came from the sea. All gods do. Everything."

"I'm from Texas." But Dobby didn't mean to argue with the shivering girl who hugged him tightly, her face turned to watch the sparkling object out of one eye.

The star flickered brightly, like a super nova, and went black.

"Where did it go?" Butter pulled away to search the sky.

"Over there." Dobby pointed up into the sky with the hand that had been rubbing her bony shoulders through the thin material of her dress. "Looks like it found its home right up there."

The Gypsy Dancer left a white wake in the black sea, engines firing and sometimes misfiring, sending puffs of thick oily smoke up toward the new twinkling star.

CHAPTER 41

"Are there sharks out here?"

"It's the ocean, racer boy. There are four hundred kinds of sharks."

"Do they all bite?"

Dante had splashed down twenty feet from the boat without dying instantly. The return swim was effortless, bringing back images of his sunset adventures in his island dreams. The splintered boat refused to sink, although only the canvas sunscreen, windshield, and top half of the control panel remained above water.

Ophelia grabbed for the radio microphone, but the electrical system had shorted out from the impact or the deluge of salt water. Next she fumbled for the emergency kit strapped to the base of her pilot's seat—now under three feet of water. She set the box on top of the instrument console and popped the latch. Inside were two dye packs, a signaling mirror, six hand launch flares, and a twelve-gauge flare gun with a single parachute flare already chambered.

Ophelia slammed the lid closed and turned to the hatches stuffed with life preservers.

"You okay?" Dante had swum right into the boat, barking his left shin on the submerged fiberglass side.

"We're in big trouble." Ophelia tossed him one of the bright orange life preservers, which he put on. He was standing in waist deep water with the floor of the boat slowly undulating beneath his feet. Ophelia clipped into her own life preserver and then lumbered onto the bow to find and jettison the anchor.

"Do you have food or water in your backpacks?" Ophelia grabbed two more life preservers and climbed back to the pilot's chair.

"A bag of granola and three packs of Oreos." Dante turned to retrieve the submerged bags from a compartment under the rear seat cushions, which began floating away. "And two jugs of Gatorade. The other bag just has clothes and a bunch of cash."

"Here, tie them both to this." Ophelia flipped him one of the life preservers. "Then clip it to the railing. If the boat starts going down, try to grab them. We'll need the Gatorade."

"You think the boat will go under?"

"It's a matter of *when*, not *if*, racer boy."

"I'm sorry I made you bring me out here." Dante scanned the horizon. No sign of land and the water looked like it might be a hundred miles deep.

"You didn't *make* me do anything." Ophelia looked around the boat as if to figure out what was left to do. "The radio's dead, but we have some flares."

"What about the boat that crashed into us? He knows we're here."

"He doesn't give a shit about us," Ophelia said. "A speed boat this far out is probably a drug runner."

"Did you see him? He didn't look like a drug runner. He looked like a crazy headhunter."

"Then he was a headhunter in a sixty-thousand dollar boat blasting dance music."

"I thought I heard music. Do you know how far the island

is?" Dante asked. It didn't take an epiphany to make him realize his life was completely in the Raro cop's hands. In the past year, his life had pretty much been handed from person to person—from doctors to nurses, and then to therapists. Even before that, he'd relied on downhill coaches to convince him to take their line through blind spots in courses where bad decisions meant piling into trees at sixty miles per hour. If not for Ophelia, Dante knew he would just crawl up above the console and take a nap until being rescued or accepting whatever other outcome presented itself. He would see if he could sleep his way through this pickle.

"If I'd known we were going to get run over, I'd have checked our position more closely. The island can't be more than a few kilometers away."

"So we can swim?"

"The current is strong, maybe five kilometers per hour to the south. It would be like trying to swim across a rip tide." Ophelia gazed longingly to the east, to where she could almost see a bump on the horizon that would be land.

"So we're drifting away from land?"

"Yeah, well, that's relative, isn't it?"

"So what's to the south of us?" Dante asked. "Where are we headed?"

"I'm pretty sure the next land would be Antarctica."

"You mean the South Pole?"

"Uh, sort of, yeah." Ophelia got busy again, lashing empty gas cans together.

"Oh, Christ, polar bears."

"I'm pretty sure they're just at the North Pole."

"I guess that's good."

"Yes, if we end up drifting six thousand kilometers, we won't have polar bears to worry about," Ophelia said.

"Are you going to shoot a flare?"

"We should wait a little, let the sun drop. Unless we start going under," Ophelia added ominously. "It'll be easier to spot.

And maybe we'll be able to see some ship lights."

"I wasn't really looking forward to it getting dark." Dante sloshed forward to balance against the co-pilot's seat. Ophelia sat against the console and faced him. The air was still hot, but the water had taken on a chill. "Do people get hypothermia in this kind of water?"

"Not for a couple of days, maybe longer. We found survivors ten days after their boat capsized twenty kilometers out. It all came down to a two liter jug of water they'd grabbed from the store at the last minute. It ended up saving their lives."

"Wow, ten days and they were fine?" Dante looked around at all that water and tried to imagine what ten long nights would be like. All those hungry things swimming in the dark right under you.

"The jellyfish are the biggest worry." Ophelia reached over the side of the boat and ran her hand through the same water that had risen up to her hips. It was the first time Dante sensed her fear. She'd finished doing everything there was to do but didn't seem to believe it. "Their faces were swollen badly. They didn't look like human faces. Both were blind from the stings."

"Blind?"

"Infections, I guess. But they lived." Ophelia kept stirring the water with one hand. "They lived, but they weren't fine."

As the sun made its final descent, the boat was slowly rotating counter-clockwise, according to the few puffs of clouds. They looked at each other, then out at the endless expanse of ocean. Having sunk at least three feet gave a new, almost overwhelming perspective. The ocean was rising around them, coming up to greet them, and maybe swallow them.

"I've never seen snow," Ophelia said, staring out into the distance beyond Dante. "I mean, except on television and in movies. You don't remember what snow is like, do you?"

Dante shook his head.

"You said your heart stopped after your accident?"

"That's what I was told."

"I helped resuscitated a drowning victim who'd been under for a good seven or eight minutes," Ophelia said. "A teenage boy. When we got his heart started, it was like a switch came on. He started coughing really hard and we couldn't hold him down. He was yelling something at us, but we couldn't understand because he still had water in his lungs and was gagging, literally foaming at the mouth. It was what you'd imagine someone with rabies would look like. And he started acting like it, too."

"This was on the beach?"

"Yeah, there were maybe a half dozen lifeguards and even more cops." Ophelia continued looking off into the darkening horizon. "He was a big, strong kid, and when he got to his feet, he was just throwing people off him, shouting the same thing over and over. One of the lifeguards jumped on his back, trying to bring him down. Amazing, since the kid had just basically been dead."

"Where was he trying to go?"

"He was headed straight back into the water. I was in front of him at one point, and his eyes were huge and desperate. We were in his way and he just had to get past us and nothing was going to stop him. That's when I finally understood what he was saying."

"Which was?"

"He kept screaming, 'I have to get back,' over and over. I'm sure it sounds like he was just traumatized and it didn't mean anything. Like a drunk gets it into his head to do something. But I know what I felt when we were trying to get him under control. And I talked to a few of the other cops later on and they all thought the same thing."

"That he liked being dead?" Dante asked, the cool water sloshing at their hips.

"You don't remember being dead, do you?"

"I remember feeling cold." Dante closed his eyes and rubbed his stubbly face. "As if having your memories erased removed the things that kept you warm. I didn't walk toward a bright white light or anything. I just remember lying there on my back, feeling everything I knew washing away from me, leaving a sense of emptiness and cold. Nothing I'd want to fight to get back to."

After a few minutes of silence, Ophelia cleared her throat. "I think it's dark enough."

The tall, blond Rarotonga cop opened the emergency kit on top of the boat's control panel and removed the twelve-gauge flare gun. Holding the small orange firearm out away from her with both hands, she discharged the parachute flare in the direction of East Pukapuka, just as the boat began to sink under their feet.

CHAPTER 42

"You got good eyes, girl," Dobby told Butter as they closed in on the spot where the flare had been fired. "Go down on the bow railing and shout up if you see anything in the water, even if it's just pieces of junk."

Dobby reached over his head to flip the switch on the three-hundred-fifty-watt searchlight mounted above the pilot house. He used the joystick next to the wheel to angle the beam straight out in front of the Gypsy Dancer. He kept the old tugboat at a crawl, searching the black water for debris or maybe an oil slick. There was no sign or smell in the air of a recent fire and there had been no second flare as they approached from the southeast. That was odd, Dobby thought, and it didn't usually mean good news. One flare goes up and then the distressed boater is supposed to send up another. Anything else might mean a quick sinking or fishermen getting drunk and screwing around, which would piss him off real good. Hell, Dobby had watched a couple of fishing charters get in a flare gun war—drunk off their asses and lobbing flares at each other's boats. All fun and games until one of the boats caught fire.

The sky was filled with stars, old and new, as the experienced salvage captain created a search grid in his head and began executing it with a sweep around the perimeter. He then set about making concentric circles, zeroing in. Dobby tooted the air horn at intervals and cracked a smile as the little savage girl mimicked the sound after each pull of the horn's rope. Meanwhile she leaned out over the bow, searching the water intently.

Not ten minutes into the sweep, Butter began jumping up and down. Dobby feared she was about to hop overboard. She screamed and pointed out into what looked like pitch darkness. When he adjusted the joystick, two orange life vests reflected brightly.

"Shit," was all Dobby had to say. There was no money and a lot of headaches attached to reeling in floaters like this. Just look at the goddamn turtle-girl, who had turned out to be all girl and no turtle. No boat meant no money for a tow and no salvage. Just two more damn hitchhikers expecting a free goddamn ride to port. Dobby killed the engine, letting the tug drift up to within ten feet of the swimmers. He had to jimmy open one of the pilot house windows and lean out to see them over the side of the forward gunwale.

"Ahoy," Dobby shouted. "Not much of a place for an evening swim, you ask me."

"Thank god," a female voice echoed off the rusted metal hull of the Gypsy Dancer. A cloud of blond hair floated all around her. There were two of them treading water in slow, wide strokes. The other, apparently a young man, seemed to be looking to her to do all the talking.

"Where might your ship be?" Dobby called down from the open window, the searchlight turning the two upturned faces bright white.

"We were hit by another boat." The woman tried to time her words to dodge the chop slapping at her face. "It kept going."

"And yours went to the bottom." Dobby rubbed his chin thoughtfully.

"Can you please throw us a line?"

"Are you hurt?"

"We're cold and tired," said the woman.

"So you are perfectly capable of swimming, as I see it. You know this ain't a ferry boat or some kind of tour charter, young lady. This is a salvage boat and I don't see nothing worth salvaging."

"Captain," the woman began, but had to struggle through a series of jarring waves before continuing. "I'm a Senior Sergeant with the Rarotonga Police."

"That's a pretty casual uniform you got on there. And I don't see no badge, missy. You maybe thinkin' about writing me a parking ticket?"

"Captain, by International Admiralty Law you are required to provide assistance, but I am begging you as a human being to help us." The woman's voice had slipped right to the verge of panic.

"It took fuel to come huntin' down the source of that flare you shot up and it's gonna cost a helluva lot more to get you to dry ground," Dobby barked. Meanwhile Butter was down on the bow working in the deep shadows, untying and then lifting the heavy rope ladder she'd barely managed to heave over the gunwale. The ladder unfurled as it fell, one end splashing into the water a few feet from where the pair was treading water.

"Thank you," the woman called up into the bright spotlight as they swam toward the ladder.

"Christ's freakin' sake, girl," Dobby complained under his breath, pulling his shoulders back in from the open window. "That ain't no goddamn way to bargain for the best price. Turnin' me into some damn charity."

The woman slid over the side of the tugboat first, followed closely by the man, who seemed to be trying to escape something he feared was following him up the ladder. He hauled his waterlogged backpacks up—one slung over each shoulder—dropped them onto the deck, then tumbled over on top of them, completely exhausted.

Dobby stood over the pair as they worked to catch their breath. The forward deck of the Gypsy Dancer was lit indirectly by the spotlight, and the captain could see Butter crouched, hiding in the heavy shadows.

"You can thank this little savage girl for savin' your skins, but I still ain't no goddamn ferry boat." Dobby stood with his feet wide and hands on his hips, his great belly thrust out indignantly. "Soon as I find this little runt's island, I'm leaving the lot of you. I'll radio your position to whoever will listen, but I got weeks of prime pickings still floating in these waters and I ain't got food or water to keep you alive."

"That's just fine, captain." The blond broad, still out of breath, began unclipping the life preserver from what appeared to Dobby to be a very healthy set of fun bags. Appears this young lady had her own pair of built-in life preservers. Dobby could have kicked himself in his own ass had he possessed the necessary flexibility. *First, I get me a buck naked primitive who's barely housebroken, now I got me a set of goddamn Barbie and Ken dolls. And all the while, there's treasures drifting away far and wide I should be reelin' in. What the hell did I do to bring on this kind of friggin' luck?*

"You!" Dobby shouted at Butter, pointing down at her hiding spot. "You get them a couple blankets and take 'em 'round to where you been bunking. You got drinkin' water in either of them bags?" Dobby asked the man, indicating the backpacks with his chin.

"Yes, sir," he managed. His face and neck looked burned and stung from what must have been jellyfish or some other nasty sea creatures. "Gatorade," he added, still gasping for air. "And enough cash to pay for a one way ride, if you're interested."

"Cash, huh? Girl!" Dobby called to Butter, who was already rummaging the cabinets in the galley for a set of old wool blankets. "Get our guests the clean ones, for Christ's sake." Then, turning back to his new passengers, he said, "Lots of shallow reefs in these waters and I ain't got a depth finder, so you two dry off and then get some rest. The little savage will settled you in and we'll figure our bearings at first light, or whenever I wake up. My price is whatever you got that you can't drink or eat and it ain't negotiable."

CHAPTER 43

Ratu slowly came to, but the world didn't make much sense. For one thing, it was upside down. For another, he seemed to be tied up and hanging from a tree.

A loud whimpering and rustling from behind him took his breath away in more ways than one as Jope's struggle caused the thin nylon rope to tighten. The two former pirates were bound together, back to back, somewhere in the middle of the wave-ravaged island.

"Quit pullin' the rope," Ratu managed, trying to expand his chest and shoulders to get some room back. "I can't breathe."

"Ratu, I thought you was dead!" Jope's voice was hoarse from all the screaming and crying he'd been doing since the bloodthirsty cannibal had caught up to them and wrestled them to the ground. Ratu had tried to fight him off but had little chance of succeeding with Jope clinging to him, refusing to let go or help in any way and screaming about not wanting to be eaten. The crazy bastard bound their wrists and ankles with the same plastic ties the cops had started using back home. Once, when a cop had tied his hands in front and stuck him in his car, Ratu had chipped a tooth trying to gnaw his way free.

"I gotta pee real bad." Jope began struggling again, but the rope was wound securely around them, cocoon-like. They were hanging two meters off the ground, slowly rotating beneath a squat palm tree at the center of what had once been a village. Smashed huts and other signs of people all pushed up against the bent-over trees. "It's making my stomach hurt."

"So pee, you dumbass, what do you want from me?" Ratu had woken up in a foul mood. The right side of his head ached from where the cannibal hit him with something hard, knocking him unconscious. His throat was bone dry from all the cocaine and hard labor building what hadn't been such an impenetrable fortress. But when he felt the lurches from Jope's quiet sobs, he softened. "It's okay, Jope, just keep your mouth closed when you piss. I gotta go, too."

"The shark-god was right; we're in some really big trouble. That crazy cannibal says he gonna eat us alive. Says we gotta tell him where we buried the coke."

"You told him we buried it?"

"Yeah, but I told him I don't remember where. And I don't, Ratu, I wasn't lying. I told him I don't care about the coke. He can have it all. I'd dig it up and give right to him, if I knew where it was. That coke been nothin' but bad news. Just please don't eat me!" Jope started sobbing again, which made the rope dig deeper into Ratu's ribcage.

"Stop crying. It's gonna be okay. Where is he now?"

"He says he's gonna swim back to his boat and get his camera. He says he makes movies of when he eats scumbags who steal from his boss."

"Oh, shit."

"Who wanna watch that kinda movie, Ratu? What kind of sick person wanna see people get eaten?" The tears and snot that streaked Jope's face were slowly being washed away by his own warm pee. "I'm such a dirty mess." Jope whimpered as he spit and coughed. "I'm a big dumb mess."

"You ain't dumb, Jope. We done some dumb things together,

but you was always a really good friend. And it was bad that I ever called you dumb. I got no right to be doing that to a good person like you."

"I hope he eats me first," Jope said, trying to stifle his sobs. "I hope one of my bones gets stuck in his throat and he chokes to death on me. Then you can be saved, Ratu."

"You're a good friend. I love you like my brother."

"You my brother, too."

Just then the bloodthirsty cannibal—covered from head to toe with some sort of batshit war paint—came stomping out of the broken jungle waving his pointed spear. The crazy bastard let out a demented yodel that drained the last bit of pee from Jope. The dude looked exactly like the weird-ass savages in the big poster taped to the window of the Suva travel agency, the one advertising the Cannibal Culture Spree over on Malakula. Ratu and Jope had passed the window hundreds of times.

The slow rotation of the former pirates had put the cannibal face to face with Jope, who shrieked, "No, please, please, please, don't eat me! I just pissed myself. Eat him first!"

CHAPTER 44

Butter snuggled between these new, warm white people, as she watched the sky change from black to purple, then get all fancy with a bunch of oranges and reds. Back on her island, she'd sometimes stay up all night and walk the long narrow path to the east side to watch the sun rise out of the sea. She might take a lizard for company, or her Habu for protection. Nobody would ever bother a little girl with a poisonous viper around her neck, especially not one that appeared to have been hacked apart and sewn back up.

A sense of calm washed over the little girl as she cuddled in these strange armpits, searching the colorful sky for some sign of a window to Happa Now. The soft touch of a woman had been confusing at first. It made her mama seem closer, but at the same time deepened her sense of loss.

Nighttime for children on tiny islands and boats out in the middle of big oceans is especially hard. On still nights, when the sea is dead calm, the sky appears endless. How could any child not feel utterly lost and alone in such a big empty place?

"What if they were wrong? What if they were lying?" Butter spoke out loud, wanting to end the quiet and feel a little less alone. "What if there is no Happa Now?" She watched the yellows begin to bleed into the orange and reds, lightening the sky and darkening the shadows around the deck. Nobody had ever gone to Happa Now and come back. Grown-ups claimed to have spoken across the great void to family members who had moved on, but she'd never heard a single whisper from Papa. If some cousin or next door neighbor who moved on could talk to you from Happa Now, then a girl's own father surely could.

Butter turned her head sideways to look at the woman, whose hair had turned brighter and more golden as it dried. What if it was just like the stories about the boogieman? Even Mama had lied about the Tooth Devil. Maybe some kids became frightened when their teeth fell out, but not her. Butter didn't need some stupid black pearl to keep from balling about a dumb baby tooth. She understood that baby teeth needed replacing. Stronger adult teeth were for cracking nuts and tearing apart smoked fish. Losing your baby teeth was necessary.

If there was no Happa Now, would her mama look anything like the parrot she'd dug up after a year in the ground? Butter hoped that whether or not there was a Happa Now, her mama's flesh and bones had washed out to sea, where nothing was wasted and nothing was left. The sea took everything back in order to make brand new things.

But here in the armpits of these lightly snoring white people, Butter felt she could deal with all these impossible questions. When the tall white man pulled away, stretched, and got up, Butter burrowed deeper into the embrace of the woman and watched him through narrowed eyes. The man walked to the east-facing stern and began to do a funny dance, bending forward and touching his toes, then twisting left and then right at the hip. Butter giggled, then shut her eyes quickly and hid her face, worried he might have heard. When she dared reopen them, the man was dancing more energetically. First, it was a silly pretend dance where he tapped his toes, swung an invisible stick and took off and held a pretend hat. Then he did a dance that looked more solemn, holding a stiff partner at the hand and hip. And Butter knew the tall white man was dancing for her because he caught her watching and winked down at her. His last dance was fast again; he'd put his hands on his knees and make silly faces. But as the sun's rays flooded over the gunwale and lit the main deck, the man quit dancing. His hands were frozen on his bent knees, as if someone had just ordered the drummers to stop.

The man stood over the giant crayon mural and whispered, "East Pukapuka," which meant nothing to Butter. His head was cocked to one side like a dog trying to figure out where a strange sound had come from. He was breathing hard from dancing.

"It's my home." Butter's voice was soft.

"It's beautiful." The rising sun put the man in silhouette, his shadow falling across the meticulous drawing.

"When Jesus wakes up, he's taking us there." Butter lifted up on one elbow, trying not to wake the white woman, but also not wanting to pull away from her warm embrace.

"Jesus?"

"The captain is Jesus. He's a god, but not a very good one."

The man walked back and knelt down on the edge of the bedroll where Butter was cradled in the sleeping woman's arms. "A big wave swept across your island."

"I know. I was there when it came for everybody." Butter's large brown eyes searched the man's face. "Jesus let the big wave happen and now he feels bad. He knows he shouldn't have done it. It took everyone to Happa Now."

"Happa Now?"

"I couldn't leave my animals behind. They need me. I opened their cages and some could fly and some could swim. I have to get back and take care of the ones that didn't get killed."

"How did you survive the wave?"

"I grabbed my turtle and held my breath," Butter said. A tear rolled down her cheek. "Jesus let my turtle die. He can't live in deep water without food."

"The captain?"

"Yes, it was the captain's fault. Turtles aren't allowed on Happa Now, just people. My turtle's just dead. But I'm not even sure Happa Now is real anymore."

"I'm sorry." The man folded his long legs to sit criss-cross, leaning back against his palms.

"Why are you here?"

"I asked her to bring me out here to find something." He paused, as if searching for the right words. "Have you ever had the feeling you were completely alone and lost in the world?"

Butter was about to mention being swept away into the open sea by a giant wave, losing her one living parent and everything she loved and knew. But the ten-year-old girl just nodded her head.

"I'm going to East Pukapuka to start my life over again." The man pointed across the deck to the mural. "That's where we were headed."

"Is this lady your wife?"

"No, I don't think she even likes me. Some really bad things have happened since we met."

"It was her boat that got wrecked?"

"Yeah."

"She's really beautiful," Butter whispered. The woman opened her eyes and began stroking Butter's long black hair away from her face, which was a Crayola mixture of Cedar Chest and Aztec Gold.

"I know."

Butter pointed to the crayon portrait at the top of the mural. "That's my mama."

"She's really pretty, too."

"Yes, she is."

"She's on Happa Now?" he asked.

"I hope so. She's with my dad, but he didn't get taken by the wave. A big shark bit him when I was little."

"Wow, I'm sorry."

"It's okay. If my animals don't need me, if they were all killed or went away, then I'm going to see my family soon, whether or not it's real."

"You're going to Happa Now?"

"Yeah, well, if I'm not needed on my island."

"How will you get there?"

"I may need help. I once had to hold a blue-footed Booby underwater. She had such a bad infection in her chest and up under her wings. She cried all the time and I couldn't help make it better."

"So you want someone to drown you?"

"The elders say it's a great honor to send someone to Happa Now, as long as you don't do it because you've been drinking wapa juice."

"Your customs are a lot different than ours."

"You've never drowned a little girl?" Butter asked. It took the man a minute to realize she was teasing.

"Jesus," he said.

"I thought about asking Jesus, but he's always drinking wapa juice." Butter's voice quieted to a hush as she looked up toward where the captain was still sleeping in the pilot house. "I think a kid needs to check out all her options before asking help from a drunk god who eats his own boogers."

CHAPTER 45

"The last thing we wanna do is come sneakin' up on a drug runner," Dobby said, handing the binoculars to Ophelia. "Them bastards are all armed to the teeth, and the one who ran you over's gotta be particularly nuts. We steer clear of them, and they return the favor. That's the way it works out here and I got no plans to change it."

"I'm not arguing with you," Ophelia said. "This trip started out as a favor to my mother. She asked me to deliver a lost cause she met on a bus near the airport, and I was about ten minutes from being free and clear."

Standing shoulder to shoulder with the captain up in the pilot house, Ophelia wiped the filthy front glass elements of the greasy binoculars on the tail of her shirt and then held them back up to her eyes. They took turns peering out one of the broken windows as the Gypsy Dancer chugged at five knots to within a few hundred meters of East Pukapuka.

Happy screams and shrieks of laughter came from down on the main deck, where racer boy and the girl were busy playing with the piles of Dobby's salvage. Ophelia had caught a glimpse of Dante wearing a dress and pillbox hat, carrying a big yellow purse. The girl was wearing a plastic Viking hat, using a sword to violently thwack everything in sight.

"That friend of yours retarded?"

"Ah, yeah, well, not exactly." Ophelia concentrated on keeping the binoculars steady. The captain had repeated his promise to radio their position once he'd left them, but it was prudent to make sure the drug runner wasn't still in these waters first.

"He sure seems retarded."

"No sign of any people." Ophelia ignored Dobby's comment. "No boats and no smoke. And it looks like the island took a direct hit from the tsunami. We had rescuers down here just days after the disaster. Whoever wasn't washed away was buried on the island."

"I seen bodies floatin' out east of the island," Dobby said, both hands on the rusty wheel. "That's where I pulled the girl out of the water. It ain't possible any of her kin survived?"

"It wasn't possible that the girl survived." Ophelia lowered the binoculars and turned to Dobby. "They estimated the wave was going two hundred-forty kilometers per hour, and was ten meters high when it swept across the island. It's wide open sea from the direction of the original earthquake. Would have been like getting hit by a train."

"I found her hangin' off the back of a sea turtle."

"She told me her turtle died."

"Yeah, a big old loggerhead swimmin' like hell trying to get away," Dobby said, shaking his head. "Thought I was gonna be rich."

"That's incredible. I saw video of the island. Some people had been caught in the trees and crushed by the wall of water. Most of the buildings were thatched huts, really primitive structures. The damage was like an enormous high tide line of trash piles. Some painted wood splinters here and there, with what turned out to be broken bodies mixed right in. It's amazing what nature is capable of, worse than I imagined."

"Coupla rainy seasons and it'll look like nothing bad ever visited," Dobby said. "That's the way it works down on these islands, and it's the same with the real big storms. It all just grows back eventually. The roots run deep."

"Except maybe for the people," Ophelia said.

Dobby took back the binoculars. "Looks like there's some wreckage on the reef." He pointed. "It's broke all to hell. Part of a hull, but it's white, with light blue trim. Your drug runner was drivin' an all black job, right?"

"Yes, black from bow to stern."

"Then he ain't here." Dobby handed her the binoculars. "Coulda been a drop or pick-up, but ain't no reason for him to hang around. He's probably headed straight out to Tahiti or Bora Bora. I say the fucker's long gone."

CHAPTER 46

Albino Paul whistled while he worked, despite a growing impatience with these two imbeciles and his inability to find the cocaine.

He'd swum back out to his boat and then motored around to the calm east side of the island, navigating through a narrow break in the reef. Now he could tuck the sleek black craft close to the beach on the leeward side of this shithole island. He was able to wade back through waist-deep water carrying the video camera and a shovel to dig for the buried cocaine. Stashing his boat was more about keeping it from getting dinged by crap peeling off the crashed fishing charter the dimwits had rammed into the reef than laying low. Albino Paul had nobody to hide from, except maybe a government bounty hunter hired to track down the maniac who had slaughtered some drug couriers at a refueling station. Few island governments would bother to invest in finding the culprit for that crime. They'd be perfectly content that all parties had moved on or were already buried and out of sight. Albino Paul didn't want any more screw-ups, and these two morons were enough of a pain in his ass.

Even the sandcastle on the west side no longer looked manmade, now that he'd kicked down the walls during his search for the cocaine bricks. He'd followed each set of footprints, dug into any small mounds, had tried each spot where it appeared the sand had been recently excavated. He kept digging up freshly buried bodies—the work of rescue and recovery crews. A few weeks in the hot sand and the sight of the corpses was hard on the stomach of even the most barbarous cannibal.

He found ample evidence that the search party had swept the island—littered containers of military food rations, crumbled cigarette packs, and the occasional deep imprints from navy deck boots.

Albino Paul wasn't the least bit sympathetic to the fate these people had suffered, even though nature—not a stronger tribe—had wiped them out. There could be pride in being slaughtered if you fought with bravery but were outmanned. The Second World War was a battle his people had no stake in, yet their land was deemed strategically important by all sides. What use were even the finest spears and most valiant fighters when metal ships and diving airplanes strafed your villages with thousands of bullets? His elders bowed down to the occupiers, laid their meager weapons at the boots of the white, black and even yellow skinned soldiers. But when these soldiers turned their backs, his forefathers stuck a knife deep and twisted hard. Five villagers would die for every attack, but that statistic had not extinguished their pride.

Here on this crappy little island, the people had done something worse than kneel down to foreign fighters with superior weapons. Allowing your people to be so easily destroyed at the hands of a god was cowardly. Gods were enslavers and their respect had to be earned. The Malakulans were not gods, but they were great warrior people, not simple, contemptible humans. By eating the hearts of their enemies and absorbing their strength, Albino Paul's people had risen above humanity. The gods knew not to screw with his people because there would be hell to pay. Maybe not at first, but one day Albino Paul's people would find a god with his back turned.

Albino Paul was certain of his final destiny in some future life. It was one of the reasons he'd embraced technology, had learned how to repair and maintain engines, had studied space travel and astronomy on a wireless laptop, alone at night in his hut.

"Resistance is futile," Albino Paul dreamed of saying once he had become a cybernetic organism, absorbing another weak race into the thriving, unstoppable collective hive. That's what his people would say once they had taken their land back from the Vanuatu government. There wasn't a *Star Trek* episode Albino Paul didn't know by heart—another benefit of the wireless Internet. The smokin' rack on that tall, skinny chick named Seven of Nine was heaven for a bloodthirsty cannibal from Malakula.

But that was centuries away, and now there were stolen bricks of cocaine to find. This current hassle was rapidly dissolving into a search for a needle in a haystack. Albino Paul was just about at the end of his rope when it came to these two morons.

"How about I track down both your mothers and slice off their tits with a butcher knife?" the bloodthirsty cannibal threatened the naked upside-down former pirates. Albino Paul grabbed the rope around their middle and spun them hard, blood and snot spraying the white sand.

"Oh, god, no!" said one.

"Weeeeee!" said the other.

The twisted rope came to a halt and then quickly began unwinding, spinning in the opposite direction.

"I'll put their tits on toast and eat them with pepper." Albino Paul stood menacingly beneath the two dizzy pieces of worthless shit, feet at shoulder width, arms crossed in front.

"We don't got mothers. Ratu's mom was a dirty crank whore who left him at the orphanage, and my dad accidentally killed my mother when he got drunk and punched her too hard."

"You fucking dipshits! I need you to remember! Was it near where you threw the coconuts at me? Did you dig the hole in a clearing, or was it surrounded by trees? Think, or I'll cut your fucking tongues off!"

"We're sorry we threw coconuts at you. We didn't wanna get eaten. Nobody wants to get eaten. Please don't eat me!"

"Shut up! Were there any big rocks around? Were you up on the bluff?"

Prolonged silence as the former pirates quietly wobbled at the end of the rope.

"For fuck's sake, don't shut up! Talk! Were you up on the bluff or not?"

"I'm pretty sure we were here on the island."

"You buried a million dollars worth of cocaine and have no fucking clue where?" Albino Paul rubbed his aching forehead. "Do you idiots remember a single detail?"

There was another long pause. "I remember it was hot."

The bloodthirsty cannibal turned and stormed off with his shovel.

CHAPTER 47

"What's up with all these birds, Ratu?"

"I don't know, but there sure are a lot of them." Ratu had avoided pointing out all the birds, which had been flying in and landing everywhere, practically carpeting the ground all around them. Tied up like this—upside down and back to back—they resembled a human bird feeder, and getting pecked to death wasn't a whole lot better than being eaten by a cannibal. He was pretty sure of that.

"I never seen so many birds." Jope pursed his lips and began to whistle and call to them. "Here birdie, birdie, here birdie."

"What the fuck are you doing?"

"Bird calls."

"You want them gettin' closer to us?" Ratu asked.

"I can do one of them big gray gooses that fly in a pointy shape."

"Don't."

Jope tilted his chin to the ground as all the shoulder-to-shoulder birds crowded closer. It was as if some were standing on one another's backs, there were so many. "You know a bird call to make them go away?"

"The trees are all filled up, too."

When Jope had rotated around to face the trees, he said, "Holy shit, it looks just like a scene from that movie."

"What movie?"

"You know, that real scary movie with all the birds." Jope wracked his brain for the title. "*Snakes on a Plane*, or something like that. They shot chickens out of cannons and some fat white guy took one up the pooper on that lousy canoe trip. Remember the banjo boy?"

Ratu recalled jumbled pieces of all the movies they'd snuck into. "Yeah, and there was that crazy fucker with a chainsaw."

"Brummbumbumbum …" Jope mimicked the chainsaw, which made some of the birds back off.

"Blood everywhere!"

"Hey, Chucky, why do you kill?" Jope asked in a deep voice and giggled maniacally.

"I'm mad 'cause I got a little doll-size pecker!" Ratu cackled hysterically, then coughed up a wad of bloody phlegm and spit at the closest bird.

Jope stopped laughing, grew serious as they slowly turned. "You remember them naked pictures of that vampire chick after she was all growed up?"

"Yeah, you showed them to me on the library computer. Then that old lady pushing around the cart of books went apeshit and kicked us out."

"I'd let a chick with knobs like those bite me, you know? Not a crazy cannibal, but that hot vampire chick would be okay." Jope was quiet for a minute. "He's comin' back to eat us, isn't he?"

"Stop thinking about it or you'll just get upset again. Think about something happy."

The former pirates were silent for a while, reflecting on the scary movies they'd watched to escape the Suva afternoon sun, empty beer bottles clanking at their feet and a serpentine trail of pot smoke climbing up through the projection light.

More and more birds arrived, searching for places to land. Flocks of all types circled overhead, sounding upset and impatient. The bigger birds came barreling down on top of others already on the ground, sending them squawking and scrambling, tiny feathers flying. Those feathers floated everywhere, coating all the men's sweaty body parts that weren't wrapped in rope.

"Something crazy is up with these birds," Jope said over the noise of what seemed like tens of thousands of complaining birds. There was a flurry of wings directly above the former pirates as an elegant pair of black-naped terns landed on Jope and Ratu's bound feet. The male immediately mounted the female from behind, humping away as if nobody was watching. "This is startin' to get really weird," Jope said.

The former pirates continued to rotate slowly, bobbing ever so slightly from the motion of the mating birds.

CHAPTER 48

D obby dropped anchor within a stone's throw of the reef. A strong current pulled the old tugboat broadside to the island.

"That your island, girl?" Dobby asked Butter, as the four stood on the starboard side of the main deck.

"That's my home." Butter couldn't tear her eyes away from the battered landscape and the strange, unfamiliar birds circling in crowded flocks over what had been the jungle interior. The entrance to the lagoon, where the hundred people of her village had joined hands to greet the big wave, was just out of view. The island's tallest tree, a majestic old coconut palm at the north end of the cove, was gone. That was where Franklin Roosevelt, the island's best climber, had held lookout for the wave after the island had received the emergency radio warning.

"The tree is gone." Butter spoke softly, tears silently streaming down her brown face, her eyes red and puffy. Lost were the families of parrots that had burrowed homes into the crotch of the soaring tree, hidden and protected within the crown of leaves. And all those tiny blind snakes, no more than a finger length, looking like shiny black worms under the deadfall at the tree's enormous base. Along with the sadness, rage had begun to take root deep in the girl's stomach as she realized the amount of hate required to do this to her home. A god all filled up with hate and anger for no reason at all. One who thought it was fun to kill, just like those rotten boys who hurt her animals. Butter clenched her fists, ragged nails digging into her palms and creating bloody little half-moons.

Butter wanted to scream at Jesus Dobby, demand he set things right immediately. But she had a growing sense that no one could do that, especially Jesus. She had witnessed him drunkenly attempt to change a light bulb by screwing it in the wrong direction, over and over, swearing, the threads repeatedly popping the bulb back out of the socket. Even a *savage* like her, as he always called her, knew better. She'd watched him finally give up and try to toss the uncooperative bulb into the sea, only his throw would come up short, and the bulb would explode against the gunwale into a thousand shards of thin glass.

Whether or not Jesus had conjured the wave, he had allowed her animals to die, and they were never coming back.

"How do we get to the island?" Dante asked.

Ophelia pointed down to a smudged yellow valise at the captain's feet. Dobby squatted, opened a red flap, extended the painter line and gave a hard pull. In thirty seconds, the self-contained CO_2 inflation system had completely filled the four-man life raft.

"There's enough cash in the backpack for Dobby to take you home," Dante whispered to Ophelia, as they walked to the far side of the deck.

"You'll die here alone."

"The doctor said I could die any second. Does this seem like such a bad place for it?"

"How am I supposed to just leave you?" Ophelia looked down at her feet. Her white canvas sneakers were stained with mud and grease.

"That's been the plan from the beginning."

"That was before I got to know just how helpless you are." Ophelia watched the captain prepare to launch the life boat off the stern. For all of Dobby's tough talk, he'd stuffed bags with dozens of cans of Spam and mixed vegetables, all ready to be dropped into the life boat.

"I'm not that helpless," said Dante, shrugging his shoulders, also watching the captain work. "Hey, I just learned how to shave and brush my teeth. I'm a fast learner."

"Your teeth are yellow and your face is scruffy. Congratulations, you've learned enough to make you look as well-kempt as the wino I arrested last Wednesday for pissing in a doorway."

"I told you we needed a bigger boat."

"Can you even build a shelter?" she demanded. She was the senior sergeant raising her voice as the captain and little girl turned to look at them.

"If I wanna stay dry and out of the sun, I better learn real quick." Dante smiled his goofiest smile. *Not retarded*, Ophelia thought, suddenly embarrassed she hadn't defended him from the captain's mocking. *He's just mostly a child all over again.*

"How will you eat?"

"I bought enough fishing gear off the captain to feed a village. And how do you know I wasn't a Boy Scout?"

"I gave him a damn good deal," Dobby called over his shoulder, sorting through a huge greasy toolbox.

Dante looked her in the eye. "I'm here, Ophelia, and this is it. I came a long way to find my peace and I'm not turning back."

"And there's nothing I can say?"

"Nothing."

"You know that means I have to stay, racer boy."

"I can look after the girl."

"It's you who needs looking after."

"This island is on the International Red Cross route," Dante said. "The girl says they come regularly."

"They brought supplies to the village every month or two." Ophelia said, shaking her head. "And sometimes they couldn't get crews together for six months. We had a relative here; we know how things worked."

"We'll have all the necessities. Butter said they even have cisterns for water."

"You tell me what a cistern is and maybe I won't think you are a hundred percent full of shit."

Dante stood quietly, watching the captain sort through the toolbox, tossing some tools into a pile and dropping others back inside.

"What could go wrong out here? I mean, other than a big wave coming along and killing everything?" Dante asked.

"That's not funny."

"We won't need the supply ships."

"Good, 'cause with no village, they won't be back."

"You have family, Ophelia, your mom."

"It's six hundred kilometers, not the moon."

"But your job?"

"That's my business," Ophelia said, pointedly. "And things are probably different on my island than where you come from. I might just be expected to stay on and look after a crazy white guy and a little village girl who's lost her family."

"You goin' or stayin'?" Dobby asked Ophelia, as the pair walked back across the cluttered deck. "Your boy's got the cash for a run back to your island, if you want. No sweat off my back, one way or the other."

"Stay," Butter whispered, still watching the island, perhaps willing the shadows to be hiding the people and animals she had known. Then, from out of the north, came an enormous albatross, its nearly ten-foot wingspan spread wide to catch the warm thermals as it glided across the sparkling water. The huge bird swept in low over the reef, nearly meeting its shadow as it hunted fish and squid near the surface. "Stay with us," Butter said loud enough for Ophelia to hear.

"Dobby, give me two hours to look around the island before you go anywhere." Ophelia helped him lower supplies into the bobbing life raft, amazed he'd given them so much.

"Two hours." Dobby checked the face of his broken watch. "In two hours I'm gone—with or without you."

Butter was the first to jump down into the raft.

CHAPTER 49

Albino Paul was seething under the broiling afternoon sun
as he crouched on top of the island's highest ground, a
small bluff not more than two meters above sea level. He was
sick to death of this god-awful place. There was hardly a scrap
of shade left because of the damaged trees, and now blisters
had broken out across his palms and along manicured fingers.
Whatever the hell had happened here should have come twice
as hard, washing the whole damn island back into the sea.

He hated the idea of abandoning this gig, and having to eat
it on so much fuel added insult to injury. A setback like this
would cost him months in his plans to buy Malakula, and his
drug dealing bosses were major hard-asses about fuck ups. Not
being able to track down a couple of two-bit ass-bandits despite
the solid GPS trail was a fuck-up of the top-shelf variety.

The bloodthirsty cannibal stood up with his shovel then
quickly dropped back down at the sight of the old tugboat.
It was anchored out beyond the reef in the same spot he'd
originally parked his boat. Albino Paul rubbed his eyes,
blinking away ghost images from the bright sun, and watched
two white people—one man and one woman—and a little

brown girl in a bright yellow dress climb into a raft and begin paddling across the reef. He figured the tugboat was just some local garbage trawler, since its main deck was piled with the typical crap floating in these waters.

"Okay, new plan," the cannibal whispered, feeling that good old adrenaline flood throughout his body. It was the rush of a hunt back on, of the sudden and surprising appearance of some very sweet prey.

The sight of the young girl at the front of the rubber raft, reaching down to touch the choppy water as the adults paddled, made Albino Paul's stomach rumble with hunger. The white people were a gift—more than any self-respecting bloodthirsty cannibal could dare hope for out here in the middle of butt-fuck nowhere—but the little one was a dream come true. Child victims were the once in a lifetime, ultimate delicacies. The prospect of eating the girl made the thought of having to gnaw on the bones of the sour smelling Fiji ass-wranglers as disgusting as it got.

Albino Paul wiped at his mouth, furrowing his brow at his wet hand. Then he smiled wide. He was drooling like a feral dog. No time to retrieve his spear; the garden shovel in his left hand would do just fine. With its forty-four inch wooden handle and heavy steel blade, it was an adequate weapon. The trio's route to the island would lead them right past the sandcastle he'd kicked over. In full hunting mode, Albino Paul minced off the bluff and bent forward with the shovel held out in both hands, making his way down to the edge of the jungle to hide among the mounds of sand.

He hated to lose sight of the life boat, but he trusted his instincts. And he could now smell these newcomers as vividly as a next door neighbor's sizzling barbecue grill.

"Come on, just keep coming," Albino Paul whispered, crawling from the last of the broken trees to the remains of the sandcastle, which consisted of three large heaps of white sand and a scattering of small round coconuts. The island reached out toward the water here and the two adult paddlers were headed straight toward his new position.

The little girl was sitting upright in the boat, just meters from the beach, looking toward the treetops. Albino Paul followed her gaze upward, back over his shoulder, wondering where all the goddamn birds had come from. The trees were jammed with cackling winged creatures. He glanced back down, briefly considering how he'd neglected to notice the dozens of birds on the ground all around him. He must have pushed through them to get down to this spot. Hell, there was guano all over the place; he could feel its slimy wetness against his skin. But Albino Paul's attention was pulled back to his exquisite target. The girl's fragile neck was so deliciously exposed, and her small pink tongue darted out to wet those pouty, juicy lips.

The bloodthirsty cannibal let out a moan that was almost sexual and immediately scolded himself for getting so carried away. A few birds hopped away from him. This was no ordinary hunt, he reminded himself. This was to be an epic feast, something of legends, virgin meat brought to him by white people. The story he would bring back to his tribe would be passed down through generations, would inspire the dreams of young cannibal boys and provide the platform for the resurrection of his people, his entire culture.

Albino Paul was shaking as he allowed the girl and then the tall white woman to stroll past his hunting position. They walked through a parting flock of seagulls, as the most dangerous of the group—the white man—secured the small rubber dingy.

"Not too soon," Albino Paul whispered, as he smelled the white man's approach from the other side of the great mound of sand he pressed into. "Wait … wait …"

When the bloodthirsty cannibal heard the tall white man's footsteps pass and then begin to crunch the dry, broken palm fronds at the edge of the jungle, he rose up from hiding. Albino Paul screamed the ancient tribal screams of his proud ancestors, making what seemed to be ten thousand birds take flight from surrounding treetops, and nearly scaring to death the tall white man who had been following what he assumed was the path of the woman and the little girl.

"Your flesh is the nourishment of my forefathers!" Albino Paul shouted in his people's ancient tribal language, although his skills were imperfect, and what he actually yelled was, "Your flesh tastes like foreskins!"

Since the only foreign phrases Dante had ever known had to do with picking up scantily clad drunk women in noisy Euro bars, there was no chance of him being confused by the lunatic's words. Whether or not his memories of foreign pick-up lines were intact, he recognized a death threat when he heard one. It came from the crazy headhunter who had tried to kill them once and had been lying in wait here on the island. As the hard steel shovel struck him squarely across the side of the head, the former world class ski racer's eyes saw that death had come for another visit.

Dante's knees were locked, keeping his stunned body momentarily upright. A stream of crystal clear images ran across his vision as he teetered on the brink of consciousness. A green winter jacket lay across the woman's lap and a woolen hat was pulled down over her ears. It was his mother, much younger, before she'd gotten sick with cancer. He looked down at his clothes and saw that he was just a boy, sitting on a bench in a huge, familiar room, where he'd been many times. Gigantic wooden beams extended just below the high ceiling, and the fireplace in front of him was tall enough to walk right into when it wasn't lit. Gray rocks formed an arch over the crackling fire.

Dante's small hands clutched a cup of cocoa, with a single

marshmallow half submerged. They were in the old ski lodge, the one his mom would take them to in the Catskills. It was her favorite place to ski because of the lodge, she'd said. The lifts were slow and the grooming and snowmaking far inferior to all of the surrounding ski areas. But skiing was about more than a quick trip up and down a perfect carpet of tilled snow. It was the twists through changing fall lines and sometimes feeling like you were a little lost that made a day of skiing special. And all its faults—including a lodge so drafty that you had to crowd the fireplace on especially cold days—were just part of the resort's character.

His mother smiled at him as he slurped at the soft marshmallow. There were no wrinkles around her mouth, just smooth pale skin. She had learned to ski in college, but neither her husband nor daughter had any interest. For Dante, skiing had been a chance to have her all to himself. No evil sister and no short-tempered father. He was just a little boy trying to keep up with his mom on winding trails, the cold air stinging his face in a good way. Dante remembered the happy screams she made, the ones that sounded like a funny sneeze. Sometimes he'd crash in the deep snow and she wouldn't notice. He'd scramble to get his skis back on and she'd get farther and farther away, disappearing around a turn in the distance. He'd be left breathing hard, struggling, suddenly alone in the cold.

The images of skiing faded. Dante Wheeler saw stars before he saw blackness, and then felt the piercing cold come rushing back all over again as he collapsed onto the sand and broken palm fronds.

CHAPTER 50

"Check out them legs." Jope's voice was full of lust, despite the dire circumstances. "You remember that place by the airport they wouldn't let us into?"

"My head hurts bad."

"All them guys wearin' suits, but I had to take a pee. Big bouncer tells me to go fuck myself, go whiz in the street. But then he went for a sandwich next door. You remember that place?"

"Yeah, I remember, Jope. You really pissed off the bartender."

"Ten dollars for two beers! 'No way fucker,' I said. 'Not unless your mama sits on my lap and holds my bottle between her titties.' "

"The bartender went next door to the sandwich shop and got the bouncer."

"Yeah, real big motherfucker. That chick hangin' there has legs just like the girl from that place."

"It wasn't a girl."

"You think all rich dudes like chicks with wangs?"

"My head hurts, Jope."

"What if there's a whole buncha shit like that we don't know about? You remember that movie where there wasn't no real food left in the world? Most of the people were poor and lived in shitholes like us. 'Cept the rich people are all eatin' the last of them fat strawberries and sayin' 'ha, ha, ha, you poor dumb fuckers, we still eatin' juicy strawberries.' "

"It had that pissed off white cop in it."

"Yeah, right, Ratu! I love that guy 'cause he didn't let nobody fuck with him. 'Take your stinking paws off me, you damned dirty ape!' You remember that? He showed them monkeys who was boss."

"It was called *Soylent Green*." More and more of the movie and that day came back to Ratu. It had been the off-season for tourists and they didn't have much cash from dealing crank. They'd snuck in through the back door of the theater as always, but nobody had cared. It was a junky old movie reel off the rack and the owner just wanted to sell some soda and popcorn. The doors were all left open because it was cool enough to turn off the air conditioners. Even a cat had snuck in and was making sounds like it was in heat. The movie was named after the only food poor people were allowed to have. But it turned out to be secretly made from mashed-up people. Ratu and Jope had spent the next week picking out people who looked like they'd taste good with mustard or mayonnaise. "It was a good movie," was all Ratu said.

"I hope that chick don't gotta wang." Jope had been looking at the leggy blond next to them with her shorts hiked to her crotch. He'd been staring at her pale thighs and just now noticed she was crying.

"That guy she's tied to ain't looking so good," Ratu said, slowly spinning to face the new pair of white people hanging just as upside-down, a few meters away. The white couple's tree was heavily stressed by more than twice the weight.

"He looks dead," Jope called to the hot, leggy blond, who only seemed to want to whimper to herself. "I don't gotta girlfriend. And I got plenty of coke I'll share with you."

"You don't have any coke, dumbass." The shark-god had suddenly appeared on a nearby fallen tree, startling the two former pirates. But the shark-god also didn't look so good. A crust of dark, dried blood had formed in each nostril, and his eyes were bloodshot and pupils incredibly dilated. He sat slumped, his great head in his hands as if it ached miserably.

"We just forgot where we buried it," Jope said defensively.

"I dug it up, you dumbass," said the shark-god. "You buried it right down on the beach and put a big rock on top."

"I don't remember doing that. Is that where we buried it, Ratu?"

"I don't remember anything."

"And one of you dipwads used another rock to scratch an arrow pointing down."

"That crazy cannibal woulda found it," Ratu said.

"Ya think? Gee, maybe I'll hide the coke and then draw a big arrow pointing to where it's buried. And the rest of my plan is to be hung upside down and wait to be eaten." The shark-god sniffled and pinched at his nostrils. Upon closer observation, the former pirates noticed his human hands were shaking badly, and he couldn't seem to stop tapping his bare feet.

"Your shark-god been hittin' our stash hard," Ratu whispered to his friend.

"He's not just *my* shark-god, he's *our* shark-god, Ratu. He's *everybody's* shark-god."

"Well, everybody's shark-god is pretty strung out on blow."

"He can help us, Ratu." But Ratu didn't think the shark-god looked capable of helping anyone, not even himself. The shark-god stank of his own poop.

"Hey, shark-god," Jope called to the man-beast creature who seemed to have fallen asleep with his eyes open. "Hey, wake up! We need you to help us!"

"I need a drink of water." The shark-god looked around, perhaps thinking he might have put a glass of water down somewhere nearby. "You have any water?"

"Hey, Blondie?" Jope called to the hot babe on the next rotation. "You don't got any water, do you?"

"Where would she have water, Jope? Jesus, she's tied up worse than we are. And look at all the blood coming from her boyfriend's head."

"Miss?" Jope tried again. The blond woman kept whimpering, ignoring the former pirates and the shark-god. "We don't mean no disrespect, or nothin'. It'll be okay, and you get used to bein' upside-down after a while. Just make sure to keep your mouth shut if you gotta pee."

"I really need water." The shark-god slipped off his perch on the log with a thud, squishing a half-dozen small birds under his human ass. The former pirates watched as he plunged one hand into the front pocket of his cut-off khaki pants, pulling out a monstrous handful of what had once been their nearly pure cocaine. The shark-god covered one nostril and then practically jammed the mound of coke up the other. The snorting sounds he made sounded like a donkey's braying.

"Holy fuck," said Jope, as the shark-god fell completely onto his side, killing more birds, his breaths coming in shallow gulps. A dozen new birds fluttered down from the tree tops, alighted on his great blue and gray head, and began to preen.

"We gonna have to find a new god," Ratu said.

CHAPTER 51

Albino Paul was giddy with anticipation.

It was late in the South Pacific afternoon and the broken trees created jagged shadows that reached across the white sand like the hands of a skeleton. A cool breeze made the two sets of hanging people gently rock as they turned slow revolutions. The woman's constant whimpering served as a lullaby, sending the two coke thieves into a deep sleep. Their snoring competed with the racket made by the birds. The flow from the white man's head wound had eased to a light red trickle. Albino Paul wondered if he'd hit the man too hard. He might not survive long enough to be carved. No big deal, though, since it was all about the child.

The tree tops were teeming with thousands of fussing birds. When one took off for a better spot, twenty new arrivals fought over the newly created space.

Albino Paul welcomed the birds as a sign of nature's approval of the seminal event he was so carefully organizing. The video camera was in position, four small fires at the perimeter corners of the sacrificial altar smoldered, and brush and deadfall had been shoveled up and carted away. Despite the makeshift setting, this backdrop was turning out to be perfect.

How many shows had he performed for the Cannibal Culture Spree? Six hundred? A thousand? Whatever the number, he was through summoning phony spirits and praying to pretend gods. The next time he squeezed the penis gourd in place, the filthy white people wouldn't be laughing and pointing, snapping photos. No, they'd be begging for mercy, ropes cutting into their skin as they struggled.

The cannibal could make out the partially visible outline of what must be the two Fijian idiots' god, sprawled next to them. A creature that looked to be half human, half fish, and completely fucking ridiculous. But Albino Paul also welcomed what he sensed was a dying deity, yet another sign of his own growing power. That he could so easily bring gods to their knees confirmed his might. How many humans could overwhelm a god without even trying?

The sickly looking half fish god sneezed twice. Its face was partially buried in sand, and small white puffs of powder billowed from each nostril.

"Bless you," Albino Paul said absently, a habit picked up from all the pasty tourists.

The sacrificial altar where the girl lay was sometimes called a tenderizing log. Victims were lashed tightly and beaten with heavy clubs. The blows filled the soft flesh with blood and worked to numb the subject's body, helping to keep them conscious while they were sliced up. The little girl was naked, spread-eagled on her back, her woven belt and bright yellow dress carefully cut away by Albino Paul. He'd wrapped a leather strap across her neck and around the thick log. The girl refused to cry for herself, as if sensing he fed on fear as well as flesh. He'd made no secret of his intentions, repeating over and over what a magnificent honor it was to sacrifice one's flesh to such a noble and glorious cause.

"You're not noble," she had told him, as much scorn in her

voice as she could muster. "You're just evil. Eating people is dirty and wrong."

Albino Paul, who'd been using a compact mirror to reapply his tribal hunting paint, marched over to the bound girl and slapped her hard across the face for such blasphemy. Birds jumped and squawked at the commotion. He heard her try to spit at him, but he'd already turned and walked back to retrieve the small mirror, pushing a pathway through the thickening carpet of birds. There might be as many as a hundred thousand now, filling the air with their talk, their growing discontent. They pecked at his bare feet and shins, but he didn't bother kicking at them. Surely the birds were spirits come to bear witness, anxious as he was for the virgin to be sacrificed.

"The birds are here to watch me eat you," he told the girl, picking up the mirror to finish applying his makeup. He watched her in the small piece of glass over his shoulder, but she just stared straight up at the cloud of birds circling above. The graceful shearwaters and petrels that soared in wide banked turns and might be the spirits of his great aunts and uncles, the sandpipers and the tattlers who might be long-dead grandfathers and stillborn nieces. The shadow of a magnificent southern royal albatross, perhaps once a village elder, swept across the sacrificial altar. It made Albino Paul's heart ache and stomach rumble. Perfect, lovely innocence lay before him, ready, waiting for him to devour her young, unspoiled meat. His penis gourd grew tight and uncomfortable, but he refused to adjust it.

He'd kept his tools out her line of sight. She couldn't see the felt knife holder he'd unfurled and placed on the tenderizing log between her open legs, the selection of knives and sharpening files out of her view. Albino Paul wanted to relish the look in her eyes at her first glimpse of his glistening carving knife, to soak in her terror as she realized what was about to penetrate her soft flesh.

He walked the sacrificial perimeter shuffling birds out of the way, dropping handfuls of powder into each small fire, making them smoke with a heavy spiced scent. It was convenient to have helpers perform these duties during the tourist shows, but now he relished each task. This was the real thing. Passing the tripod-mounted video camera, he flicked on the "record" switch and checked the viewfinder to be sure the girl was centered.

Albino Paul took a deep breath and surveyed the marvelous scene. He ran through a last minute checklist in his head, deciding there was nothing he'd forgotten.

"It's time," he said, shrugging off a bird that came in for a hard landing on his right shoulder, leaving small scratches where it had tried to gain purchase.

He was smiling as he approached the girl and the sacrificial altar from the end nearest her lovely head. Albino Paul reached down for the thick club he'd selected earlier for tenderizing her and held it up to the gods, his bright white eyes full of energy.

"I offer the flesh of this virgin to the mighty Malakula gods!" Albino Paul called in his forefathers' ancient language, although what he actually said was, "I drink the laundry water of fat Malakula brides!"

Albino Paul brought the club down with a whoosh, striking the little girl across the chest and stomach. The heavy thud knocked the wind out of her. Her back arched from what must be excruciating pain, and although her mouth was open, she was unable to draw breath.

This new racket woke the former pirates from their fevered slumber, and the white woman began to scream bloody murder. Above, thousands of birds jeered and took flight, distressed and confused, sending guano flying everywhere. A young kingfisher bravely stood his ground beneath the noise and commotion at the sacrificial altar, tilting his head sideways, his long beak inching toward the knot on the leather strap holding the girl.

Albino Paul straddled the log, his polished penis gourd

hovering over the girl's head like a pointed rocket, and brought the club down again and again. The white woman pleaded for him to stop, to come take her instead, but Albino Paul continued tenderizing the lovely virgin.

Despite the pain and lack of air, Butter's eyes were open, fixed on a spot high above, a tiny wrinkle in the thin clouds over the island the dancing white man had called East Pukapuka. For the first time in her young life, she was looking at the doorway to Happa Now. And although she couldn't quite make out the words chanted by her dead friends and family—the plaintive cries that might have been "Olly, olly, oxen free"—Butter smiled with contentment and the knowledge that her papa would soon be tossing her back up into the air, despite warnings from Mama that he was going to drop her on her head. Butter was now certain Happa Now was real and much closer than she'd ever imagined.

The terrible man reached forward and grabbed the longest, sharpest knife from between her legs. She watched him glance toward the camera he'd set up on metal sticks and make a bowing gesture toward it. He reached down and pinched a section of baby fat on her soft stomach. With his other hand, he brought the knife close to her skin and seemed to brace himself to begin cutting. Butter could see and feel how badly his hands were shaking. He seemed frightened. Maybe he didn't know how relieved she was at this moment, how much she welcomed being sent to the next life.

Butter looked away from the man and his knife, searching the air for the butterfly that would take her to Happa Now.

A few yards away, splayed out beneath where the two former pirates were both blubbering over what the awful cannibal was doing to the little girl, the once mighty shark-god raised his snout from the warm sand. Bloodshot eyes glared at the cannibal and the long knife that was inches from the child's flesh, about to begin slicing. Dakuwaqa cleared his sore throat and gnashed his thousands of razor-sharp teeth. Just before his heart exploded inside his human chest, he uttered two final words. Jope and Ratu both heard the spoken order and immediately began to struggle against their ropes, but to no avail. The thin nylon cords didn't budge an inch, and they stopped their fruitless wriggling when they realized the command wasn't intended for them. Instead, the shark-god's dying command was directed at the now half-million birds that had gathered all around the island of East Pukapuka.

"Sic 'em!" the shark-god ordered the birds. And, by god, they did.

CHAPTER 52

Technically it wasn't the birds that killed the bloodthirsty cannibal named after The Smiling Pope. Sure, he was dive-bombed, pecked, and swarmed by a blizzard of feathers and thorny beaks, but he managed to stumble down the path to the beach and wade out to his boat. The cover of gnarled trees and the club he managed to hold onto and blindly swing had given him some hope of escape.

Blood seeped from small gashes all over his body. The boat's steering wheel was slick from his gore. Albino Paul's right eye had been easy pickings for a kamikaze pigeon. Several fingers went to the doves and boobies. A large blue heron swooped down and snatched away his penis gourd, doing enough damage to his testicles to ensure he would never reproduce, even if he survived this onslaught.

Turning due east, Albino Paul slipped through the narrow passage in the coral reef and jammed the throttle wide-open. Even the speediest birds fell back, unable to keep up with the roaring engines. With his lacerated palm, he slapped at the stereo's "play" button and Gloria Estefan's magical voice erupted from the three speakers not punctured by bird bombs.

Just as the speedometer topped a hundred-sixty, the bloodthirsty cannibal looked up through his cracked and spider-webbed windshield to catch a brief image. His boat was set on a collision course with a mostly rusted, black and red metal ship.

"I don't feel so good," Albino Paul's said. They were the last words he ever spoke in this life.

Jesus Dobby looked down at the flash of gleaming black speed boat hurtling directly toward his bow. He caught a glimpse of huge white eyes and a face painted with comically pointed teeth. He'd seen the face before, printed on colorful posters for a cannibal tourist attraction on one of the islands. Oddball tourist attractions weren't new to anyone hailing from the Lone Star State. Dobby had seen billboards telling people to come visit the Eiffel Tower, Stonehenge II, and the toilet seat museum down in Alamo Heights. Right off I-27, between Lubbock and Amarillo, resided a life-size crucified Jesus Christ in a glass case.

But this tourist attraction was going like a bat out of hell and Dobby had no hope of maneuvering the tugboat out of its path. The captain's conscience had convinced him to u-turn an hour earlier. He just couldn't abandon the damn turtle-girl, the pain in the ass white woman, and her retarded boyfriend. He'd had the queerest feeling, like someone was whispering in his ear to get his saggy gray ass back to the beat up island.

"Sounds like Gloria Estefan," were Dobby's last words spoken in this life.

The head-on impact with the Gypsy Dancer caused a tremendous fiery explosion, followed by a black mushroom cloud that chased the souls of Jesus Dobby and the bloodthirsty cannibal toward their next lives. Both boats sank to the bottom in seconds. For hundreds of years they would provide hiding places and hunting grounds for countless species of tropical fish.

CHAPTER 53

"I feel like she's safe, that she's out of danger," Butter's papa told his wife, a little out of breath, the pair once again in the throes of their recently rekindled love. This time, they were doing it doggy style.

"Don't stop!" Anonymous pleaded.

"Sorry, the image kind of came to me out of nowhere."

"You stopped." She rested her sweaty forehead on the bedroll.

"And I don't think we'll see her for a long time."

"You think that retarded ski racer will keep an eye on her?" Anonymous had crested the knoll of orgasm for the second time but wasn't ready to call it quits, patiently waiting on all fours for her husband to refocus.

"Well, she does have the cop. And I get the feeling she's a very down to earth woman." Clarence resumed his work from behind, slowly at first. But then, as his worry over his daughter faded, he noticed something strange.

Just as the God of Weather was responsible for the moderate temperatures and low humidity, the God of Time had been responsible for everything running a bit slower because Butter was about to be eaten by the cannibal. Colossal negativity reached the afterlife in waves, emotional tsunamis, the type of thing that prompted a resident of Happa Now to sluggishly wade out into the blue water, face the sweeping horizon, and channel a message across the great void to the previous life. "Knock it off, already! It took me four days to brush my teeth, for crying out loud," would be a typical admonition from the afterlife.

As peace and harmony replaced nagging despair over the dangers that had threatened their only child, everything around them began to speed up. Clarence's thrusting hips were a stormy ocean, powerful, a flurry of motion. Their bodies slapped together, damp skin sounding like a flag in a gale force wind. And Clarence wasn't even trying very hard.

"She seems smart and sweet." Anonymous was again enjoying the lustful rhythm of her husband.

"And those legs are something else!" he said.

"Do you really want to discuss her legs right now?"

"Sorry, honey."

"I know you're sorry." She craned her neck for a kiss. "I really missed you."

"I missed you, too." Clarence paused to reposition his knees on softer bedding.

Anonymous closed her eyes, wiggled her brown bum. "I'm starting to get close again."

Outside the love hut sat Happa Now's two newest residents, backs propped against low-growing coconut palms, facing each other in the pleasant, partly cloudy, eighty-two degree afternoon. Jesus Dobby was rubbing his scalp, which had itched for as long as he could remember from a chronic case of head lice. But here in this shady spot, it just tingled slightly. The nasty little bumps were now smooth and cool to the touch.

"Do I know you?" Dobby asked.

The man sitting across from him was wearing full-body war paint, with big pointy white teeth drawn on his cheeks. His necklace appeared to be made out of fragile bones, almost like fingers.

"Oh, yeah, no, I get that all the time." He was rubbing his stomach, a puzzled expression on his face, as though trying to decide if he was hungry. Now, a thin coat of nervous sweat broke out all over his painted body, turning his black skin shiny.

"Nah, I'm pretty sure we've met." Dobby squinted his eyes while absently pulling at the curls of the mat of gray chest hairs under his crucifix made of buttons. He remembered grabbing at the little savage girl's gift just before colliding with the black speed boat. The last thing Dobby remembered was thick black smoke swirling upward, all around him. He'd had the feeling of riding a bucking bronco, then of getting sucked inside a giant vacuum cleaner. "I'm sure I know you from somewhere."

"Yeah, well, I got one of those faces," the man said, rubbing and smearing a few giant white teeth. Then, as if to change the subject, "Those two sure are goin' at it, huh?"

From inside the love hut there came a guttural moan from the man, followed by the frantic, out of breath voice of the female who was reaching her third orgasm in the last half hour. To the two suspicious former acquaintances, it sounded like a cat was in mortal distress, but everyone knew animals weren't allowed on Happa Now.

"Olly, olly, oxen free!" screeched the climaxing woman. Neither Jesus Dobby nor the painted man could suppress childish grins. The cannibal put his palm in the air and the cranky old captain leaned forward and high-fived it.

DISCUSSION QUESTIONS FOR BOOK CLUBS

The Turtle-Girl from East Pukapuka touches upon a wide range of topics both serious and absurd, realistic and surreal. Its characters are the products of American and native cultures. The following questions are intended to help your group begin the conversation.

1. The birds were drawn to Bigness and were the first to see the wave coming in the opening chapter. What drew the birds back to East Pukapuka? Was it Albino Paul's presence? He saw their arrival as a positive sign, but would the birds have attacked him if the shark-god hadn't given the order? Or were they only present to witness his form of Bigness?

2. There are quite a few competing religions in the book. Did you find any of them offensive? The gods in this book are all imperfect. How do they compare to the gods that you have read about throughout history? What about our mainstream religions? Was the Shark God meant to be real?

3. Did you feel sympathy for the people of East Pukapuka as the wave approached, or did you see their deaths as another step in their journey? Had your attitude changed by the end of the book?

4. Happa Now is the afterlife that awaits anyone who dies in East Pukapuka. Does it compare favorably with the Christian notion of heaven? Butter was told people can communicate from Happa Now; did you see evidence of that in the book?

5. The gods attempted to create a perfect afterlife on Happa Now but were too far removed from the human experience and missed the importance of domestic pets. Do other religions believe there are pets in heaven? As a child, did you believe your pet would go to heaven? How do you feel about pets and the afterlife now?

6. Butter loses a great deal of her trust in adults when she discovers the Tooth Devil is only a parent and not a creature from the ocean depths leaving black pearls in wooden spoons. Does the Tooth Fairy leave money or other prizes under your child's pillow? Do you recall your own reaction when you discovered that these mythical creatures of childhood—the Tooth Fairy, Santa Claus, the Easter Bunny—did not exist? Was your faith in all things unseen affected?

7. Ratu and Jope deal drugs, shoplift, steal a boat, take advantage of innocent tourists, become pirates, yet are sympathetic characters. What characteristics make them likeable? Or not?

8. Dante's family doesn't visit him in the rehab center,

and his teammates only make a token appearance at his bedside. His family ties are broken. Why? Is his transformation and quest real, or were they planted in his brain by the travel channel?

9. How does the portrayal of women in this book affect your reading of the story? Butter is a girl, not a woman, but is she already aware of the disadvantages of her gender?

10. Does racism play a role in Albino Paul's motivation to resurrect his people's history of cannibalism? Albino Paul is a character who does some very bad things, but do you view his character as entirely evil?

Student artists from Western Wayne High School, in South Canaan, PA, submitted their vision of a turtle-girl in a contest under the direction of Art Department Chairman Justin Hayden. The call for entries asked students to provide illustrations of the following scene from the book:

> *The Turtle-Girl from East Pukapuka* is an adult literary novel by Cole Alpaugh centering around a 10-year-old girl whose tiny South Pacific island is ravaged by a tsunami. She escapes by clinging to the shell of an old Loggerhead sea turtle, but is alone and adrift in the open ocean. The girl is unconscious from being bitten by a habu viper for which she'd been caring. She is naked except for a thin woven belt, and is thin, with long black hair. The turtle is swimming hard, trying to save the girl who had nursed him back to health after he'd been struck by a boat. She's seen as the world's first Turtle-Girl by the salvage tugboat boat captain who spots their small wake while hunting flotsam treasure, mistaking the duo for a freak-of-nature that could bring him a fortune if he can capture her.

Alyssa DeKenipp and Allie Poltanis were the winning artists. Their work is presented on the following pages.

Painting by Alyssa DeKenipp

Painting by Allie Poltanis

Cole with some of his current and former soccer players
in Northeast Pennsylvania.
—Photo by Amy Alpaugh

Cole Alpaugh began his newspaper career in the early '80s at a daily paper on Maryland's Eastern Shore, where he covered everything from bake sales to KKK meetings. He moved on to a paper in Massachusetts, specializing in feature essays. His stories on a Hispanic youth gang and the life of a Golden Gloves boxer won national awards. At his most recent newspaper job, a large daily in Central New Jersey, he was given the freedom to pursue more "true life" essays, including award-winning pieces on a traveling rodeo and an in-depth story on an emergency room doctor. The doctor's story ended when the physician brought back to life an elderly woman who'd once been his children's babysitter. The essay was nominated by Gannett News Service for a 1991 Pulitzer Prize. Cole also did work for two Manhattan-based news agencies, covering conflicts in Haiti, Panama, Nicaragua, El Salvador, and guerrilla raids conducted out of the refugee camps along the Thai/Cambodia boarder. His work has appeared in dozens of magazines, as well as most newspapers in America.

Cole's first novel, *The Bear in a Muddy Tutu*, was published by Camel Press, an imprint of Coffeetown Press, in 2011. Coming Soon from Coffeetown: Cole's third novel, *The Spy's Little Zonbi*.

Cole is currently a freelance photographer and writer living in Northeast Pennsylvania, where he also coaches his daughter's soccer team.

You can find Cole online at www.colealpaugh.com.